Three brand new stories from three talented authors!

Featured authors include Rayka Mennen—Oops!—
All Vince Anderson wanted was a decent assistant who
knew the right end of a pen. Instead he gets Leena, bright
eyed, smart and also his landlady and a witch. He falls head
over heels in love. But can he trust his attraction to her isn't
manipulated by her powers?

Leena Mackay had enough to worry about with a
mortgage payment she couldn't make and a sister intent on
casting crazy spells. Why did her boss have to rent an
apartment in her house and turn out to be the only guy who
could make her lick her lips?

Can she convince him that their love transcends the
earthly and the supernatural?

Liz Hunter—Dang Crooked Arrow—Tara Avery
pegged Harrison Howard as a playboy and ladies' man the
minute he walked into the florist's shop. So attracted to the
'hottie' shop owner, Harry barely noticed Tara and the four
children with her. Inexplicably, Tara and Harry take
another look and suddenly saw each other with new eyes,
and it was love at first sight.

Only thing is, Tara can't abide Lothario's lifestyle,
changing his lady of the week at three month intervals to
coincide with his sales route. And no way did Harry want
to step foot into a relationship with a woman and four
children.

Despite their reservations and with a little outside interference they can't help but fall in love.

Phyllis Campbell—Crazy Cupid—Fashion designer Kenya Whitaker is leery about the strange and poorly dressed man she meets, and she's even more skeptical when he explains he's from the future. She refuses to help, but the offbeat, sexy man charms, and shows her what love is really all about.

Eli's very existence is threatened and he needs Kenya's assistance. The man she's supposed to marry has locked Eli's father in a mental institution. Joshua Montgomery must be released and put in his rightful spot as president of Montgomery Aisle. If Eli fails, he'll not only lose Kenya, but life will cease to exist.

Champagne Books Presents

Stupid Cupid
A Valentine's Anthology

By

Phyllis Campbell,

Liz Hunter &

Rayka Mennen

Stupid Cupid

ISBN 1897261063

OOPS!

Copyright © 2006 by Usha Menon

DANG CROOKED ARROW

Copyright © 2006 by Donna K. Smith

CRAZY CUPID

Copyright © 2006 by Marie Higgins

February 2006

Cover Art © Chris Butts

Produced in Canada

Visit us online at www.champagnebooks.com

Champagne Books
#35069-4604 37 ST SW
Calgary, AB T3E 7C7
Canada

Stupid Cupid

Prologue

"Thas'ri Bunny, my arrows. My arrows make people fall in love. No, no I am serus, real serus, they do."

A long, deep, resonating belch climbed up from the depths of the little cherub. Easter Bunny's ears shot straight up and his body quaked with shivers of disgust.

"I think you've had enough Cupid."

"I'm okay Bunny, I can fly." A twitch in his left wing nearly toppled Cupid to the floor. "I'm not drunk! I prove it to ya, jus watch."

"It's okay, really."

"Watch Bunny."

With agility and perfection of form that belied the mass inebriation that obviously racked the little man, Cupid whipped an arrow into his bow and drew back. Without warning another gassy expulsion caused his aim to falter as he released the drawn string. The result was certainly unexpected.

The satisfied grin on Cupid's face was wiped clean when Easter Bunny burst into an uncontrollable fit of laughter. The errant shaft had split into two as it was meant to. Each one struck a target as had happened countless times throughout his illustrious career.

Slobbering, Cupid wiped his mouth with the back of one paw and drawled out his shocked, drunken surprise, "Tha can't be good Bunny."

"Oh my goodness Cupid, you have one seriously warped sense of humor."

Sitting in a corner booth, wrapped so tightly in each others arms that they were almost one body, sat a six foot Nubian princess and a three foot midget Eskimo with no teeth.

"That does it Bunny, I'm goin' home."

Oops!

Rayka Mennen

Champagne Books

Calgary, AB Canada

Rayka Mennen chooses to write romance because she believes in the power of love to heal. She welcomes you to her world of romance, laughter, magic and even a little mayhem. Also a nurse scientist, she remains committed to her research in cancer prevention/early detection. She had no idea her writing career would take off as it has and she's becoming an expert juggler of both careers—but she wouldn't give up a moment of either.

Books by Rayka Mennen

Operation Playboy

Bound By Destiny

Don't miss any of our special offers. Write to us at #35069-4604 37 St SW, Calgary AB Canada T3E 7C7 or visit us online at www.champagnebooks.com to sign up for our quarterly newsletter.

Dedication

To KM for your unfailing support of my writing career.

To PR & MK for your friendship; may your love story
continue to inspire.

Prologue

Despite a blinding headache, Cupid peered out the window of the rent-controlled apartment where Easter Bunny lived. The sun shone in his eyes with a brightness that almost seemed gleeful. By Jove, of course! They probably knew about his screw-ups by now. And of course, ever since he'd stolen those herds from Apollo, his brother was on the lookout for a way to get even.

"Pshaw. Go away," he mumbled.

"No way," Apollo shot back. "I gotta see you fix this."

Cupid groaned. He'd better get in touch with Dionysius to find out how to deal with this hangover. At least that's what Easter Bunny had told him it was--this feeling that his head might explode.

He opened the window then flexed his wings before flying out into the early morning. There was only one thing to do--get this awful pain taken care of, then come back and fix the havoc he'd wreaked the night before.

One

Today of all days, someone had cast a klutz spell on her! And she had a pretty good idea who it was. This spell casting practice by her sister could land them all in big trouble.

Leena set the plates down on one end of the counter with great care, trying not to make a sound; or drop the whole damn lot. The account exec droned on behind her as he addressed each still shot on the screen, telling the gathered team why this was the best way to advertise the next miracle vacuum cleaner.

Why in the hell her boss wanted a full meal served in a room that was darkened for the presentation she had no idea. Phyllis had these strange starts at times. She grimaced at Val, the other office assistant, who rolled her eyes and proceeded to walk down one end of the table, a tray of desserts in her hands.

Leena picked up the stainless steel coffeepot. Jeez, it was heavy! She glanced around the table. A couple of people had their coffee cups right-side-up, which meant they wanted coffee. Should she ask the others? But that might disturb the presenter. With another silent curse sent her boss's way, she headed for the guy with the open cup at one end of the long table.

As she made her way up the table behind Val, people began turning their coffee cups over or shook their heads at her. Good, maybe she could get this over without a mishap.

She came to the new guy, Vincent Anderson, who neither looked at her nor had his cup upright. *Arrogant--*.

She stifled the thought and let out a tiny sigh as the presenter concluded. Someone called out for the lights to be turned on; everyone began clapping. She leaned down to him and caught a whiff of his after-shave, giving an appreciative sniff. It reminded her of sun-splashed porticos on a Jamaican island resort. Not that she'd ever been to one. But that's what the firm's last ad campaign had been about.

"Would you like some coffee?"

"What? Sure." He turned back to clapping and with another sigh, she turned his cup over and poured.

Leena later decided that it was the combination of the bright conference room lights coming on suddenly and the klutz spell at work. She blinked and the lid of the coffeepot swung open, cascading coffee down into the cup and onto his lap.

"Ouch!" She set the pot down as he scrambled back from the table. Grabbing his napkin, she dabbed at his legs.

"Oh, God I'm so sorry. Are you hurt?" She pressed the napkin against his thigh hoping to soak up the coffee.

"Geez. Dammit." He seemed to be trying to control himself. "I'm fine. Just a few drops. Really. Listen, you can stop that now." He caught her around the wrist and she stilled when she realized she was patting his...well, his *thing*.

"Sorry" she mumbled, backing off as the heat rose up her neck and face, along with strange tingles that shot up her arm.

"It's okay. Most of it went on the floor anyway."

Stricken with embarrassment, she glanced up at him. His hazel eyes glinted with amusement and something else. "I--."

He cut her off. "It's fine. Maybe you could bring another napkin and cup for me?"

"Oh, sure." She rushed back to the sideboard and unwrapped an extra set of cutlery wrapped in a cloth napkin. She turned, bumping her elbow into a hard body part. She realized it was his abdomen. Dang it! The man had followed her.

"Sorry," she mumbled, backing into the table behind her. She handed him the napkin and looked down at her feet.

"Thanks."

She watched surreptitiously as he dabbed at the front of his khakis. He had a nice forehead and she loved the way an unruly lock fell over it.

What the hell was wrong with her? Mr. Unruly Lock could very well get her fired. In the three weeks he'd been there, he'd fired two assistants and had made the copy ad gal cry. And Leena needed this job like she needed to breathe.

Vincent handed the napkin back to Leena and stood there, his attention on the speaker. Jeanine--blond, beautiful and a man-eater. Good luck with that, she thought.

Glancing over she realized what he'd said was true. Most of the coffee had spilled on the dark carpet. The few splashes on the table were mopped up already. By him?

She secured the lid of the wayward coffeepot and gingerly poured coffee for the remaining two people, trying not to glance at Vincent or his thighs, so nicely outlined by those khakis. She should probably offer to pay for the cleaning, but she really couldn't afford it.

Back by the food, Leena rested against the wall. She and Val would wait a few more minutes then leave and come back for clean up after the meeting.

The screen still showed a shot of a nice-looking man in jeans and a white T-shirt, lying back on a sofa. He held a smiling toddler up over his chest. This was the first run of an idea pitched to the vacuum cleaner guys and she could tell they liked it. The general story was of a man who had more time to play with his kid and cook dinner for his wife because of the fancy vacuum cleaner that made cleaning a cinch.

The whole scene vibrated with good-will--the American dream, happily every after and all that jazz. Ha!

She eyed the photo with skepticism when something occurred to her. The scene wasn't quite right. What was it? She focused and it hit her. She tried to hide a grin as she muttered. "It won't work."

"Why not?" asked a quiet, deep voice almost in her ear. She started and turned, realizing too late that Mr. Hot Shot was still standing next to her. She blanched. Her sister, Carly, would hear about this latest spell gone wrong.

"Oh, nothing. Just talking to myself."

"About what?" he insisted, his steadfast hazel eyes catching her gaze.

Why me?

Couldn't he just go back to his place and leave her alone? Surely he had an employee to fire or some other horrible thing still left to do? When it looked like he wouldn't drop it, she improvised.

"I was just considering how I might get the stain off your pants. And I thought about getting you a wet napkin. But I decided that would only make it worse." She cast about for something more to say. "Salt. Yeah, that's it. I'll get you some salt to sprinkle on it."

"You were watching that photo. Now tell me what about it won't work."

Vincent's eyes roved her face. Such gorgeous eyes-- green one minute and light brown the next. Leena shook off the thought. Focus. That's what she needed to get through this day. His after-shave wafted over her again and she almost groaned. Better just tell him and get the hell away.

"That photo. He's supposed to be married, right?"

He nodded, his eyes bright and curious. "Yeah?"

"Well, he's not wearing a ring."

"So--oh hell, you're right." He grinned at her. "Wow! Sharp eyes."

She shrugged. At least he wasn't yelling at her or something.

"Wanna tell them that?"

Was he nuts? "No thanks. I've got stuff to do." She gathered a stack of plates and headed toward the cart set unobtrusively in the corner by the door.

"Then, mind if I say it?"

"Be my guest," she shot over her shoulder, stepping carefully away.

~ * ~

Vince shook his head in amazement. All these talented people in the room--well some were on the light side of talent--and no one had caught it. He caught Jeanine's gaze and responded to her flirty look with a strained smile. She'd caught his eye when he first got here. But not anymore. Too blatant. A few years ago, maybe. Not now. Now he appreciated subtlety and women who did not act like they would spread themselves over him at the slightest encouragement.

Like that assistant. Pretty woman. He'd been surprised he noticed her. She wasn't his type with all that curly hair and rather sixties manner of dressing. Linens and earth tones. But her brown eyes sparkled and she seemed to bring the light into a room with her.

With an inward roll of his eyes at his poetic thoughts, he walked back to his seat. Maybe it was time not to be so picky. He hadn't been on a date in almost a year.

Phyllis, the president of the advertising firm he'd just joined, clapped her hands to get everyone's attention.

"Thank you all. Looks like this one's a wrap." She gestured to the vacuum company guys who nodded and smiled. They must have indicated their approval while he chatted with the office help. He caught his boss's eye and she nodded toward the door, holding up all five fingers. Okay, he'd see her in her office in five minutes.

His pants didn't look all that bad, just a few dark spots. It was Friday after all and he had no other meetings. He could stay in these 'til he went home.

Phyllis joined him in the outer room of her suite.

"Come into the office." She waved him to a chair and shut the door. "So what did you think?"

"Of what? The presentation? Good work."

"Really?"

"Yeah. We could jazz up our presentation style a bit. But otherwise, I thought the team did well."

"I know what you mean. Can you help them with that?"

"Yeah. I was thinking we should do mock pitches a couple of days before they're actually due. Just to some of us in the office. I'll send a memo around. That is, unless…"

"No, its all yours." She laughed. "That's why I'm paying you the big bucks."

He grinned. She wasn't really. When Phyllis and her husband divorced, he kept all their major accounts and she split off and started her own ad firm. A year later, she was doing well but not great. He'd been looking for more of a challenge than managing the big corporate accounts he had at his last company. And so she negotiated with him--a share of the profits and free rein to whip her young team into shape. He took it and so far he'd enjoyed it. But it had only been three weeks.

"Just one thing," Vincent added. "That last still, where the model's on the sofa. He's not wearing a wedding ring. But the whole scene revolves around his married life--wife, kid, hearth and home."

"Good catch. This is exactly why I hired you. Well, the vacuum guys wouldn't have caught it, but if it had gone into production, someone might've complained."

He couldn't take the credit. There was far too much of that in this business anyway. "I didn't catch it, actually. It was that assistant."

"What assistant? Yours? You don't have one anymore."

"I didn't want an assistant who spent more time checking out her make-up and adjusting her neckline around me," he said mildly. "No, the one who served the food. The curly-haired one."

"Leena?"

He shrugged because he didn't know her name. "Maybe. Kind of earth mother look."

"That's Leena. Really? She caught it?"

He nodded. "Well, if that's all, I've got stuff to do."

Back in his office, he sorted through his mail wishing he had an assistant. Vince returned a few calls and began work on a new ad campaign for one of his own major accounts. The cosmetic company was marketing a set of skin-care products for the older woman.

He didn't hear Phyllis until she cleared her throat. Starting, he looked up from his computer.

"How's it going?"

"It would go a lot faster if I had an assistant. I've got two major campaigns to pitch."

"What do you want exactly?

"Just someone who wants to work. Efficient, quiet, gets the job done. Has some familiarity with the process of making ads."

She ran a hand through her short hair. "I may have a short-term solution. How about Leena?"

"Who's--. Oh, the office assistant?"

"She's sharp and all those other things. Try it out," she interjected before he could speak.

"A few weeks. She needs something full-time and would have left us if she didn't find it here. I don't know what her circumstances are, but I think she needs the money."

"Look, I don't want any baggage."

"Vince, just because she needs the salary doesn't mean she'll bring her baggage to you. If she even has any. Just try it."

It might be better than his current situation. "Okay. I'll try it but I'm making no promises."

"Great. She gets off at five. I'll tell her to stop by."

He nodded, got himself a soda from the little fridge under his desk and went back to work, trying to find his rhythm again. A few minutes or hours later--he never knew when he was buried in idea development--he heard a knock on the door.

That woman, the assistant, stood there. He couldn't remember her name but she looked so vulnerable that he stood to welcome her.

"Hi. I hear we're working together."

She nodded.

"Come in," he continued when she hovered at the door.

She stepped toward his desk. "We haven't been introduced. Leena Mackay."

"Vince Anderson." He wondered why she seemed so unsure. Then he remembered his reputation since he'd started working here. "Glad to have you to help me out." He sat back in his chair. "We can get started on Monday morning. I'm usually in before eight, but if you can't get in by eight?"

"Oh yes, of course I can. Thanks. And sorry about this afternoon."

"Forget it. No harm done." She stood by the corner of his desk, clutching an enormous shoulder bag. "Well, see you Monday then?"

"Oh, sure. Thanks again." She swung on her heel and he watched in horror as her bag caught his open soda can, knocking it over, spewing the contents across his desk.

Two

Leena marched into the ramshackle, old three-story house, slamming the door behind her. The cats, lying on the tiles in front of the fireplace, jumped up, squealing.

"Sorry guys. Didn't mean to startle you. Caaarly!"

She ran up the stairs as she yelled for her sister. "Carly, you come out here this minute. What the hell have you been doing?"

She burst into her sister's room without knocking, something she would never normally do. "Carly!" Today qualified as a grand exception.

Her sister's room looked like a storm had recently passed through. Books everywhere. Of course being a teenager she also had the requisite clothes on the floor.

"What?" asked Carly mildly.

Uh-oh. It wasn't a good sign when Carly went all meek.

"I want to know what you did last night."

"Slept?"

She failed to see the humor. "Carly, I'm warning you. I'm at the end of my rope here. Did you or did you not cast some sort of spell that went wrong?"

"Aw, man. It didn't work?"

She sat on the bed almost too angry to speak. Taking a couple of deep breaths, she told herself to calm down. Or

Carly would go into her stubborn mode and nothing would get accomplished. She expelled the air out through her mouth, slowly.

"Since I don't know what you were trying to accomplish, I can't say if it didn't work or not. Just tell me what you did. Please?" she pleaded.

Carly hefted herself against the headboard, eyeing her warily. Leena laid a hand on her sister's jean-clad ankle. "Just tell me, sweetie."

"Well, there was this spell."

Didn't it always start this way?

"What kind of spell?"

"One that made a person's natural tendencies come out strongly."

This was worse than she'd thought. "All their tendencies?"

"Er…yes. I think so. Anyway, I just tried it out on Puff. He said it was okay."

Carly had an uncanny knack of communicating with animals. Maybe the damn cat had really said it was okay.

"Honey, except I don't think it worked on him."

"Then why are you so mad?"

"Because, I'm pretty sure it worked on me!"

"Oh, man! I'm sorry, Leena. What happened?"

Leena gave her sister a pared down version of the day's events, starting with knocking the car's alignment off by hitting the pavement and the final event--spilling soda all over her new boss' desk.

Carly expressed contrition but she didn't know how to undo it. She did promise to look through the book of spells before dinner.

"Come down in about an hour. It won't be much-- pasta."

Leena walked downstairs and into the kitchen where the cats were already sitting expectantly by their bowls. She set some water to boil, fed the animals, and threw some penne pasta into the pot. After heating up some left over marinara sauce, she rummaged about and found some salad fixings. This may be the last time they had fresh vegetables for a while.

Any way she looked at it they were in deep trouble. Her jewelry business was sporadic. Maybe she would do better if she had more time to attend craft fairs and do more promotion. But with her two jobs, she couldn't afford the time. She needed the job to pay the mortgage and keep food on the table. But they'd managed until Mom had left for the commune. Without her mother's added income, the money she'd put aside to rent a small store in Garrison Square to sell her jewelry was now all gone.

Last week, after much soul searching, she came to the conclusion that she had to get a full time job with health insurance. What if something happened to Carly? Or to her? Phyllis was a godsend, offering her the full-time position at the firm. Although she wasn't so sure about her new boss. She wondered what he thought of her. Any redemption she made for spilling coffee on him by catching the omission in the ad shot got lost in the soda episode.

She wasn't that klutzy. It had to be Carly's spell that made her slight clumsiness exacerbate. Wondering what else it would enhance, she groaned and checked the pasta before collapsing on a chair.

Maybe someone would rent their apartment soon. The last person to come by--actually two young college students--hadn't worked out. They looked a little wild and she had a sixteen-year-old sister in the house to watch out for. So she told them she would check out their application but there were a few people ahead of them.

Was it a good idea to rent out a portion of their three-story house? She hashed it out with herself, just as she had with her neighbor, Gina. What other choice did she have? It would give them the extra income they so desperately needed.

She called to Carly to come down for dinner. Over their meal she confirmed, as expected, Carly didn't know how to reverse the spell. And, it would take about a week to wear off. She only hoped she still had her job by the time it did.

~ * ~

Vince strode down the driveway of his new house, pausing to take in the neighborhood. Still a little work to be done here. But for the most part, the old three-story, walk-up town homes were all rehabbed. Judging by the For Sale signs, the rest would catch up soon. He liked the quiet tree-lined street the minute he drove through. Two blocks of a quiet oasis in a city teeming with people and life.

Maybe he would check out the other homes before he went back to work. Settling his sunglasses on his face, he strolled down the street, taking in the bay windows and tiny gardens. Halfway down the block, he frowned at the ramshackle house on his right. Dingy brick and a sagging roof over the porch. They better get that fixed before winter. The garden however, was a riot of fall colors. A tree with dark red leaves leaned charmingly over a corner of the porch. In his mind's eye, he saw the place, spruced up, a fresh coat of paint over the front door, the railings replaced.

He stopped and stared at the For Rent sign. Should he? After all, he was on a month-to-month lease at his current Lakeshore condo. If he could rent this place for a few months, he could supervise the rehab on his house. He memorized the number and turned back toward his car. He would call them first and see what the situation was. From the car, he called the number and spoke to a young lady-- sounded like a teenager. She made arrangements with him to come by at three that afternoon. And she seemed to think that a six month lease would work.

At five to three he rang the bell as he glanced around the yard. The house was still sturdy. Structurally, it didn't need much work. Mostly cosmetic it seemed. No one answered and after a couple more rings he decided to walk around to the back. He heard the door open and swung back. No it couldn't be! Fate wouldn't be quite such a jokester.

~ * ~

Leena stared in dismay at Vince. What was he doing here? For one wild moment she thought her sister had done something again. Then she realized Carly didn't know Vince.

"Mr. Anderson? What are you doing here?"

He seemed to have difficulty speaking. "Er…that was my question, too. Please don't tell me you live here?"

"Yes, I do. But why is that a problem? Oh my God! Have you come about the rental? Oh no!"

Life wasn't getting any better. When Carly had said a potential renter was coming by, she hadn't bothered to ask his name. Dammit!

"I have."

"But why?" she wailed. "I'm sure you have a fancy place somewhere expensive."

He chuckled. "I do have a place. I don't know how fancy it is. May I come in?"

"Oh, sure." Feeling like she was letting in her doom, she stepped back and gestured for him to follow her. Why had she worn her oldest jeans and this old top today? Well, not because she expected her handsome boss--the one she spilled things on--to show up.

At least the house was neat, if old and worn. Waving him to a chair she sat, conscious of her torn jeans and stomach-baring little top. He, on the other hand, looked like he stepped out of the pages of GQ, in his khakis and green T-shirt. The color reflected in his eyes, making them brighter, more intense.

"Well. I'm not sure what to say."

He seemed amused. His mouth quirked up at one corner. "You could tell me about this apartment you're renting out. It is an apartment, correct?"

"It is. Well, of sorts. Two rooms and an attached bathroom. You would have to share the kitchen with us. I'm sure this wasn't what you were expecting. I'm sorry, Carly should have told you over the phone. My sister," she added. "That's who you spoke to."

"Wait a second, not so fast. I would like to see the rooms. Not having a kitchen wouldn't really bother me. I would just need to store some breakfast things, that's all. I eat out most of the time."

"Really?" When was the last time she had a meal outside? That wasn't fast food anyway. "I have to warn you, I have a sixteen-year-old sister, too. And she's a typical teenager." Why did she feel so compelled to warn him off?

"I was a teenager once." He shrugged and his engaging grin pulled a reluctant smile from her.

Sure, but had he been a witch-teenager from hell? She didn't think so. If he got wind of any weirdness about her, it could signify the end of her new job. Not something she should chance when they needed the extra money. Realizing he was waiting for an answer, she made a snap decision.

"Okay then. Let me show you around."

She pushed Puff away from the door where he sprawled and led him into the hall and around the stairs. "I have to warn you, my sister is currently using one of the rooms as her study. I'll fumigate…er…clean it before you come of course." Better watch her tongue. Who knew what kind of sense of humor he had.

"Of course." The laugh in his voice told her he appreciated the joke.

She led him into the small apartment-like section of the house. It even had a separate entrance but she'd have to fix the second step leading up to the door and clear away the weeds. Thank the gods that no witch paraphernalia lay around, just piles of books. She stepped to one side and let him inspect the rooms, even as she eyed the visible titles to make sure they didn't say something like *how to send a warlock to Uranus*. The apartment was pleasant enough and had often served as the base for their mother's long term visitors.

Leena tried to see it through his eyes. Bamboo shades covered the two large windows, one in either room. In the bedroom, a wrought iron queen sized bed dominated one corner while a rustic white dresser and matching bedside table took up the center wall. No closet but the large wardrobe with doors should suffice. The second room was smaller but included a wicker sofa and loveseat, a small TV and a bookshelf. Clean, but very basic.

He poked his head into the bathroom, then backed out to the second room where she waited. "If the price is still what your sister said, I'll take it."

Torn between elation and trepidation, she hesitated for a second or so. Was this wise? But she really didn't have time to weigh pros and cons anymore.

"The rent's the same. But can you tell me why you want to rent here?"

"I own a house down the road. Bought it about two months ago. But the workmen are there. Some renovations still need to be done. So this way, I can live in the neighborhood and be close by to check on things."

Reasonable explanation. "Which house did you buy?"

"Seven fourteen."

"The lovely place with the green door." Probably the color her face was--with envy. "When do you want the place?"

"By next weekend would be great. If that's okay with you?"

She sighed. No it really wasn't, but what was a gal with such debt to do?

"That's fine."

"So how about the lease? Should we go over it now or do you want to give it to me at work?"

The lease? Oh heavens, she hadn't even thought about that!

"How about I bring it in on Monday?"

And just like that she heard the doors clanging shut behind her; the click of the lock, and she knew there was no turning back. With a mental roll of her eyes at her doomsday prophecies, she gestured to him to lead the way out. Then, she wished she hadn't. This man had a backside view that would make a nun take notice.

"The kitchen's that way." She waved him to the left and tried not to eye that excellent behind. What was the matter with her? Must be hormonal. She refused to entertain the thought that Carly's spell was bringing out latent sexual needs. "This is it. Feel free to use the fridge, the stove, anything you want really. We try to each do our own dishes." She hesitated, then rushed in. "Carly and I try to have dinner together most nights. About seven. You're welcome to join us if you like." With his rent they would be eating a little better and she couldn't very well be having dinner when he was in the kitchen.

"Thanks. That's very generous of you. But I'm usually at business dinners and such. I might just stock up on breakfast things."

"Okay." She didn't know what else to say to him. And she had work to do. She started on a new line of jewelry today that she was hoping to market for Christmas.

Besides, he looked too good and her hormones were wondering what it felt like to touch him.

"Great. I'll see you at work then, bright and early. And no more spills, I hope."

She winced. "Sorry again. That was--."

"A mistake, I know. I was just teasing you."

~ * ~

Vince rubbed the back of his neck. The tension always seemed to gather right there. And he was plenty tense. They were launching two new accounts and he was going after the biggest account he'd had yet. He heard rumors that a well-known car manufacturer was not happy with their current advertising firm. He discussed it with Phyllis and they decided to go for it. It had taken calling in a lot of favors--he almost had no pink slips left with anyone--but they had a meeting with the car company two weeks out. Now he just had to get moved into Leena's little apartment, then he could concentrate on their presentation.

They decided to throw everything they had at the company. Three teams were working simultaneously to develop separate themes for the new branding. It was a gamble but he wanted to showcase the talent in the company.

He glanced at his watch--Eric was late. Dammit. He pressed speed dial on his cell phone.

"Hey, where are you?"

"Just leaving the house?" Eric sounded completely unrepentant for someone who was an hour late.

"Dammit, Eric!"

"What? You on some deadline to move? I thought we had the day."

They did. But Eric said he'd be there at ten and--he had to lighten up. Taking a deep breath, he said. "No deadline. But you did say ten."

"Oh hell, you should know that means eleven by now."

He should. How he stayed friends with Eric, as different as they were, was a mystery to everyone, including them.

"Just get here soon okay?"

They were going to unload some of his antique pieces at his new house and lock them in an upstairs room. And he needed Eric's truck for that.

Three hours later, Vince wiped his brow. This was it. All the furniture he wanted from his old place was upstairs in the house being refurbished. His clothes and computer and stuff were all in the apartment. Standing on the wood step by the outside entrance to his little place, he waved Eric off. The stair looked newly repaired but not too sturdy. He might have to take a hammer and a few more nails to it.

Wondering where his landlady was, he locked up and drove to the grocery store. Better get everything he needed, then settle down to work. Leena gave him the lease--one that looked suspiciously like one of those free ones you downloaded off the internet--last week. He signed for six months and she looked surprised. Maybe she wanted a year's commitment but he hated going into something for that long without really testing out the situation.

She hadn't said anything, just made herself a copy and gave it back to him. All week, she'd been calmly efficient if a bit tentative. There were times he wanted to tell her to snap out of it--that he wasn't going to bite her. And others when he wanted to do just that--grab her close and bite softly on that turned up, stubborn chin of hers before kissing her senseless.

Vince had never really been attracted to someone like her before and he couldn't explain it. Maybe it was the quiet intelligence behind her questions, or that way she had of cocking her head to one side and looking at him through a tangle of hair. Just once, last Wednesday, he stepped back from bending over her sketches and knocked into her. When he steadied her with his hand, he got a fist full of the silkiest curls he'd ever touched. It took all his control not to slide his fingers against her scalp and--.

He grimaced and cut his thinking short. The biggest project of his life was waiting completion and here he was mooning over his assistant. Like any gauche teenager.

Wow! A parking spot right in front of her house. He pulled in and unloaded his groceries. Still no sign of Leena or her sister. A nice-looking woman, with red waist length curls, had waved to him earlier from the house to the right. Other than that, no sign of any life. He supposed the cats were around somewhere, too. He chuckled as he remembered their names--Puff 'n Stuff.

He met the sister, Carly, a couple of times during the week, when he stopped by with some things. A cute teenager, she hadn't said much the first time, but asked a lot of personal questions the next. Like was he married, did he have a girlfriend, did he like cats? He put it down to her age and answered, no, no, and yes.

The two enormous cats lay sprawled on the kitchen floor. Neither deigned to do more than raise their heads to look at him. He stepped over them gingerly, put his beer and milk in the fridge and noted how empty the shelves were. The pantry door stood ajar making it easy to figure out where to store his cereal.

Trying to get a response from the cats was like dragging a truck with a rope. Impossible. They simply flicked the ends of their tails and ignored him. He wandered back to his rooms and settled down with his laptop, jotting down ideas for his team's ad campaign. Each team had three people, and each was to come up with an ad for the two new cars to be launched. His job, in addition to his ad, would be to give a killer presentation that tied it all into one long-term ad campaign.

Doors slammed above him then footsteps thundered down the stairs. The murmur of voices passed his door but he ignored them. Let Leena come find him if she liked. He wouldn't seek out her distracting presence.

At six, he took a break and stretched. It was slow going and he just wasn't inspired. Maybe he should go for a run. Or better yet, grab a beer and watch the game for a while.

Vince walked into the kitchen wondering if they'd left again. He hadn't heard anyone in the house for a while. The damn cat--one of them anyway--lay across the doorway and he stumbled so as not to step on it. Stifling a curse he hopped into the room and stopped short.

Leena sat with her head on the breakfast table, her pose one of utter dejection. A smothered sob confirmed she was crying. What the hell?

"Er…sorry. I'll come back." He tried to back out in haste not wanting any of her hassles. But she raised her head and looked at him. Sucker that he was, he couldn't leave after seeing those tear-drenched eyes. He sighed and stopped his retreat. "What's wrong?"

"Oh, I'm sorry. I didn't realize--nothing--I mean--just a bad day." She fumbled in her bag for something and pulled out a ragged tissue and wiped her eyes. "Please get what you need. I was leaving anyway."

He moved to block her headlong rush out of the room. "Leena, tell me what's wrong. Maybe I can help. Maybe I can't, but you might feel better if you talked to someone."

All Vince wanted to do was take her in his arms and hold her close. Wanted to make all the bad stuff go away, make her smile again. That desire hit him with the force of a defensive-back's tackle and he almost reeled. Whoa! How did this woman make him feel like this?

"I can't. I mean--you can't help."

Her doleful sniff wrung his heart. "Come here." Almost propelled by a force outside him, he reached for her slowly. She gazed at him with wide eyes but didn't back away. Vince pulled her close and cradled her head against his chest. He needed this like he needed a bout of the flu right now. But he couldn't help himself.

Like he'd come home after a long, hungry stint away, his body relaxed around hers, curving around her in protection. His fingers rifled through her curls as he made soothing noises. She didn't move away, but his hug seemed to have set her off again because she cried for a few more minutes before giving a couple of choking sobs. Her arms crept around him and he couldn't deny the sense of rightness about holding her like this, comforting her.

He soon became aware of the softness of the body he held; the curve of her waist where his hand rested; the spicy-flowery scent of her hair. Her warm breath tickled his skin where his polo neck T-shirt lay open. Yielding breasts pressed against his chest and the stirring in his pants told him he was headed for full mast.

Three

Leena's awareness of the strong, hard body curved around her grew every second. Slowly, like the delicious feeling of wakefulness after a long night's sleep, her body awoke to the nuances of his muscled chest, so comforting. The solid feel of his arms around her. How long had it been since she'd been held like this? Like there was someone to share the burden with her, someone to take care of her.

Dangerous territory her mind warned. But her heart, savoring the feeling of being cared for, refused to listen. She held her body still, afraid to breathe too hard, afraid to move, in case it broke the spell. Her arms began to ache with the strain of holding them lightly against his broad back.

Vince spoke into her hair, his breath warming her scalp. "You okay?"

She nodded, not trusting herself to speak. Relishing the sensual awakening of her own body in reaction to his, she moved infinitesimally closer and stifled a gasp. He was aroused! A most impressive bulge nudged her stomach.

"See? I told you you'd feel better if you told me about it," his deep drawl rumbled through the chest so close to her face.

Of course it felt better. Especially with the evidence of his want so clear. Telling him only--. *Telling him*?

Damn, I haven't told him yet.

And when he found out, she doubted their little interlude would continue. She pulled back with a sigh about the same time he stirred. Looking up into his face was her first mistake. Her second was looking into his eyes. More green than hazel, his gaze captured hers, full of hot desire and illicit temptation. Witch or not, she was still human and no human gal could resist that look. Not when she hadn't had sex in over five years.

Primal instinct took over and she rose on tiptoe even as he bent his head. Their lips met; his warm and firm, moving with slight pressure over hers. A wave of lassitude swept over her; she sagged against him. Little shards of sensation that began in her face shot down her neck and chest. The big hand on her waist slid up and his fingers brushed the outer curve of her breast. More warmth turning into heat spread through her torso and limbs until they all honed in on her secret core. Moisture seeped in blatant response to his coaxing mouth and clever hands.

Never had a kiss affected her quite like this. The thought bounced around somewhere in a coherent corner of her mind. What would happen if he used his tongue?

As if he heard her, Vince flicked the tip of his tongue over the part of her lips. She opened to him as naturally as a flower to the morning dew. With a little grunt of satisfaction, he entered her mouth. Her senses swam, every nerve ending singing in response to the rhythm he set. She met him stroke for stroke, bolder than she'd ever been in her life.

Leena's aching calves reminded her she was on tiptoe and she tried to find a more comfortable position. Still in tune with her, still kissing her, Vince walked backward and sank into a chair, pulling her sideways onto his lap.

Utter bliss. She cuddled closer, running her fingers through his wavy brown hair. She luxuriated in the feel of his broad shoulders beneath her hands. At last he pulled back from the kiss, leaving her bereft. But only for a second. In the next instant, he buried his face in the curve of her neck and brushed his thumbs over her nipples. Leena couldn't stop the shudder that raced through her as she arched her back so her breasts pressed into him.

Wanton? Oh yes! Never had losing control felt so good. Never had the rewards for being bad been quite so fantastic. It seemed like a fantasy coming true. After a week of working with him and lusting after him, what a prize!

He mumbled something against her neck and she focused on the sensation of his warm breath on her skin. Then with something like a sigh, he drew back a bit until she could see his face. The look he gave called to her, like a moth to a flame. The open hunger, the sheer confidence that his desire was returned was a heady combination. It may have been five years since she'd experienced this, but she hadn't forgotten the feelings; the rush of desire. She caught his look and returned it, emboldened by the feel of his erection against her and his slightly ragged breathing.

"This wasn't what I planned when I tried to comfort you," he said.

"I know." And she did know that.

"But it's happened and I don't know what to do."

"I would have thought you'd know. Don't tell me you need instruction?" She listened to herself as if in a dream. Where was she getting the courage to say all this?

He chuckled. "No thanks. I'm well-versed in what comes next. What I don't know is if you are."

Did he think she was that inexperienced? Embarrassed, she tried to pull back but Vince held her fast, his hands linking behind her back. "I don't mean what you're thinking. I meant are you ready for the next step?"

She nodded, mute, not trusting her voice. The next step. Did he mean more kissing, more--. Oh, *that* next step. Was she ready? She met his gaze and knew in that instant she'd be a fool to turn down what she knew would be the best sex of her life.

"Tell me," he ordered in a soft voice, never taking his gaze off her.

"I'm," she cleared her throat. Great, she sounded like a frog telling him to have sex with her. "I'm ready."

"No regrets?" His eyes bored into hers.

"None." Well, she may have some but she suspected they would have to do with not being able to do this again.

Vince leaned back in the chair, bringing her toward him with his hold. "Take off your shirt."

"What?" Startled she dropped her hands from his shoulders.

"Unbutton your shirt for me." His voice dropped a notch with the demand.

Hesitant, yet driven by a demon she could not name, her hands moved to her top button and she undid the first, then the next. Vince brought one hand to her face and traced a gentle line over her cheek with his thumb. The gentle caress spurred her on.

Still holding his hot gaze, she undid the third one and his finger traced a line over her lips. She flicked out her tongue and caught the tip of his index finger. His eyes went from hot to molten green in an instant. Gratified by his response, Leena undid the fourth button knowing her breasts and her bra would be visible. She glanced down, glad she'd worn one of her lacy black bras. When she looked up again, his eyes had dropped to her chest.

With a boldness she didn't know she possessed, she quickly unbuttoned her shirt all the way and pulled the ends open. She couldn't see his look, but his breathing quickened. He slid the material off her shoulders, caressing the bare skin he exposed. Leena felt that touch in every nerve ending, all the way to the center between her legs. She wanted to clamp them together to stop the tingling.

"Now the bra. Unhook it." His rough whisper compelled her response.

Not allowing herself to think, she slid the front hook apart and her breasts sprang free. She sensed rather than heard his swift intake of breath. God, it felt good to rouse this man, to make him want her.

"Beautiful. Just like I knew they'd be."

He'd been thinking about her breasts?

Giving her no time to process the remark, his hands grabbed hers and moved them under her breasts. With his fingers beneath hers, he made her cup them and lift them up. Like an offering to him. The sensation of her own hands and his on her flesh sent shivers down her spine. She shifted on his lap and he removed one hand to slide it under her thigh and tug it over his hips. With all her focus on the flick of his thumb over her nipple, she automatically straddled him, her free hand sliding under his tee to warm itself on the smooth skin of his back.

She barely registered his fingers sliding under the elastic waistband of her pants and over her tush. How could she when he hefted her breast higher, capturing the tip in his mouth, his teeth worrying the aureole gently? She moaned as she arched further into his mouth, wanting more than this teasing touch. He took the hint and closed his lips around her lightly. She wanted more, she wanted hard. So she pushed against him and this time he took her fully into his mouth, suckling deep. She almost sobbed from the relief and the sensations that washed over her.

Her own hands roved over his back and her hips started a rhythm all their own. It was only when Vince released her breast and began kissing his way over to the other one that she realized his fingers had slid all the way to her moist entrance. His palm firm against her bottom, he followed the dance of her hips. He clamped down on her nipple and at the same time, slid a finger up her slick passage.

The way his hand pressed down on her brought her firm against his own bulging desire. He parted her folds ever so gently and she squirmed, wanting more. Just as he'd known her desires before, he seemed to sense them now. His tongue circled her nipple and two fingers stroked, now deep, now shallow, almost slipping out in the wet evidence of her own desire. She bucked her hips against him, clutching his shoulders. Vince stroked faster.

He let her nipple go and growled, "That's it, baby. Show me what you want."

And she did. With no other thought but the need to do as he asked, she tightened her thighs around him. "Vince…" she panted.

"Let go, babe. I'm here to catch you."

No one had ever said that to her before. All her being narrowed to the area between her legs as he found the crest of her craving and rubbed. Secure in the knowledge he was there, she stepped off the mountain and cried out at the incredible sensation of free falling. When thought returned, he was guiding her back to earth, his lips on hers, one arm wrapped around her body, holding her tight and close.

~ * ~

Vince couldn't remember the last time he'd made out like this. He liked his sex, long, hard and with an edge. But for the longest time, he'd lapsed into the mundane. A date, a kiss, a roll in the bed. Even the last long relationship he had for almost a year--a record for him as Eric would say-- had gotten boring toward the end. But this! This brought back the old excitement, the sheer joy of having a woman wrapped around him, wanting him with every fiber of her being, wanting him now and always. He pushed that last thought away. What a strange thought during his best sex in years. And they had only just begun.

Her hair tickled his nose as she burrowed her face into his neck and he tried to stifle his sneeze but couldn't. He did manage to turn his face away from her.

"Damn. Excuse me," he mumbled.

"Bless you." Her breath slid along his neck, sending little tentacles of sensation wandering down his chest and to his groin.

He smoothed her hair down on top of her head and she sat up. The movement brought their hips aligned closer. And of course his throbbing sex responded with all the vigor a man could hope for. Vince framed her head in his hands, pushing her curls flat.

"Sorry, your hair--."

"I know," she interrupted. "If I thought it would lay back down I would cut it."

"Don't. It suits you." Besides making his libido twitch every time she let it down.

Leena dislodged his hands and gathered her hair in a knot at the back of her head. One twist and it settled in a bundle low on her neck. Better this way. When they were in bed, however, he wanted to see it spread over his pillow. But right now he cared for nothing except taking this to its natural conclusion.

Linking his fingers with hers, he brought his face close. That dreamy look in her eyes, the mark of a woman sated, made him want to make it happen again and again. This time however, her mouth reached for him, her lips feathering over his until he captured them in a hard kiss. The warm, honeyed taste called to him, heady, inviting him to take more and more.

They broke the kiss to allow her to pull his T-shirt over his head. The soft swell of her breasts pressed into his chest and the lace of her bra scratched a nipple. More than anything, he wanted to shuck his clothes and lower her slowly onto him, already knowing how he would slip and slide in all that wetness.

He fought to control the storm raging inside, wanting her as ready as he was. Leena rode the rising crest of his desire with him, her hands searching over his stomach, tugging at the elastic waistband of his gym shorts. Needing some leverage to raise up so she could slip them off, he braced an elbow against the table. Giving silent thanks for all the push-ups he did, Vince raised his hips and almost lost his balance as a door slammed and a voice called out for Leena.

Damn! He threw a desperate glance at the open kitchen door. No way would either of them get to it before her sister came in. And then, as he watched, the door slowly closed shut. His jaw dropped. What a lucky breeze to show up at this moment. Somewhere in the back of his mind, a thought fought to make its way to his consciousness. No wind ever shut a door with such deliberation. The soft click of the latch galvanized him just as Leena scrambled off his lap.

"Ouch." She must have hit something on the chair.

"What the hell?"

"Get dressed," she hissed at him.

He looked around for his tee and found it under the chair. She had her bra clipped and buttoned her shirt, cursing softly. He had just managed to pull his shirt on when Carly tried the door handle.

"Hey! What's with the door? Why is it locked?" she called out.

"It's not." Leena moved to open it and faced her sister. "You know how it sticks sometimes."

"It does? I didn't know that." Carly pushed her way in. "Lee, you'll never guess. I talked to Gina and she said I had to--." She saw Vince and stopped. "Oh!"

Turning to her sister who was busy stacking some papers on the breakfast table, she grinned in a way that made her look about ten. "Oh, I see. That's why the door was stuck."

They both hastened to correct her.

"What do--," Leena questioned.

"The wind--."

Carly held up a hand, palm out. "Oh, puhleeze. I'm sixteen, not six. I've had sex ed."

Leena sputtered as Carly continued. "Just use one of the other rooms next time and you won't get interrupted. Anyway, this is great. You're both here, so I only need to say this once. Gina said--. Wait a minute." She turned to Vince. "Did you say the breeze shut the door?"

He nodded in the face of the little whirlwind facing him. "That means you--." Carly turned to Leena, her curls bouncing every which way as she gave a little hop. "That means you did it. You used your powers. You're back. Oh, Lee, I'm so excited." She fell on her sister hugging her, talking all the while.

Vince gaped as Leena tried to extricate herself. Then Carly's continued words penetrated the fog that seemed to envelop him.

"Your powers," Carly said. "You used them at last. Does this mean you'll teach me? Now you can undo that awful spell I cast on both of you."

What in the hell was she talking about? Was she saying *Spell*? As in witches and stuff like that? *Spell*? He ran his hands through his hair in frustration.

"Carly, stop." Leena pulled herself free, sheer panic on her face. "You don't know what you're talking about."

"What's the matter? Gina said it would only work if you two were meant to be together and looks like you are. You were making out, weren't you?"

Leena let out a groan like a wounded animal. "Carly, shut up. Vince I'm sorry, she's just trying to irritate me with one of her make-believe lies. She does that you know."

"Oh come on, Sis. How long can you hide this?"

"Carly, I'm warning you--."

Vince found his voice. "Would someone tell me what the hell is going on?" He felt like he'd entered the twilight zone. They continued arguing, oblivious to him. "Hey!" He smacked a hand down on the table. They both jumped and fell silent. "That's better. Now, what the hell just happened here?"

Leena looked at him, her eyes huge and stricken, as if he'd hit her instead of the table. He shoved aside the guilt at making her look that way. "What," he enunciated every word, "is going on?"

Leena's throat worked but the only sound that came from her was a groan.

"Carly? Want to try explaining?"

"Er...Lee?" She turned to her sister, questioning.

Leena found her voice. "Just tell him how you like to pretend."

Carly rolled her eyes.

"No, I don't think so, Leena. I want to know exactly what she meant by casting spells and how that damn door shut. And what she meant by you using your power. Sit," he ordered the two of them, waving to the chairs. Then, softening his voice when they both flinched, he added. "Let's talk about this calmly, okay?"

They both sat, although he suspected Leena did it more for her own sake than because he ordered her to. She looked ready to collapse. He took a step toward her then checked himself. First they had to sort this out.

Vince propped a foot on the bottom rung of the chair nearest him, leaning an arm on his knee. "Okay, any time you're ready."

Carly looked mutinous like only a teenager could, and Leena sat there looking like her world was crashing about her ears. What was wrong with them? Of the two, he figured he could break Carly faster. So he turned on the charm, that famous persuasion that won him some prime accounts.

"Carly, I can tell you came in here with some news. Something about a…a spell?" He felt stupid even saying it. And I know I saw that door shut without a da-- any wind around." He gave her a slight smile. "And you're right. Your sister and I were…getting to know each other a little better." He ignored the choked sound from Leena. "We've just started working together and we have the biggest presentation our company has ever done coming up in a couple of weeks. I thought some time talking in a more causal setting would help us work together better. I was just getting myself a beer." He walked to the fridge and paused. "Leena, how about you?"

"God, yes please," she choked out.

Vince twisted the caps off two bottles and brought one to her. "So, Carly, what did Gina tell you?" When she didn't answer, he smiled at her. "Look, I just want to understand what's going on. How can I help if I don't know what's happening?"

"Really? You want to help?"

"Yes. It's what I was trying to do earlier with Leena."

"Okay then." She cocked her head to one side in a gesture so like her sister he almost laughed. But he mistrusted the calculating look in her eyes. "Did you pay a deposit?"

He blinked at the change in subject. "Deposit?"

"Yeah, like when you signed the lease. Gina told me we should have asked for a deposit."

He was getting a little tired of *Gina said*. Actually though, he had wondered about that but hadn't thought it his job to ask. "So?"

"So, I think you should pay us one." They needed money--that much was clear. Given the dilapidated condition of the house and renting out rooms.

"Okay. It's usually one month's rent. That okay with you?"

"Yes." She eyed him. "Can I trust you?"

He met her look evenly, held her gaze. "Yes."

Leena might have moaned again but he couldn't be sure. He was almost enjoying sparring with this spunky girl. After a moment of studying him she nodded. "Okay."

"So, now you'll tell me what's going on?"

"Yeah."

He sighed, holding onto his temper. "So talk."

"Carly, don't. I can't afford to lose this job," interjected Leena.

"Its okay," she assured her sister. "I've found us work." Carly turned back to Vince.

"You see, we're witches."

Four

Whatever Vince expected it wasn't that.

"You're what?" He shot a glance at Leena but she had her head buried in her hands.

It was Carly who answered. "You heard me. We're witches. Only, Leena doesn't want to be one. She says I shouldn't either. But we have to find a way to make our payments. And that's why Leena has to take a full time job and give up on her jewelry business."

He latched onto the only thing that made any sense. "Payments?"

This time it was Leena who answered. "Mortgage payments. We're about to lose the house. That's why I was upset when you came in. That and--."

"You're kidding right?" Vince replied.

"I don't kid about money, Vince. Believe me," she snapped.

"Not the money. About this…this witch thing."

"I wish I was. Nope, this is the real deal."

He had to sit. "There's no such thing. As witches I mean. Do you guys think you belong to some WICCA group?" That had to be it. They, for some odd reason, wanted to be known as witches.

"We don't belong to a conclave. No WICCA, nothing. Because she won't let us." Exasperation tinged Carly's tone.

"That's right. Because all it's brought us is grief. And you should be focusing on your studies, getting a professional degree so you won't struggle like we have," Leena shot back at her sister. "Carly, go upstairs please. Vince and I need to talk this through."

For a minute he thought Carly would rebel, but she caved under her sister's steady look. "Okay, but Gina said--."

"Tell me later," interrupted Leena. "Now please just go."

"Don't forget that deposit." Carly pointed a finger at him and he just managed to stop himself saluting. Even with all her weirdness, the kid was likable. So he grinned and waved at her.

He turned to find Leena watching him, eyes wary. A part of him wanted to dismiss it all as imagination. But she was too serious, too solemn. If it had only been Carly, he might have been inclined to shrug it off. But Leena's reaction gave it a ring of authenticity. Still it was too fantastic to believe.

"So what's this really about?"

"Just what I told you, Vince. Witchery, witches, the paranormal, call it what you want. It's still the same thing. Carly and I were born witches. When I was younger I actually believed in my calling. But now it's all I can do to make ends meet. That's why I took the full time job and rented the rooms to you."

Something jogged his memory. "Earlier you said something about the mortgage payments upset you. And something else but you didn't finish. What was that?"

She took a deep breath, needing to fortify herself it seemed. Fidgeting with the papers on the table, she mumbled, "Your car."

"What about my car?"

"Oh hell. I hit it as I tried to park behind you."

His Beamer. She hit his Beamer! With an effort, he controlled his rising anger. "How bad?"

"Bad enough. I hit the back fender, broke the light. Don't worry, I have insurance." She looked at him and he willed himself to ignore that hesitant look. Part of him wanted to say it was all right, while another side seemed to be getting madder by the minute.

"Okay, we'll deal with that in a minute. Now what was that Carly said about casting spells? Did she do something to me? Come to think of it, I've felt weird all week." *Not as weird as calmly discussing being a witch with his landlady.*

"God, I hope not. She's been practicing spell casting. Obviously she has no idea what she's doing. She cast some sort of spell on the cat but it backfired and hit me. That's why I've been so nervous all week, spilling things. I bet it's why I hit your car, too."

There it came--the excuses. It wasn't my fault.

"Sure," he drawled. "So what did she do to me?"

"I have no idea. We'll have to ask her. If I know anything about her, she's hovering in the hallway. Carly," she called out. "Get in here please."

Carly slipped in confirming she'd been hiding outside the door. "What?"

"What did you do to Vince?"

"Noth--." Again that steady look from her sister. "Okay, okay. Stop giving me that look. I thought you guys would make a good match, so...so I...." Her courage seemed to fail her.

"Its okay, honey. Just tell me. I'll fix it." Leena obviously knew how to get her sister to talk.

"Well, I cast a joining spell."

"Oh no!"

What the hell was that? Leena's reaction alarmed him even more. "What is that?" he asked, his voice rising in panic.

"A joining spell is kind of a love potion type of spell. It's supposed to make two people...er...wan--I mean, desire each other."

Her trepidation took on a whole new meaning. "You mean--." He broke off, not knowing how to phrase what they had done in front of the teenager.

"It worked, didn't it? I knew it. You guys were making out weren't you?"

"Carly, go to your room."

"Carly, you should leave."

They spoke in unison and she looked at them in disgust. "Great. Gang up on me. I'll be up in my room."

"Really in your room this time, not behind the door," Leena said.

Carly huffed her way out the door and thumped up the stairs, talking, presumably to herself.

Vince took a long swig of his beer, wishing he had something stronger. "So all that earlier was because she cast some love spell on me?" That explained his strong attraction to someone not his type. The surge of anger became stronger.

"I'm not sure what she did. Until I talk to her I can't say for sure. But--"

"So what, Leena? Did you add something to what she did? So I'd sleep with you? Forget you hit my car? Maybe pay you more money in rent?"

He hated being manipulated. Loathed the thought that someone had controlled his actions. If such a thing was even possible. Maybe she had planned this all along? Righteous anger filled him and he went with it. "Too bad it didn't work. I'll expect your insurance information in the morning. You'll have to find some other sucker, Leena."

Ignoring the stricken look on her face, he stalked out the door.

~ * ~

Leena trudged wearily up the stairs to her sister's room. She had no time to process what Vince said, his reaction. All she knew was the incredible sense of loss and shame that pervaded her being. How could she have been so cheap? And that's what it felt like. Having sex with him on the kitchen chair. She quelled the excitement that threatened to take over as she remembered the sensations of being on his lap, coming apart in his arms. She'd never acted that way before. Did it have something to do with Carly's spell? There was only one way to find out.

Their mother had had affairs and jaunted about town with little regard for two impressionable girls at home. When she began going away for days on end, Leena had become both mom and sister to Carly. They were close but she hadn't been able to curb Carly's enthusiasm for their heritage. She, on the other hand, wanted them to have a normal life, wanted Carly to grow up and have a real job. Something professional so her sister would be financially secure. Unlike Leena herself, who hadn't been able to go to college. She sighed as the wisps of dreams long buried teased the corners of her mind.

Carly sat against the headboard in her familiar pose, her expression half-mutinous, half-scared.

"Oh, honey. Come here." Leena didn't have it in her to yell at her sister. After all, Carly thought she was helping. In Carly's mind, learning to use her powers would solve all their problems.

Her sister hugged her, choking back a sob. "I didn't mean to mess things up. I really didn't."

"I know, baby, I know. You want to help." She'd reserve her lecture for later.

Once Carly stopped crying, Leena settled back on the foot of the bed and asked. "So tell me everything you did. Start from the time of the first spell last week."

"Okay. Well, you know about that. After that, I didn't do anything. I couldn't find a way to reverse it. Then I met Vince last week--he came over a couple of times to drop things off. And he was, like, so nice. I thought he made a good match for you."

"Why do you think I need to be paired up with someone?"

"You're unhappy all the time. I can see it. You worry about the money and the house and me. I thought you should have someone to take care of you."

Leena agreed in theory. Not so much about being taken care of, but how nice it would be to have someone to lean on, to laugh with, have great sex with. A vision of Vince, caring and hot, looking at her as he held her hair back, came unbidden to mind. She blinked to clear her head.

"It's not for you to choose someone for me, Carly. It has to happen naturally. Spells like this don't last. Not unless people have an attraction for each other and are…are suited to each other. Vince and I, we're very different people. He's a big time ad executive. Do you know the kind of people he has dinners with?"

Carly shook her head. "Well, they're big time, too. And I would never fit with that kind of life."

"But you guys were making out, weren't you?"

Leena sighed. How to circumvent this one? "We weren't making out." She waited a second for the proverbial lightening to strike. "We kissed, that's all." No way was she telling Carly what actually happened in there. "And it was most likely because of your spell. Nothing else. I have to work with the man. And we really need the money from this job. It even has health insurance benefits. Do you know what that means? It means we can sit back a bit and not worry as much about how to get things paid. Besides, what if he decides to break his lease? We don't have the money to sue him or anything. And boy, do we need that rent money right now." She decided to leave the issue of the deposit alone. If he paid it, it would be a great help. If not, she'd muddle along like she had in the past.

But first she had to get Carly to stop trying out spells. She knew her sister well enough to realize that a simple request would not work. Carly was stubborn as they came. And those damn cats probably encouraged her.

"Carly, I want to make a deal with you. I want you to stop spell casting during the school year. In the summers, I'll work with you. If you finish high school, you can apprentice with someone. Someone who knows more than I do."

Carly mulled it over, cocking her head to one side and chewing her lower lip. "Why can't I just apprentice with you?"

"Because I never had any strong formal training. If you want to do this right, you have to learn from someone really good." Unlike their mother, she silently added. She'd always been careful not to denigrate Mom in front of Carly. They rarely discussed their mother anymore and she had no idea of how Carly really felt. "Is it a deal, Carly?"

"I know someone I can learn from."

"Good." No way was she going to get side-tracked without extracting a promise from her sister. "But first, tell me you promise?"

"Every summer 'til I finish school? That's three whole summers."

"Yes, every summer."

"Okay."

"Okay, what?"

"Okay, I promise not to spell cast during school."

"And in the summers you'll only do it with me."

Carly let out an exaggerated sigh. "Okay. I promise that, too."

"Good. Now get your homework or whatever done. Didn't you say you had an English paper due?"

"History. And I already did it. You read it Friday night, remember." Carly gave her classic roll of the eyes.

"So you did. Okay." Leena stood and stretched. "Well, I have to go look through the books and figure out how to reverse these spells."

"I'll come with you." Carly scrambled off the bed. "I promise I won't do anything. I'll just watch."

Leena hesitated.

"Please?" Carly added. "What's the harm?"

"Oh, okay." The harm had to do with the fact that she hadn't used her powers in over three years. And here she was doing it twice in one day. At least Carly had forgotten about the kitchen door incident.

Carly trailed her to the room that had been their mother's workroom. Leena dusted off the *Spell Work Book* and the *Book of Powers*. She instructed Carly to find the spell she had cast while she sat down to refresh her memory about using her powers. Calling forth her witch-side negated any chance of a normal relationship with Vince. They were worlds apart. The dark, cursive writing blurred as tears filled her eyes and she swiped at them in irritation. Had she ever had a chance with him? It was just one sexual interlude.

"Lee?" Carly's hesitant voice pulled her back from the abyss of self-pity she was about to enter. "If you're upset that you don't know how to do it, I know someone who can help."

All thoughts of Vince and his sexy hands flew out of her mind. "Who? And how do you know someone like this anyway?" Panic threatened to take over. Who had Carly been talking to? There were all sorts of insane witches and warlocks and demons out there.

"Gina."

"Who's Gina? Wait, *Gina*? As in next door? What the hell did you do now, Carly?"

"Okay, before you blow up, just hear me out. I talked to Gina. They're witches, too. Her whole family. She said she could help but that you needed to talk to her first."

Leena slumped back in her chair. "And why were you talking to her about this?"

"I sensed it, that she knew magic, I mean. And Puff 'n Stuff agreed. So I just asked her about it."

"You mean you just marched up to our nice neighbor and asked her if she was a witch?"

"Duh, no! I talked about magic and witches and finally Gina asked if there was something specific I wanted to know. And that's how it happened. And she was much nicer about it than you," finished Carly, her posture defiant.

"Sorry." Leena knew she'd been very irritable with Carly recently. "What kind of witch is she?"

"I don't really know. She said something about Tier One?"

Leena whistled. Tier One witches were very powerful and usually born into the line. Their mother had been a Tier

Three and Leena herself had progressed enough to enter Tier Two, but never had.

"What exactly did she say?"

"She asked me to bring you over tonight. That's what I was trying to tell you when you locked me out of the kitchen." Carly's dark eyes flashed in triumph.

While she may not entirely trust Carly's intuition just yet, the cats she did trust. Leena shook her head. "Fine, let's go then." How wonderful if someone could extricate them from this mess.

Leena traced her sister's footsteps to Gina's house next door, lagging as doubts assailed her. There was no sign of Vince though the lights were on in his room. She heard him go out and back in. Must have checked on his car. Maybe it wouldn't be so bad, she consoled herself.

Gina opened the door looking beautiful as always. Her green sweater, the neckline dipping low in front should have clashed with her red hair but didn't.

"Hi, you two. I'm so glad you came. I was worried when I didn't hear back from Carly." Her husky voice ended in a laugh.

"We had to sort some things out." Leena hesitated, her innate cautious nature not letting her trust completely.

"Of course, of course. Come in."

"If it isn't too late--"

"God, no! It's Sunday night. I'm at home and bored out of my wits. Besides it's only nine."

She led them through the living room. Leena caught glimpses of an attractive arrangement of a futon and chairs and a gleaming coffee table before they walked into what was obviously a study.

"I thought this might be more comfortable." Gina waved them to a brown leather sofa. "Please sit."

Carly and she sat side-by-side, with Gina on a loveseat opposite them. "Tell me how I can help."

~ * ~

Leena crept into the house trying not to wake the cats or anyone else. Exhausted after the bout at Gina's house, she had one more thing to take care of before she crawled into bed. Carly had been sent to bed a while back. Once Gina confirmed the story with Leena, she suggested Carly leave them alone. When Carly protested, Gina firmly informed the teenager there were real and serious consequences to using magic negatively. And that she thought Carly should take some time to think about those consequences.

Leena wished she could deal with Carly as effectively. Of course it helped that her stubborn sister stood in some awe of Gina, who did turn out to be a Tier One witch from a long line of powerful witches. Carly had left and Gina helped Leena reverse the spells. At least she watched as Gina did most of the work. But she'd been called on to use her rusty powers and concentrate, add her energies to Gina's as they called the working spell back.

They first handled the spell Carly had cast on Leena. They made it turn back its course. That was easier because Carly had it so jumbled it had no real coherent force. Gina directed its energy pattern to a rabbit haunting the tiny vegetable garden in her backyard. Then they focused on the joining spell. This once was much harder. It seemed like something held it back, not releasing it.

Gina said it could be Vince's own feelings were now so entangled that it made it harder to call the spell. Or that something else was involved. Because it didn't send any malevolent signals back, Gina decided to ignore it. She thought they were successful but there really was no way to tell until she met Vince and observed his reactions. And Leena wanted to see him like she wanted Carly to cast another spell!

She wrote her car insurance information on a piece of paper and scribbled a note with it:

> *I'll have the insurance company contact you tomorrow. But just in case, here's the information. Sorry--Leena.*

She debated about adding the apology then figured he deserved it. A light shone from the space under his door. She bent and slid the white envelope through. She waited by the door. First, the creak of a chair, followed by footsteps toward her. He must have moved to pick it up. No further sound followed, no opening of the door, no opportunity to see him again.

She swallowed a sob and fled up the stairs. Once under the covers, the tears came hot and hard and for a long, long time.

> *Cupid stood in the shadows, watching the girl sleep, the stain of tears still on her cheek. He tried to keep that damn spell with Vince, but they'd been strong and he knew they would just keep trying, so he let it go. So they were as different as...as night and*

day. But his arrows had found them. By Jove, why couldn't humans just do as they should?

Five

The incessant beep penetrated his sleep-fogged mind. Vince slapped at the alarm clock and opened on eye. Damn! It couldn't be six already. He groaned, dragging himself through his morning ablutions. He eyed the door leading into the house. Even though he couldn't hear anyone stirring in the house, he didn't take the chance of running into the sisters. He left by the outside entrance.

In the morning light he examined his car again. It really wasn't that bad--scraped bumper and a broken taillight. He fingered the paper he'd stuck in his pocket. Such a forlorn note. Her footsteps paused outside his door as if she expected him to come out. But he'd been in no mood to deal with her last night. Refusing to feel guilty, he drove to the nearest coffee shop and ordered a double espresso.

Vince was the first one at work. He got an hour of solid work done before a couple of the assistants filed in. Glancing at the clock, he wondered if Leena would show up. She had fifteen minutes. At five to the hour, he heard someone in the outer office and guessed it was her. After a half-hour of straining to hear what she was doing and trying to ignore her presence outside, he gave up the fight and strode out of his office.

There she was, hair tied back in a neat bundle, although wayward curls were already escaping to gather around her forehead and nape. He cursed that now familiar tug in his groin.

"Good…" she cleared her throat. "Good morning. I started on the research into their previous ads. Unless there's something else…"

He hated how tentative she sounded. But he had no one to blame but himself. Why did just being around her make him forget *he* was the wronged one?

Sounding brusquer than he meant to, he replied, "That's fine. Bring it to me when you're done."

He caught the flash of hurt in her eyes before she nodded, bending her head to the computer screen. She should set that thing at eye level. And what did he care if she got an aching neck? Besides, he still had a headache.

Vince got practically nothing done in the next two hours--beyond a few doodles. The events of the previous night filled his thoughts. Not the least of which was the delicious interlude in the kitchen. At one time he even found himself wishing Carly had arrived a half-hour later. Hell, even fifteen minutes later and he could've experienced what he knew would have been a damn hot ride. He adjusted his crotch and forced away the images of Leena on his lap, sated and dreamy. Instead he focused on the news he got later. Witches? Witches!

With a humph of disbelief he turned back to the drawing board--and found himself sketching a woman with wild curly hair entering a car. He balled the sheet of paper and threw it in the wastebasket.

Dammit! If they had put some sort of spell on him, he wished to hell they'd take it off. He just couldn't operate this way. When she knocked, he was still staring at a blank sheet.

"Yeah?" He swiveled to face her.

"I put those ads together. Do you want to see them now?"

He sighed. "Yeah, sure."

"If you don't mind, I'd like to tack these up on the wall. Or maybe your whiteboard?"

He waved his assent, watching her lean up to tape legal sized sheets at about his eye level. Her soft, blue linen pants outlined her behind when she reached up. The white top molded the side of her breast just like he wanted to. He curled his hand around the arm of his chair. Damn, damn, damn!

Oversexed, Vince! Stop acting like a teenager.

When she began pasting printed words beneath each picture, he leaned forward. After taping the last one, she turned and waved him closer. Vince rolled his chair to the whiteboard and raised an eyebrow. "Well?"

She flushed. "These are stills of the ads for the car manufacturer for the last 3 years. Beneath each one are my impressions of the image being conveyed and the quarter's earnings for the company."

"That's more than I asked for."

"I know," she twisted the side of her pants into a pleat. "I just thought this might give you a better picture of their sales. I can take the extra stuff down."

"No, let it stay. I didn't say it wasn't good." He studied the wall. Her impressions were on the mark, concise words conveying the overall image of the ad--American Dream, Mid-life Crisis. Yup, they certainly did market segmentation in the last year.

"Where did you get the earnings?" He could guess, but he wanted to know.

"Annual reports. Stock market archives." She continued that nervous pleating of her pants. Feeling sorry for her-- she was so obviously tense--he waved her to a chair. "Why don't you sit down and take notes?"

He elaborated on her impressions, noting when sales went up or down, what images were associated with better figures. Of course there were other factors to consider, but this was a great start. Already he could see a couple of images in his head.

He outlined one for her and they tossed ideas back and forth. She picked up on subtleties he would normally have seen faster. Granted her opinion was mostly uninformed from an ad man's perspective, but she brought the layman's viewpoint to the table rather well. They continued until a loud rumble from her stomach reminded him it was past lunchtime.

"Sorry." she looked so embarrassed and so damn cute it took all his control not to haul her into his lap and kiss away her concern.

"Don't apologize. Want to go to lunch and continue this?"

She looked uncertain. "Actually, I have errands to run and I brought a sandwich with me."

Aware of an unsettling disappointment, he gave a short nod. "Fine, I'll see you in about an hour, then. I'll need to get some letters out."

"Okay, thanks." She bit her lower lip looking like she wanted to say something more. Then she gave a slight shake of her head.

Sitting down to lunch at the bistro around the corner, he caught himself running a thumb over his lower lip.

~ * ~

Leena collapsed into her chair, willing herself to calm down. Now that he'd left, she had the shakes. After holding herself in all morning, she probably owed herself this mini meltdown.

Sitting with him, talking to him today had been one of the hardest things she'd done. Each time he waved his hand she saw him touching her. Every time he smiled she felt his lips on hers.

She practically inhaled her peanut butter sandwich and settled in to make some calls. First the insurance agent. She gave him the details and begged them to call Vince as soon as they could. Then the bank. Finding a way around the mortgage payments was not as easy, but at least now she had an appointment with someone for Friday.

To take her mind off the events of the previous day, she quickly typed up the notes from their morning discussion and emailed it to Vince. Phyllis stopped by and commented on the dark circles under Leena's eyes. Waving it away to allergies, she tried to anticipate what Vince might need. She made notes about some letters the previous assistant had in her *IN* tray, then redid her budget on her yellow writing pad. No matter how she looked at it, they were in trouble. Even with Vince's rent payment. Besides, who knew how long he would stay.

Funny how she still wanted him. She made a mental note to ask Gina how long the residual effects of the spell took to dissipate.

He came back in exactly one hour and she spent the afternoon jumping every time the phone rang or he walked by. By evening she had a raging headache.

Thank goodness Carly was with a study group tonight. She raced home, made herself a plain omelet and escaped to her room. Carly came home about nine. Leena was still awake when Vince came in--way past midnight.

The rest of the week was pretty much the same. The only difference was that he ate some cereal in the kitchen and made some coffee before leaving the house. She stayed in her room until he left. By Friday afternoon, her headache was permanent and her body throbbed with tension.

~ * ~

Vince leaned back in his chair, letting his shoulders relax. She left early, mumbling about an appointment. Thank goodness! Anymore of this and he had two options-- fire her or shut the door and make love to her on the floor.

They hadn't discussed her claim of being a witch, the spells, nothing. Her insurance guys had called and he got them to agree that he would get the car fixed at his dealer. He didn't bother to tell her when the agent came to appraise the damage.

Grimacing at his cowardice, he tried to put her out of his mind. They'd come up with a list of keywords to add to the presentation. Where were they? Not in his email inbox. Leena must not have had time to type it up.

Stretching, he made for her desk and rummaged about until he located the yellow pad she took notes in. Flipping through, he smiled at her doodles of palm trees and what looked like boats on the water. The next page made him pause. It looked like a budget and before he realized it was personal he skimmed the numbers. Must be her personal budget and judging by the columns, things didn't look good for her. Underneath the four figures with the minus sign she'd written--*sell house?*

Quickly, he moved a few pages down and found the keywords. Taking the pad back to his desk, he typed them into a document then replaced the notebook.

Feeling guilty for looking over her personal accounts, he still couldn't get it out of his mind. He remembered his deal with Carly. He should have given her a check for the deposit. It wouldn't solve Leena's problem but it might help in the short term. Better yet, he should just give her cash. Before he could analyze this urge to help Leena, he copied his presentation onto his flash drive, stuffed the papers he needed into his briefcase and left. He had to make it to the bank--he couldn't withdraw that much from an ATM. Maybe, just maybe this might ease his lust, too. The desire he experienced around her was eating him alive.

Back at Leena's house, he left the money in an envelope on the kitchen table with her name on it. Next he ordered a pizza and settled down to work, leaving his front room door open half way.

Sure enough, Carly stopped by. "Hi. You're back."

He grinned at her. "Yeah. How was your week?"

"Not bad. Not bad at all. Met this guy."

Uh-oh. He didn't think he could handle teenage confidences. He just wanted information about Leena from her. "Cool. So did I." He winked at her.

Carly rolled her eyes. "Okay, I get it. You don't want to hear it." She sidled into the room, hefting her backpack on one shoulder. "Whatcha doin?"

"Working on my presentation for next week."

"Yeah, Lee told me about this big thing at work."

Big thing. He supposed that was a good way to describe it as any.

"Hey, I ordered some pizza. Want to join me?"

"What's on it?" She asked, cocking her head to one side.

He couldn't help laughing. "Meat lovers. It should be here in the next ten minutes."

"I'll be back by the time it gets here."

True to her word she showed up just before the bell rang. They chowed down and he found himself laughing at her artless conversation. She seemed a good kid. And boy could she talk. He found their mother had left a few years ago and Leena had taken over raising Carly; that Leena had given up being a witch at the time her mother left.

Despite his skepticism, he asked more questions. And heard about witches in general and their powers and Leena's deal with Carly to teach her over the summers. He'd spent some time yesterday looking up this very issue on the web. Turned out some people really did think they had powers. He was inclined to believe it was in their heads. But how could he explain his obsession with Leena? And his see-sawing emotions? Wanting to take her in his arms one minute and run like hell the next.

"So what happened with the spell you mentioned? The love potion."

She had the grace to blush. "Didn't Leena tell you?"

He shook his head, his mouth full of pizza.

"They reversed it."

"They who?" he mumbled.

"Gina and Lee."

Ah, the mysterious *Gina said*. "So, who's this Gina?"

"My neighbor. She's the best. She helped Lee set it all right. Wouldn't let me stay. She actually sent me to bed."

Something her sister should probably do more often. "So this…this spell doesn't work anymore?"

"Nope," was the blithe answer. "I'm stuffed."

He forbore to agree that she should be. She'd certainly ate like a normal teenager.

"Can I put the rest in the fridge?" he asked.

"Sure, I'll give you something to put it in."

They stuffed the remaining slices into a plastic container. Soon after, Carly wandered off to watch TV and he sat on the wooden step outside his door drinking a beer. And thinking.

Lord, but his mind was in a jumble. Could she really be a witch? And how stupid did he seem for even considering it? Yet Leena had seemed so sincere. And Carly seemed to totally believe.

He glanced up at Gina's house. She apparently was the attractive redhead next door. He toyed with the idea of marching up to her door and demanding an explanation.

Grimacing at the direction of his thoughts, he finished his beer, stood up to stretch, and wondered where Leena was. What a way to spend a Friday night. He wandered back to the kitchen for another beer.

Of course he didn't have to be home alone tonight. There were a few people he could have called for company--there were even a couple of women on that list. But he had no interest in being with them.

One curly haired woman who said she was a witch consumed his thoughts.

~ * ~

Leena threw her keys and the mail on the kitchen table. A glass of orange juice fortified her. She wasn't really hungry enough for dinner. The hard slatted back of the chair provided some relief for her aching back. Amazing how much calmer she felt now, compared to when she left the bank earlier this afternoon. Knowing that the bank could foreclose on the house had been a nasty surprise.

On an impulse, she'd stopped at the salon belonging to Gina and her cousin. She desperately needed some advice and Gina and Kat had been more than willing to give it. They went out for drinks and talked through Leena's situation. The women couldn't have been friendlier or more supportive. They welcomed her to the sisterhood, as they called it, with mango mojitos. She must learn how to make that drink!

And they helped her reach her decision to sell the house. She had no great love for it. Her mother had written it over to her and Carly before she left. Mom was somewhere in Alaska, last they heard, following her latest love. The house was a liability to them. But with the value of real estate having gone up like it had in their neighborhood, Kat thought Leena would get a good price. She'd even called her husband, who consulted on development work for the city, to ask his opinion and he agreed.

Tomorrow she would talk to real estate agents after she discussed this with Carly. She was pretty sure Carly would go along with the plan.

With a sigh of relief, she began to leaf through the mail when she noticed the white envelope with her name. She read the word *Deposit.* Inside was the equivalent of one month's rent.

Oh no! Vince hadn't really thought she would hold him to that deal with Carly. And why not give it to her in person?

The clock on the wall behind read 9:42 p.m. She would just have to see if he was still awake. She finished off the juice as she thought about her week: tiptoeing around him, holding her breath, praying he wouldn't brush against her. Trying to ignore the long looks he gave her when he thought she wasn't looking.

She stalked up to his door with the envelope of money. The door stood ajar. When no one answered her knock, she pushed the door open and stepped in.

"Vince," she called, standing just inside the door. "Hey, Vince, are you there?"

She heard a muffled curse. "Leena?" He walked in from the bedroom. She choked and sagged against a thankfully firm wall behind her.

"What are you doing here?" he asked holding a towel closed at his waist. She was far too busy following the line of dark hair that disappeared under the towel's edge.

Six

Leena gulped and prayed for the strength to act nonchalant. "Oh, hi. I'm sorry I didn't realize you were in the shower."

"That's okay. Did you need something?"

Despite herself, her eyes roved over his shoulders remembering how she clutched them just a week ago.

"Leena? You okay?"

"Huh?" She pulled her eyes back to his. "What? Oh, yes, I'm fine. I'll stop by in the morning." She half turned, reluctant to leave the delectable sight.

"Wait. Please stay. I'll be back in a minute."

He disappeared into the bedroom and she heard the faint sounds of a drawer opening. He was back in less than a minute. Much to the disappointment of that newly-found wild side of hers, he'd pulled on shorts and a T-shirt. She let out a tiny sigh, trying to dispel the regret.

"What's up?" he asked with that sexy half-grin that tantalized her all week.

"Er…nothing really." She clasped her hands together and the envelope crinkled in her hand. "Oh! I came to return this." She held it out to him.

"The deposit? Why?"

"You can't imagine I would hold you to that."

"It's a normal part of a rental agreement. So you forgot to ask me for it when we signed the lease. Big deal."

"But--"

"But nothing," he interrupted. "Your sister is a better business woman than you are, you know that? I'm not taking it back."

"You have to."

"No."

They stared at each mutinously. Her lips quivered as she realized how ridiculous they must look. Glaring at each other like a couple of five-year-olds. He must have seen the humor because he grinned at her.

"We could do this all night."

She could think of much better things to do with him all night. "I don't think so. Will you really not take this back?"

"I really won't. Now you want to sit and talk about something else?"

Something else? What could he mean? She reminded herself of the last time they talked about personal stuff. He said some really mean things. But somehow, here in his room, in the muted light of a table lamp, it didn't matter that much.

He walked toward her with slow steps, his look warming her. She found that wall again, pressed her back against it for support and closed her eyes. One deep breath and the fresh scent of soap and that delicious after-shave assailed her. Her lids flew open to find him close enough to touch, his hands splayed on the wall on either side of her.

She should have been uncomfortable with him looming over her. But all she knew was the rising excitement as her senses awoke. The heat of his body so near to hers called forth an answering warmth from her own. His face descended even closer and his breath fanned her lips.

"Leena?"

She answered the unspoken question by lifting her chin. Her eyes closed as their mouths met, clung. Such a sense of homecoming. She didn't stop to analyze but gave in to the raw need that stalked her all week.

Of their own volition, her hands crept up around his neck, rifling through the damp hair curling on his neck. His own seized her shoulders and pulled her close.

Warm tingles turned to heated shards coursing through her body as he pressed closer and closer, until she wasn't sure where he began and she ended.

Hands fumbling with the buttons of her shirt, he began walking backwards, pulling her with him with the sheer magic of his mouth. His tongue stroked hers in a wild rhythm, a prelude to the inevitable primal dance to come.

He stopped and pulled back from her only to wrench his tee over his head. Leena used that moment to wave her hand at the door, which shut gently. He didn't notice.

Vince framed her face with his hands. "Are you in this all the way?" he asked, his eyes catching hers in a look that made her shiver in anticipation.

"Yes," she whispered. It was the only answer she could give. Here was a pull far greater than her will. "Yes, if you are."

He groaned and captured her mouth again, even as he shoved her shirt off her shoulders. Leena shrugged out of it. She spared a thought for the older, rather plain bra she'd worn, then dismissed it. Somehow she didn't think he cared.

"I'm in, babe, all the way. It's what I've wanted all week," he murmured against her neck, his breath tickling the sensitive spot on the side.

She shivered. "You, too?"

At that he pulled back and looked down into her face. "It was the worst torture."

"I know," she replied, her tone soft. "Believe me, I know."

"Let's not waste any time."

Vince fell back on the sofa. She stopped, confused. Until he smiled in a way that heated her blood to boiling. "Shall we go back to where we left off?"

God, yes.

She nodded, suddenly shy.

"Then take your bra off. And your pants."

He sat back, hands behind his head. It took all the courage she had to do it, but she did. The open desire in his face encouraged her and she reached behind and unhooked her bra. Ever so slowly, she slid the straps down then held the cups in place with one hand.

"Take it all off," he ordered softly, his voice rougher than usual, before he ran his tongue over his lips.

The memory of that mouth on her breasts spurred her on and she dropped the bra on the sofa next to him. His breath hitched as he held out his hands to her.

~ * ~

Vince used her outstretched fingers to pull Leena down onto his lap. He winced as she landed on his erection. If he didn't watch it this would be over in the next second or so. Marveling at how quickly she could bring him to fever pitch, he raised her hips slightly, adjusting her position.

Sliding his hands in slow torture up her sides, he drew out the moment before touching her breasts. The slight arching of her back told him what she thought of his pace.

With a chuckle he closed his fingers around each breast, molding, glorying in the feel of those perfect mounds. Just a little too big to fit into his palms, they spilled out, her nipples standing, plump and ripe. Hefting her flesh in his hand, he lowered his head until his breath fanned the strawberry colored aureole. She whimpered--a small sound that nevertheless filled him with satisfaction. Good, she wanted this as much as he did.

He licked one nipple then blew on it and a shudder ran through her. She arched again and this time he took her in his mouth, suckling hard, just like she wanted the last time. The sound of raw need that broke from her egged him on even as she clasped his head in place with one hand, the other roving over his shoulders.

Splaying his hands under her arms, he lifted her higher. She came up on her knees, pressing herself against his stomach. Vince moved to her other breast, murmuring encouragement as she rubbed against him.

The small whimpers and mews that broke from her, sounds of satisfaction and need nearly sent him over the edge. Her delicate touch strayed beneath the elastic waist of his shorts.

He unbuttoned her pants and shoved them down, his hand searching for her; over the silky material of her panties, between her legs where he found the cloth damp and cool. His fingers slipped past it, sliding in the wetness. He parted her folds carefully and inserted one finger, circling, testing. She bucked against his hand, her ready response releasing the storm he was trying so hard to contain.

God, she was so ready. Vince thought he might burst out of his shorts. All he could think of was her sinking down on him, taking him into her, covered in all--. He didn't have a damn condom with him.

He was too far into this to stop now. Her fingers circled him, holding him firm. He clenched his jaw and gritted out, "I don't have protection."

Her fingers stilled then she whispered against his mouth. "So let's do it this way for now."

He could have resisted, almost, until she started pumping him with steady strokes. On her knees, her body bent slightly so she could reach him, thighs open to his hand. He wished there was a mirror in the ceiling so he could see her like this. Not a sight he would soon forget.

Then all coherent thought fled as she brought her lips down on his, her tongue searching for his, moving inside his mouth, echoing the rhythm of her hand. The pressure built and he was barely aware of his fingers setting their own tune in and out of her. She stiffened and convulsed around his fingers losing the beat for a moment.

He groaned into her mouth, but she picked it up again in an instant. The tension in his body built and stretched thin. She broke the kiss and bent to his chest, her tongue licking his nipple. When she bit down, he went rigid before he surged against her hand, the dam breaking. Never had he found his release with a woman this way. She continued to hold him gently as he pulsed in her hand before slumping back against the sofa, two fingers still inside her.

~ * ~

Thighs trembling, knees giving way, Leena sagged against the comforting, solid chest before her. He captured her inarticulate cry with his mouth. A gentle kiss but with remnants of their passion lurking behind it. Slow and sweet, he explored her mouth, nipped at her lips then soothed them with his tongue.

She clutched his shoulders wanting a reprieve, yet never wanting this to end. When he lay down on the sofa and arranged her to half-sprawl over his body, she acquiesced, marveling that he had any strength left. She closed her eyes to better absorb the sensations still bracketing her body, her mind.

When she awoke it was to the unfamiliar feel of a body wrapped close to her. Without opening her eyes she took in the delicious feeling of a hard arm holding her close, of hair roughened legs entangled with her. The scrumptious scent of man, aftershave and sex threatened to overcome her and she opened her eyes, lifting up from the hard pillow of his chest.

The tender kiss on top of her head seemed out of character for him. So far she'd only seen his passion and his anger. But the tenderness was there, in the way he held her, in the hand linked with hers. Still semi-aroused, the length of him nudged her inner thigh.

If she could have conjured up a condom she would have. Hating the thought the night might end without the ultimate experience--his body joined to hers. Although, he didn't seem inclined to ask her to leave.

"Awake?" he asked, his voice a rough whisper.

"Mmm." Not entirely, not yet she wasn't.

"Feeling okay?"

She came awake at that. Okay? What would he ask next? Are we expecting snow in Chicago this winter? Of course she was okay. In fact she was more than okay--she was sated yet aroused, still sleepy, somewhat hungry, and in love. She held herself very, very still as she realized what she had just thought.

Throwing it around in her mind, she expected the phrase to knock against the walls she thought she had around her heart. Turns out they either crumbled or weren't there because her heart swelled in a mix of love, elation and trepidation. Oh no! This was just sex to him--she was so sure of that.

His spoke again, not whispering this time. "Hey, you okay?"

She levered herself up off his chest, leaning one elbow on the bed. Convinced her love would be written all over her face she didn't really want to look at him. But he deserved an answer. After all, how many men could say they satisfied a woman without even going all the way?

The uncertainty in his eyes made her chest ache. All she wanted to do was comfort him. Let him know he was *the man*. Marveling at how, in her moment of crisis, her instinct was to comfort this man, she shook her head.

"What? What's wrong?"

He thought she was answering him! "No, I'm fine. I'm okay. Better than okay."

"Even though…" His trailed away and again that hint of vulnerability tugged at her newly discovered love.

She ran a finger along his jaw, loving the rough stubble that lined it. Oh hell! She was in trouble all right if she began mooning over the man's beard.

"Even though," she stated, firm in her resolve that this had still been one of the best ever.

He captured the finger straying over his lips. The gentle bite, the tiny lick of his tongue made itself known to every fiber of her being.

"You know, I don't even think we shut that door. God, I've never lost control like this."

She didn't like the frown gathering in his eyes. "Don't worry, I closed it."

"Really? When?"

She hesitated wishing she'd left well alone.

"Not that thing again? Like in the kitchen?"

She sighed and nodded.

Note to self: Do not mention you can move objects without touching them while cuddling in bed with the sexiest man you've been with.

End of cozy interlude. She sat up grabbing for the sheet to cover her breasts as Vince hefted himself up in bed.

"Tell me this isn't true. This is some sort of joke, right?"

"I wish it was, Vince. I've never wished so hard as I have this week that all this was a joke."

He rubbed a hand over his face and through his hair.

"Vince, it really is true. I do have powers, that you can't explain with science or…or rational thought."

"What kind of powers?" He pulled himself up and swung his legs over the side of the bed, twisting to look at her.

His withdrawal hurt more than she wanted to admit. "Moving inanimate objects." His confusion showed in his face. She glanced around the room to find a tennis racket in its cover, leaning against the corner of the wall. "Look at that racket over there." She focused and made a short sweeping motion with her hand. It fell with a tiny thud and lay on the floor.

"Damn! How did you do that?"

"With my mind."

"Shit! I can't believe it!"

She understood his skepticism, she really did. But it still hurt. Leena scrambled off the bed then wished she had located her clothes first. He must have brought her into the bedroom sometime during the night. She dove under the sheets again as he pulled on a pair of jeans. Of course he would leave the waist unbuttoned, making him look sexy as hell.

"Are my clothes in the other room?"

"I'll get them."

He came back in seconds and handed her the white shirt and linen pants she wore yesterday. Ignoring the lack of underwear she dressed in a hurry, her movements awkward under the covers.

Once fully clothed she stood and faced him. He seemed like a man lost, his gaze searching hers, for what she didn't know.

"We have to talk about this. It's just not possible."

She willed herself to be gentle and not snap at him. Explaining herself was something she had never had to do before.

Because you kept everyone at least a city block away from you.

Ignoring her inner voice, she said. "It *is* possible. It's just not something you thought was possible. Or even knew could happen. We're all afraid of the unknown to some extent."

"Should I be afraid of you?"

"God, no. I don't hurt people, least of all you." She stopped, afraid she'd said too much.

"Okay." He paced to the small window then turned back to her. Pitch black outside. It must be well into the night but she didn't want to distract herself by looking for a clock. "Let's see if I've got this. You *are* a witch. As is your sister. According to her this is something you're born with, like a genetic birth defect or something."

Despite the fact that she had often cursed her heritage, all of a sudden she didn't like his choice of words.

"It's not a disease. It's a part of me, of us." He raised a brow. Wanting to smack it, she hastened to add, "Carly and myself. So I haven't used my powers in three years. It was mainly because I didn't want Carly to think that was her way out. I wanted her to make the right choices, get an education so she would be financially secure. Then, if she chose to be a witch also, I wouldn't have stopped her."

Now, how to explain life with her mother? How she flitted from one man to the next, thinking her minor powers would win her favors. Or, the constant lack of money, of making do; trying to raise Carly to be a good human being with choices Leena herself never had. Not that she resented Carly or having to take care of her. But the regrets still milled about at the back of her mind.

A wave of tiredness crashed over her. Maybe the middle of the night wasn't the best time to have this discussion.

"Can you show me how you did that? Moved the racket?"

"I'm not sure I can actually show you. But you can watch me if you like." Maybe if he understood this better.

Shelving the thought that she was clutching at straws, she moved to stand in front of the racket. She concentrated and made a small movement with her hand. The racket slid a couple of feet along the floor.

"That's amazing."

She shrugged. She didn't exactly want a prize here.

He stalked back and forth by the window. "What else can you do?"

Might as well get it all out. "If I concentrate really hard, I can put a suggestion into your mind. That doesn't mean you'd do it. You'd have to want to do it. I can't force you to."

"Show me," he replied, his strained voice evidence of his tension.

Leena looked at the face that had become so dear in so short a time. His lips went to work as he chewed on the inside of his cheek. She'd seen him do that when he was worried or tense. Remembering the feel of his mouth on hers, she thought, *I want to kiss her.* She focused all her energies at sending that thought winging into his mind.

A moment later his eyes widened. "I've just had a very strong urge to kiss you."

She nodded satisfied. Then she noticed the dawning disgust in his eyes.

"So that explains why I have the hots for you."

Seven

Vince cursed when his foot hit a dip in the pavement and he stumbled. Slowing his pace, he swiped the sweat from his forehead but kept jogging. But he couldn't seem to outrun the look in Leena's eyes when he accused her of manipulating his desires. Of course he hadn't meant it to come out quite like that. Ha! How many men said that at least once in their lifetimes?

The knowledge that the woman he had just been to bed with, the woman he had been anticipating having even better sex with, could move inanimate objects with her fricking mind would throw anyone off kilter. He ran past her house, then his and around the block again.

Last night she walked out of his bedroom without any argument. The only thing she'd said in a strained, low tone was *I would never do that to you.*

Well, yeah. He wanted to believe that. But what other explanation could there be for this explosive attraction between them? Granted he had good sexual relationships in the past. But this…this was special. Even when he wasn't with her, he thought about her a hundred times a day. A flash of something red would remind him about the way the highlights in her hair glinted in the sun. Her lilting voice outside his office never failed to draw a smile, even though he hid it. Her light step in the hallway outside his room made his heart skip a beat in anticipation. This had to be unnatural.

He slowed to a walk and trudged back to his apartment, using the outside entrance to avoid seeing anyone. Not that Leena had been around. All day Saturday she'd been missing in action. Convenient--so he couldn't even apologize. She wasn't home when he fell asleep, neither was Carly. And this morning when he woke there was no one around except the cats. Today they chose to watch him unwaveringly as he ate his cereal and drank coffee.

A quick shower later he prowled the increasingly claustrophobic living room. Deciding he would get no work done in this mood he called Eric and agreed to join him for a game of tennis.

He met Eric at the courts and they played drills for about a half-hour before taking a break.

"So what's the matter with you?" Eric asked, taking a swig of water.

"Me? Nothing," Vince answered. "Why?"

"For one, you haven't noticed the blonde bombshell who's been eyeing you."

"What? Where?" He followed the jerk of Eric's head with is eyes. Hmmm. Pretty. Bombshell? He thought not. Now if she'd been a brunette…

Thankful that Eric interrupted his thoughts he paid attention. "See? That's what I'm talking about. You have no interest."

He shrugged.

"And you look like you lost Lassie at the last stop light or something."

He did? Well, he hadn't slept at all. "Didn't get much sleep."

"It's more than that. Hell I've known you since you were five."

"Leave it, Eric."

"Oh, so there's something to leave? Who is it? Gotta be a woman."

"Why? Could be work."

"Nope, this isn't work. You've got that look. Hell, I've seen it on my brothers. So who is it?" Eric leaned back against the wood bench and settled down to listen.

Vince eyed his best friend with irritation. Eric wouldn't let it alone. Probably the cop in him. "It's a long, bizarre story."

"You got somewhere to be?"

"Hell, no."

They ended up at a bar a few blocks away, skipping their regular haunt Millie's, where they knew too many people. Between beers he told Eric the whole story, leaving out the details about the sex. That information was his alone to savor.

"And that's it. Haven't seen her since."

Eric whistled. "Man, that's some story."

"Hell, yeah," he agreed, drawing lines on the condensation on his glass. It reminded him of how Leena had traced lines on his chest with her fingers and he hastily abandoned the project.

"So what're you gonna do?"

"Hell, man. I don't know. I don't even know what I want."

"How 'bout the sister. She good for information?"

"Yeah. But that won't help. I can't ask her if her older sister forced me…manipulated me to have sex with her."

"She forced you?" Interest peaked in Eric's eyes.

"Oh, can it. Not like that."

"So what's your problem exactly? Pretty woman. Great assistant according to you. Wants to make love to you. I'm assuming the sex was good, too?"

"Great," answered Vince absently. He winced as Eric let out a shout of laughter.

"Figured as much. Oh, man." Eric wiped his eyes, looked at Vince and lost it again.

"Glad I can entertain you," bit out Vince.

"Man, I'm sorry. It's just…it ain't like you. Falling for a witch. That's rich. Hey, that was poetry." Eric shook his head, laughing.

Vince glared at him, murder in his eyes. If Leena were here, he'd ask her to make something fall on his friend's head.

"Okay, okay. I'm done." Eric chuckled and swiped at his lids.

"Thanks. I was getting ready to brain you."

"Yeah, I thought your patience might not last much longer."

They swigged beer and stared at the TV. The game really didn't register with Vince. What the hell came next?

"Hey, didn't you say something about a neighbor?" asked Eric finally.

"Huh? What neighbor? Oh, yeah. Her sister Carly said their neighbor helped…call back the spells or something like that."

"Go talk to her."

"Who? The neighbor? 'Course not. I can't just barge into someone's house asking about their witch neighbors."

"But, if what they're saying is true, and I'm not saying it is, then this woman is a witch, too. Maybe she can explain what's going on."

"I don't know." What if asking questions got Leena into some sort of trouble?

"Just think about it."

"I will." Vince drained his beer and stood. "I gotta get back. Long day tomorrow.

"Need a ride back?"

"I'm good."

"Let me know how it goes. If you need this woman investigated or anything, I'll call someone in her precinct."

"Let's wait on that. See you later." Vince raised a hand in farewell. He drove back to the house, nursing his throbbing head.

~ * ~

Leena put down the phone and took a deep breath. She wrapped her arms around herself to hold off the chill taking over.

"You okay?" Gina asked.

"Yeah."

"Honey, you don't look okay. Here, finish your tea."

Leena took a grateful sip of the hot liquid, then a couple more. Slowly the warmth crept through her frame. And with it came the conviction that she made the right decision.

"Better." She never would have guessed Gina would become such a good friend in so short a time. She'd been there, like a solid frame, helping Leena choose a realtor, calling on her large family for help.

Gina's cousins Pete and Kat, and Kat's husband, Jake were all coming to help her get the yard cleaned up and little things done around the house. And perhaps the best thing of all, Gina and Kat had offered her a job in their salon. They needed someone to man the front desk. Besides, with Kat going on maternity leave soon, Gina would need help with the overall running of the place. The money wasn't as good as the job with Vince, but without the house mortgage they would manage fine.

The phone call had been to Phyllis. Leena spent half the night Saturday and a good part of Sunday tying up loose ends at the ad firm. She knew they had that big presentation coming up. So she did as much as she could to help him and Phyllis prepare. Beyond this, it was really up to Vince and the others to get their ad shots done and their graphics cleaned up. She told Phyllis she had to leave for family reasons. Phyllis had been surprised and a little irritable, but not unkind.

But she really couldn't face Vince day after day. Bad enough she might have to run into him at home. If they found a buyer, she would have to find a way to work with him to cut short his lease. She could cross that bridge when she had to. Right now, she didn't want to think about

Vince. The pain and hurt she kept at bay threatened to overwhelm her.

She finished her tea and caught Gina's sympathetic gaze.

"I'd better go. I have a lot to do around the house before I start working for you."

"With me, with us. Remember I'm expecting some of your jewelry for a Halloween show."

"I haven't forgotten." Gina and Kat sold jewelry and pottery from local artists in their salon. What a bonus that was for her. Maybe her luck had finally turned. *Except in love*. "I'll see you on Tuesday."

"Take care 'til then. The guys will be by tomorrow afternoon. Pete is off tomorrow and Jake is between consulting jobs."

"Thanks. See you soon." She stepped toward the door.

Gina added softly. "And if you need me to talk to him, just say the word."

She stopped, facing Gina. The warm sympathy in her gaze brought the sting of tears to Leena's eyes. She ran back to give Gina a hug.

"Thank you, Gina. For everything. I'll be okay. Really I will."

By ten the next night she really had begun to believe she'd be okay. The realtor called saying she had an interested buyer. Gina's family showed up en masse, and the guys promised they would be back tomorrow to fix the crown molding in the dining room and the fireplace mantel. She left a note for Vince telling him about the repair work. She hadn't seen him yet. And that was fine with her.

There were times when she wanted to find him and sock the living daylights out of him for thinking her capable of such a horrible thing. Other times, she simply missed him so much she wanted to curl up in a corner and cry.

But she kept chugging on.

Like the little engine that could.

Eight

Vince folded his clean laundry, giving his jeans a morose look. Friday afternoon and here he was washing clothes. Well, he had nothing better to do.

Their presentation to the car client had gone so well, he had the day off. Phyllis should be signing off on the deal today. If only he could find Leena to share the good news with her, tell her how much her preliminary work had helped him.

But no, Ms. Leena with the witchy powers had done a disappearing act. He never could find her at home. Now Carly he had run into a few times, excitedly talking about selling their home and Gina's family helping them fix the place…and Leena's new job.

Vince tried to act nonchalant but he itched to know more. But he wouldn't stoop to get information from her sister. Why had she made herself so scarce? Surely they could talk this out? Maybe he was wrong about this thing between them stemming from her manipulation. God knows, he still wanted her, even not having seen her for at least a week.

The memory of the hurt in her eyes and her strangely still figure stayed burned in his mind. If nothing else, he wanted a chance to apologize for being so rude. Mostly he wanted to see her, make sure she was okay, that these decisions were really the right ones for her.

A thud startled him. Someone laughed and called out something. Boy, those guys had been over every day fixing up the place. She deserved the help and he was glad her friends were doing this. But a little part of him couldn't help wishing he could have shared in the work.

Oh hell, staying in here only made the feelings of loneliness and regret worse. He might as well go to his house and do some work. Maybe sweating it out would help him sleep better tonight. Or sleep at all.

He pulled on a shirt over his tee and slipped his cell phone into his pocket. Taking the back entrance so as not to run into any of Leena's helpers, he turned a corner into the backyard and stopped short. Two strange men and Gina were grouped around the small table. Another woman he didn't know sat on the porch, a drink in hand.

He nodded to them. "Hi, you must be Vince," said Gina. "I was hoping I'd get to meet you."

She was? "Hi. I'm guessing you're Gina."

She waved. "Vince, meet my cousin, Pete, and Jake…my cousin-in-law. That's Kat another cousin, on the porch."

Vince shook hands with the men and raised a hand in greeting to the attractive, long-haired lady.

"Getting a lot of work done here."

"Yeah. Place sure needed it," Pete said.

"Amen to that," Jake added. "Hey, Vince, grab a beer. The cooler's on the porch. I know it's early but we're on vacation today."

"In Jake-speech that means no kids," joked Kat from her chair.

They seemed a friendly bunch. And just maybe Leena would join them.

"Sure thanks. Leena around?" he asked in what he hoped was a casual tone.

"She'll be back later," Gina replied. "Well, Vince help yourself. Pete and I will be right back."

Vince walked to the porch. The woman named Kat opened the cooler. "Beer?" she asked and handed him one when he nodded.

He couldn't help grinning back at her. Up close he saw she was pregnant. He twisted the cap and drank.

"So, hear you're renting the place," Jake commented, coming up the steps to join them.

"Yes. Just until my house is done."

"Oh, are you building something?" Kat asked.

"Refurbishing actually. Just down the street--714."

"On this street? Really? Is that about a block south?"

"Just about."

"Oh, don't tell me--714. I think I know it. Jake, it's the one with the green door. Isn't it, Vince?" She turned to him, her long, curly hair swinging.

"That's the one."

"We wondered what the owner was doing."

"Mostly the downstairs. Got workmen in. I'll paint the upstairs. Not much to do there that I can't get done." He hesitated then added, "Stop by there sometime and I'll show you around."

"We'll do that, man. It'll be our turn next. We've sort of outgrown Kat's condo." Jake tilted his head at the woman and she grinned.

"Jake, don't even talk about doing something like refurbishing with those two around. Our kids," she said to Vince. "Two boys."

"With way too much energy," Jake added. "And that reminds me, I want to get done so I can enjoy the rest of the evening without them." He swooped to give Kat a kiss and she touched his cheek, her hand lingering. "You doing okay, sweetheart?"

"I'm fine. Go do what you have to."

"Nice meeting you, Vince." He walked off whistling.

"The boys are with my parents tonight. It's a rare treat for us," Kat explained.

He nodded. "So this is your third?"

"In a way. Actually, my second. Our oldest is Jake's son from his first marriage. And this will be it," she added firmly, taking a sip of her drink.

Vince stayed, strangely reluctant to leave. Something about this woman was so soothing, so restful. The sheer contentment in her face made him feel at peace...and envious.

"You're troubled, aren't you, Vince," she asked, her quiet voice wrapping around him.

"Excuse me?" Had Leena told them?

"No, she didn't really share the details."

How the hell--

"But I know she's troubled and so it seems are you. See Vince, I can sense your feelings. I'm a witch, too."

He stared. This sweet, pregnant woman was a *witch*?

"We're really quite ordinary people in general you know. And we can't help being born into this way of life. Just like Leena can't help it or change it. It's her destiny."

He gulped down some beer, not sure what to say.

"You see, I think I know what you're feeling. Jake went through the same skepticism when we first met. He was kind of scared of it all, and worried about his son. And for a while he just didn't believe. Some day, ask him to tell you the whole story. The point is he put aside his disbelief and his suspicion. And once he did that, he was able to relate to me. We've been married for almost five years. And I swear to you, we've both never been happier."

He raised a brow.

"I'm not telling you to go propose to her." She laughed, a husky sound that drew an answering smile from her husband as he went by, lugging a section of fence. She blew him a kiss. "I'm suggesting an open mind. Right now you don't trust her. First, witches really aren't allowed to use their powers for personal gain. And while some do, the consequences are pretty bad. Second, Leena's been fighting not to use her powers." She glanced at his face. "I don't want to interfere. If you want me to stop, I will."

"Go on. Please." He wasn't even going to ask how she could be so dead on about his feelings.

"Go with your gut, Vince. Not your head, your reason. Just your heart. Just try it--just once and see what happens."

"I'm not sure what you mean."

"Right now you're questioning her ability, her very existence. You've never believed in the paranormal. So how can you trust her, given all that disbelief?"

He gaped. Was she reading his mind?

Jake spoke up from behind Vince. "Floored me, too. Just go with it, though. She's got an amazing ability to sense your feelings."

Vince jumped, not having heard Jake come back.

"I'll tell you one thing, Vince. For me, opening my mind was worth it." He rounded his wife's chair and clasped her shoulders. "I'm not given to sentimentality. But I can't imagine my life without Kat. She's saved me in more ways than one." He dropped a kiss on her head. "And I could have easily lost her because of my inability to accept her for who she was."

"Boy, that's a lot coming from you. What turned you so romantic?" She chuckled. "That's some endorsement, Vince, from my usually reticent husband. Here, take my hand."

Vince hesitated, giving Jake a quick glance. He nodded.

Taking her fingers in his, he allowed her to grasp them. She reached for his other hand. "Close your eyes and concentrate. I'm going to make you see how I feel. How we feel." His eyes fluttered shut and he absorbed the feel of her cool touch.

A tiny flutter in his chest, almost like a little butterfly testing its wings gave him a slight start. The sensation grew, gradually, until it seemed to consume his chest. At first he couldn't identify it--then he realized what he felt was a complete and utter peace. Sheer happiness like he'd never really experienced before. He smiled, couldn't really stop it. Was this what she could give him?

He almost protested as she withdrew from him. His gaze met her knowing one. "Remember that feeling. And then you can decide if it's worth taking a chance for it."

Vince nodded, not sure if he should thank her or not. Still feeling a little stunned, he rubbed a hand over his eyes.

"You have a lot to think about, Vince," she said.

"I know it's intense, man. Go take a breather."

He looked at Jake in gratitude, raised a hand to them both and walked away. He strode around the block several times before settling down to brush primer over the walls in one of the upstairs rooms of his new house. This was the room he chose for his bedroom. The large bay window faced west, giving the room a warm glow this time of the afternoon.

Glancing around, he mentally placed his wrought iron bed facing the door, his antique dresser by the opposite wall. What would she think of his furniture? Did she like old things? Or did she prefer the clean, simple lines of something more modern?

He blinked as he realized his brush dripped on the floor. With a curse, he dropped it in the pan and sponged the excess paint up.

Man, she had him tied up in knots. He sat on the floor, back against the wall and tried to sort out his feelings. Other than this supernatural power stuff, he liked everything about her. He'd come to respect her quick intelligence, her attention to detail. Just the sound of her voice was enough to send his pulse into overdrive. He loved how she cared for her sister, raised her, so matter-offactly. She'd be like that with anyone she cared about he guessed. Her loyalty--

Had he just said loved? He stood and walked to the window, gazing out at the overgrown backyard. Another image appeared, wavering, over the scene in front of him. A garden, flowers and a lithe woman tending to the plants. The sounds of laughter floated up to him. He blinked and saw once more, the old landscape. But there was no escaping the vision he held in his heart. The truth that somewhere along the line, he'd fallen in love. And that, somewhere on that journey, his heart had stopped caring about who she was and what she could do.

His chest tightened as he realized he might have lost her for good. To smother the fear, he picked up the brush and began painting again, his mind racing. No, he couldn't let that happen; at least not without a good fight on his part.

The soothing motion of brushing primer on the wall calmed him somewhat. His arm rose up, then down, then sideways. He grinned as he realized what he'd done.

Nine

"Yes, Ms. Reese. We do have a twenty-four hour cancellation policy. If you cancel after two on Thursday, we will need to charge you for half the amount. See on Friday then."

She listened to the woman agree, thanked her and hung up. Rubbing her ear, she took advantage of the rare silence from the ringing phone and marveled at the scene in front of her. Three women waited for appointments. There was someone at each of the five manicure stations. The rest of the place hummed with activity.

If it weren't for her wayward heart, she could have honestly said she hadn't been happier. The house sold for the asking price, the closing was a week from today. They had a month to move out, and Leena already had apartments scouted out. After paying the mortgage, they would have a little left over to set up a cozy nest egg.

She sent up a silent prayer of thanks for her new friends Gina and Kat. The salon turned out to be a great place to work. She met new people almost everyday. And her jewelry sold so well, she started staying up late to make more. Even with the percent she paid the salon, it looked pretty lucrative.

Now if only her heart wouldn't leap every time a tall, wavy haired man walked by. She sighed and turned back to the computer.

"Hey, I'm ready for the next one," asked Kat from beside her in a low voice.

"Hey, you. Mrs. Sexton, in the red," Leena muttered, then turned her laugh into a cough as Kat turned toward her and grimaced. The very low-necked sequined top and tight pants with a cabbage rose pattern should have alerted the fashion police.

"Lee, will you check into those display stands we talked about? I didn't have time last night."

The previous evening they'd discussed ordering some for the new artist who would do a show of her pottery. She had several large pieces and they weren't sure how sturdy their present ones were.

"Sure. Busy night?"

"Jake had to check out some broken water main and I had the honor of getting the boys to myself all evening."

This time Leena laughed out loud. She'd met Kat's boys--adorable but with enough energy to send a mini-rocket into space.

"Go, I'll check it out."

She clicked on the icon that took her to the internet and printed out some specs. Then because they were still in a lull, she logged into her new email account, the one Carly had insisted she set up after she left the ad firm.

Five new messages. Probably from Carly and from the self-help listserv she signed up for. She clicked on *Check Messages*. Later she would swear that her heart came to an utter stop before it raced like it would burst out of her. In the *From* column she read *vince@adcom*...

Oh god, what did he want? She scrunched her eyes shut then opened them. The subject line said, *Please Read This*.

A deep breath, then another fortified her somewhat. She double clicked, but the line stayed highlighted and nothing happened. Her fingers hadn't worked fast enough. With a swipe of her hand on her pants she tried again. This time the message opened.

> "*Leena, The attached photo is really how I feel.*"

What photo? Where was it? She scrolled down the page until she saw where she could open the attachment. Somehow, the feeling that her life would never be the same again came unbidden to her mind.

Seize opportunity. That was yesterday's self-help message.

She went through the motions of opening the document. A photo with a whitish background began a slow download. A thick pale green, curved line appeared. She shut her eyes, knowing she would probably get nauseous if she watched it appear.

One, two…she counted the seconds in her head. She got to twenty when a voice startled her.

"Just check in with Leena and she'll set up your next appointment."

Gina stood there, concern written all over her face. Warmth crept up Leena's neck. Had they thought she was sleeping?

She tried to act nonchalant. "Sure. It's for a facial and…"

"The Urbanite package," Gina broke in.

Gina hovered as Leena entered the appointment in the computer. The photo automatically minimized when she clicked on appointments. Because it hadn't downloaded fully yet all she got was an impression of white and green lines. They said goodbye to the client.

"Okay, what's going on? You looked like you were headed to your electrocution." Gina came around the counter.

"I…I was just waiting for something on the computer. A photo to download."

"And this photo is something bad?"

"Yes. Well, no. I don't know."

"Lee, what is it?"

"It's…oh, Gina. It's Vince--he sent me an email with this picture. Said the photo was how he felt. I was waiting for it to come up on the screen. And I'm scared."

"Of what, honey?"

"What if it's an awful picture? That he hates me or something?"

"Yeah, right. He's going to go to all the trouble of sending you a photo that depicts how much he hates you?"

"Well, when you put it that way."

"Just look it at. Want me to go?

"No, please stay. I need some moral support."

Taking a huge breath in, she clicked to maximize the photo. And forgot to let it out.

She barely heard Gina. "If that isn't the goofiest, sweetest thing I've seen. If you decide not to go with this guy, send him my way, okay?"

The pale green heart on the white background wavered before her gaze. Inside, shaky letters filled the heart. *Vince + Leena.* The words blurred as tears filled her eyes.

"Wait! What's that along the bottom?"

Leena blinked and read the caption aloud. "I'm really sorry for being a jerk. Second chance?"

She blinked away the tears.

"So, what's the verdict?" Gina asked.

"So…I guess I'll talk to him." If she could hold back from jumping his bones when she saw him.

"Go talk to him. Now!"

"But, we're still open for the afternoon. How--"

"We'll cover. Hey, gals," Gina called out. "Leena's got to go take care of her relationship issue. Can we cover the desk?"

"As long she comes back looking happier, I'll do anything," said Sandy, one of the manicurists, with a laugh.

"That's it then. Go," ordered Gina. "Oh, would you mind leaving that photo open? I want to show Kat."

She would do anything for these women. Who knew she had such good friends just waiting to be found?

She closed out her email but left the photo minimized and waved goodbye to the group. This called for opening her purse a little. She took a cab home instead of the bus. In the kitchen she paced, phone in hand.

What if he didn't really mean it? So why would he send the email? Could she call him at work? He tended to stay really busy. Fully realizing her procrastination for what it was, she sat on a chair. Exasperated with her dithering, she forced herself to think in rational terms.

She loved the man, even if he was slow on the uptake. What did she stand to lose if she didn't contact him? Could be everything. But if she did, and he didn't respond like she wanted him to, needed him to, then she was back where she was now.

His brave…and sweet gesture deserved more than a call. She wanted to settle this now and in person. What if she called and he wasn't there? Then she'd leave a message, and end up chewing her nails until he got back to her. At least this way, she would be doing something, not waiting around, trying to calm the flutters in her stomach.

She drove to the office.

"Hey, Leena. What are you doing here?" The young receptionist asked in surprise.

"Just needed to finish up something. Is Vince in?"

"Yeah, I'll call him."

"It's okay. I need to get some things from my desk anyway," she lied. "I'll stick my head in and see he has a minute."

Feigning nonchalance, she walked to her old office. Everything looked like it had before she left. Even his door stood ajar like it usually did.

Leena put a hand to her belly and knocked.

"Yeah, come in," he called.

A stone seemed to drop in her stomach, leaving a hollow feeling there. She pressed against the area then stepped in. He stood leaning over a new drafting board.

She cleared her throat and he turned. If she had any doubts, they fled before the light in his eyes, the sheer welcome on his face.

"You came!" He took a step toward her and stopped. "Leena?" Uncertainty took over his expression.

"Hi, Vince." He looked so familiar and so very dear.

"Hi." They stared at each other then spoke at the same time. He said, "You go first."

If there was ever a moment to seize opportunity, this was it! Leena went for it. "I…got your email."

He nodded but didn't say anything.

"Er…I saw the photo." What now? Why didn't he say anything? Sweat trickled down the back of her neck. "And--" She just couldn't go on without some hint from him.

"And?" He quirked that brow, still remaining still and so far away from her. "And what, Leena? Do you accept my apology?"

She nodded. "Of course. It was a heated moment. We were both felling a little…intense."

He rolled his eyes in agreement.

"So what now?" he asked, walking to his desk and leaning a hip against it.

"I don't know. What do you want?"

He rubbed a hand over his eyes and she noticed the tired lines on his face. "I'd like us to start again. We had something great. Until I screwed it up. And I want to know if you're open to that."

She had to know. "What's different now, Vince?"

"Well, I did a lot of thinking. And realized I was a fool to turn my back on something that had so much potential just because it was…unfamiliar."

Leena tried to absorb what he'd said, letting the good feeling that his words brought, sink into her mind.

"Do you think this…we have potential?"

"Oh, hell yes! A lot of potential," she said. "A whole lot."

He opened his arms and she rushed into them, crowding him back against the table. Leaning back and opening his legs, he cradled her between them. With his hands on either side of her head, fingers threading through her hair, he brought his mouth to hers. Like coming home all over again. She stopped thinking and simply felt.

She cherished the familiar comfort of his chest against hers and the summer-evoking scent of his aftershave. His firm lips against hers, the clever tongue plundering her mouth. His heat surrounded her as he wrapped his arms around her, then broke the kiss.

"Thank god! I was trying to set up Plans B and C and D."

"What were they?" She smiled into his hazel eyes so full of love.

"Didn't have any yet." He grinned back. "I'm really sorry."

"Shh. It's over. Let it go." She reached up and kissed him. "I'm sure we'll have plenty of other things to work out."

"We will," he murmured. "But, if we're willing to, we could get past any issues."

"We could." A thought struck her. "Vince, I have to take care of Carly still."

"Of course," he replied. "I wouldn't expect anything different. I want you. All of you in my life."

~ * ~

Cupid grinned as he sat on the rooftop, legs swinging, watching the celebration below. He liked dropping in on them every now and then. It was Carly's graduation day and the whole gang was in Vince and Leena's backyard celebrating.

He followed the couple he considered one of his successes as they took platters back into the kitchen. Cupid materialized in the breakfast nook.

"I can't believe she made it. I didn't think I would survive it at times," Leena said, rinsing off a plate.

"Leave it, babe, we'll do it later. I know what you mean. And it's probably not over, is it? There's college and more boys." Vince gave a mock sigh. "I may actually not survive it after all."

She laughed and moved to his side. "Oh I think you will. In fact, I have a feeling you'll find yourself with other things to focus on besides Carly's boyfriends."

He drew her into his arms. "I will? Like what?"

Cupid sighed. Yeah, their own kids--twins in fact-- would keep Vince and Leena busy. He flexed his wings for the journey back. Maybe he'd stop by Easter Bunny's and tell him the news. They should probably raise a glass to Cupid's success story.

Crazy Cupid

Phyllis Campbell

Champagne Books
Calgary, AB Canada

Best selling historical author, Phyllis Campbell has changed direction and is now expanding her talent into the contemporary market. She's written four historical romances for Champagne books and is non-stop in writing more. She's been an avid reader of romance since her first year of marriage in 1985 and she still can't stop writing happy romantic endings.

Phyllis is a member of several online critique groups and romance writer groups including Romance Writer's of America.

Books by Phyllis Campbell

My Heart Belongs To You

My Knight, My Rogue

Always, My Love

Mistletoe Magic

Don't miss any of our special offers. Write to us at #35069-4604 37 St SW, Calgary AB Canada T3E 7C7 or visit us online at www.champagnebooks.com to sign up for our quarterly newsletter.

Dedication

I'd like to dedicate this story to my critique partners at Critterpals, and especially to Rayka Mennen for following the story to the end. I also want to thank my fans for encouraging my writing.

One

She was using him.

That could be the only reason for her doubts about her forthcoming marriage.

Kenya Whitaker pressed her back against the brick wall, hiding from the guests inside her soon-to-be mother-in-law's house. She took a deep breath, filling her lungs with the cool February night's air, hoping to clear the several glasses of champagne she'd consumed already tonight. If she had to put up with more of Lisa Montgomery's fake friends wishing her a happy future with Terrel, she'd be tempted to start grabbing the whole bottle of alcohol instead of the goblets Lisa's butler passed around. Kenya tried to be polite, but if she saw one more plastered-on smile, heard one more person call her darling, and endured one more cold-fish handshake, she'd do something completely out of character and scream. Swinging a bat around the room just to clear out Lisa's friends tempted her more than ever.

She giggled. The champagne was definitely taking effect.

With her thoughts scrambled, and suffocation overwhelming her, she ran her hand over the back of her neck. It had been excessively warm inside the crowded house. Careful not to disturb the French twist she'd styled her mass of hair in this evening, she patted it to make sure it still held together. Rolling her head, she worked out the kinks in her neck, wishing the knots in her shoulders would loosen, too. *Why can't I enjoy this party?* Deep down she knew the answer…yet she wouldn't admit it, because that meant admitting defeat.

From inside the glass patio door next to her, voices grew louder. Her heart thumped against the wall of her chest and she skidded away toward the shadows hovering around the rose garden. She lifted her long black skirt to her ankles to take larger steps due to the tight-fitting length, and hurried toward the garden. Before she reached the edge of the patio, the gazebo caught her eye. Kenya changed directions and headed toward the get-a-way slightly hidden by the canopied oak trees.

Once inside, she wiped dust off the cushioned benches and sat. She closed her eyes and let the cool air touch her bare arms. Because of the high-neck collar on the satin dress, she was unable to feel the same comfort on her throat. She wasn't complaining. This design was her best selling dress since she'd started her business. In one month, she'd sold over a hundred and fifty dresses.

So why aren't I happy?

Kenya touched the collar that hooked in the back. She enjoyed the way the material flowed around her breasts, leaving her arms and back completely bare before gathering tightly at her waist. The high slit on the long, beaded black gown displayed most of her right leg and high-heeled matching shoe.

She looked toward the house and sighed. She couldn't stay out here forever. Eventually, someone in the party would notice her gone. After all, this was for her and Terrel. What were the chances her own fiancé would miss her?

A light wind blew across her face, moving the tendrils by her ears. She lifted her face to the breeze and closed her eyes. Tree limbs scraped the top of the gazebo but didn't override the chirping of night sounds and croaking of frogs in Lisa's pond.

"Pssst."

She snapped her eyes open, glancing around the shadowed yard. *That didn't sound like a frog.*

The sound grew louder. "Pssst."

Unless it was a frog on steroids. She stood and walked over to the edge of the railing. In the manicured shrubbery a man's form appeared. Doubting her sight, she blinked, looking again. This time the figure stood, making the shadow larger. *Had the frog turned into Price Charming? Unlikely.*

She gasped. "Who's...out there?"

The bushes moved again and he stepped out. The shadows hid his identity well. Her heart raced as she blinked to clear her distorted vision. *It could be Prince Charming...*

"I'm looking for Kenya Whitaker."

She hitched a breath. *He talks!* "What do you want with her?"

"If you're Kenya, I want to know if your father is Edward Whitaker, the writer of the book, *Away in Time.*"

Her pulsating heart slowed and she took in a deep breath. Another fan of her father's no doubt. Although she wasn't an avid Science Fiction reader, she would always be polite to her father's fan club. "I'm sure you know that answer or you wouldn't be out here."

He stepped closer--close enough for her to see how he was dressed. He certainly didn't look like any Prince Charming she knew. By his rugged appearance, he couldn't be one of the guests from the party. As a fashion designer, she knew his black, overly-large short-sleeved cotton shirt and black Levis wouldn't blend well with the tuxedos the men inside the mansion wore. The strange man resembled a hoodlum. And why wasn't he wearing shoes? She crinkled her brow. Her fashion tastes kicked in, making her want to teach him how to dress. But then she'd have to touch him.

His hair was almost as black as his clothes, and it hung to the end of his neck, barely brushing his shoulders. A shaggy goatee shaped his mouth and his square jaw. Her in-the-latest-fashioned sense roared into high gear, and she itched to find a pair of trimmers to help him with that.

"I take it you're Kenya Whitaker then?"

"Yes."

"My name is Eli."

"I'm assuming you're not one of Lisa's guests."

"I'm not," he said.

"So what are you doing out here?"

"I was watching you, hoping for a private moment alone."

Her heart rate climbed a notch higher. "Why?"

"Because there's something very important I need to discuss with you."

She arched a brow. "What's that?"

He shook his head. "Can we meet after the party?"

Oh sure! Do I look like I meet with strange men after parties? She hoped not. "Why can't we talk now?"

"It's not a good time. Too many people are around. I don't want our conversation to be interrupted."

She gulped the golf ball-sized knot in her throat. *Or he doesn't want witnesses.* "That's not a good idea." Her voice trembled. "Just tell me now."

He released a heavy sigh and folded his arms. "If you insist."

"I do."

A smile stayed on his scruffy face, and the skin around his eyes seemed to soften. Even his shoulders relaxed. Too bad her pulse wouldn't do the same.

"I came to tell you your family is in grave danger."

Her heart jumped to her throat. "Wha--what do you mean?"

"If I can't put a stop to something that's going to happen soon, something tragic will happen to your family."

"How do you know?"

A heavy sigh came from him as he ran his fingers through his unkempt hair. "Believe me, I know."

She cocked her head. "Has anything happened now?"

"Not yet."

"How will I know when it happens?"

He growled, folding his arms over his chest. "Miss Whitaker, will you please stop asking questions for now and listen to me?"

She nodded, twisting her hands against her stomach. "Sorry. Please continue."

"You may think this sounds funny, but if I can't stop you from marrying Terrel, your family will be in grave danger...in the future."

It took a moment for her to register what he said, but as soon as her fuzzy mind unscrambled his sentence, she let out an uncontrolled snort. Gaining control over her reaction, she straightened her shoulders. "You're kidding, right?"

"No. I'm more serious than I've ever been in my life." He took another step closer and leaned against the frame of the gazebo.

"Why are you telling me this?" She scowled. "What makes you think you know what's going to happen in the future?"

"Oh, believe me, I know. And I also know what's going to happen thirty years from now."

"Ha! How can you know what's going to happen in thirty years? Are you a psychic?

"No. The reason I know is because…" He bit his bottom lip.

In anticipation, she held her breath.

"I know because..." He scratched under his ear. "I'm from the future, and I've come to stop you from making the biggest mistake of your life."

She blinked, not believing what she'd heard. *The future?* Without a doubt, he was completely crazy. *So what am I doing outside in the dark with a crazy man? Am I that bored?* For the first time tonight, she couldn't wait to get back to the party, but he blocked her path. "Listen, Mister--"

"Eli."

"Okay, Eli. I must admit, you caught my attention with that family warning thing, but now I think you've probably got the wrong woman. Besides, I need to get back to my engagement party. I'm sure Terrel is looking for me as we speak."

"Or maybe not." He shrugged. "In fact, I think your fiancé is probably the center of attention, surrounded by beautiful women who want to sleep with him, and men who can't wait to kiss his ass."

She pursed her lips at Eli's remark. How dare he presume to know more about Terrel than she did? *Although he did hit the nail on the head.*

"It doesn't matter. I need to get back." She glanced over his body, taking in his shabby attire again and cringing. Poor guy needed to be slapped up side the head with a fashion stick.

"Kenya," he said, reaching out to touch her hand.

Gasping, she pulled back. Her high-heeled shoes caught in between two boards and tipped her off balance. She flayed her hands, hoping to grasp onto something to keep her from falling. But two strong arms caught her before she hit the ground. She clung to his hard body. Dizziness assailed her, and she cursed herself for drinking so much champagne. Either that or it was his sexy scent of spice that made her lightheaded.

As he pulled her upright, the front of her body rubbed against his. Tingles danced over her skin, making her heart flutter. *Good grief! What in the hell just happened?*

"Kenya," he said again, his voice lower than before. "I am from the future, and I can prove it. And I can prove your father is in danger."

She swallowed hard. "How?"

After letting go of her, he reached in his baggy jeans' pocket and pulled out a red and green flashing gadget. "This is what I used to come here."

Biting her bottom lip, she held in a laugh. "Uh-huh..." *I'm surprised he didn't come in a time machine that looks like a car.* "And what exactly is your time?"

"I've come from thirty-one years in the future."

She bit her lip from laughing again. "Really, Mister, do you think I'm going to believe this?"

"Kenya, please call me Eli."

"Fine. Eli, forgive me, but I'm not buying one word you're saying."

He narrowed his eyes. "I thought you of all people would understand. After all, your father did write a book about time-travel."

"That doesn't mean I believe in it." She chuckled. "Besides, that story is fiction."

Eli shook his head. "You don't know how wrong you are. That book tells more about the future than any book I've ever read. I think your father was inspired to write that."

Her wobbly legs forced her to sit on a bench. An ache started in the base of her skull and she rubbed the tender spot. "Okay, Eli, let's just say for humor's sake that you're from the future. What's so important you had to come at this time of night to tell me? And how is my father involved?"

"I couldn't figure out any other way to meet you, and what I have to say is very important. Talking to you alone is the only way I can get your help."

"Oh, so the truth comes out." She nodded. "You want my help with something."

"Yes."

"Like what?"

During his pause, the full moon hit his gaze as he glanced over her face, then to her hair, and down her dress. When his stare rested on her chest, her bosom tingled and she crossed her arms to hide the sudden rise of her unbound nipples. When his eyes finally met hers again, he smiled. Why was his sexy grin doing weird things to her stomach?

"My purpose in coming here is to stop you from making the biggest mistake of your life--and in the process, I'm saving both of our futures from being destroyed."

"Go on."

"Terrel isn't a very good man. Just like now, he's greedy, cunning, vindictive, and enjoys ruining people's lives. Terrel will soon create a computer system that literally gives him access to everything he wants in the world. Thirty-one years from now, *that man* will control everything from the banks, to the airport, to the police department. With one stroke of his finger on the computer's keyboard, he'll decide your fate."

"So my soon-to-be-husband is a computer hacker?"

"Not just any hacker. Terrel is the master of all hackers. He knows his way through any computer ever programmed."

She shook her head. "This is too implausible."

"Wait, there's more."

"Like what?"

"This morning when I left my time to come here, he was devising a plan to take over the nuclear warheads all over the world. He'll try to take over the world, and in the process, he'll destroy everything. He's evil, Kenya. People in my time fear for their lives. That's why I'm here. To stop him."

A painful twinge began in the back of Kenya's head, working its way up her skull. She closed her eyes and reached back to massage her neck, trying to ease it before it became a full-blown migraine. But Eli's words echoed through her mind and wouldn't leave. *Terrel is corrupt?*

"What does my father have to do with any of this?"

Eli stepped closer, leaning his hip against the railing. "In my time, he's trying to stop your husband. Terrel has kidnapped him and is probably torturing him."

Eli reached into his other pocket and withdrew a ring. She squinted to see it better. When she recognized her father's school ring, she gasped. Besides his wedding band, her father never removed his college ring.

"Where'd you get that?"

"This is what Terrel sent to my battalion of men to prove he had your father. Along with it was his...finger."

She gasped and covered her mouth. Staring at the ring, her mind buzzed with logic...or tried to. But although Eli's story was so far-fetched, the fact that he had her father's ring--the ring he'd never taken off--proved something. Didn't it?

He sat beside her and the wooden bench groaned. His pleasant scent enveloped her as she lifted her gaze to look at his shadowed face. When had he gotten so close? Even in the night, she knew his eyes were pleading for help. She scrunched her forehead as the headache grew.

She scooted closer to the edge of the bench. "And what exactly am I suppose to do about all of this?"

"Don't marry Terrel Montgomery."

She shook her head. "Oh, and everything will change just like that?" She pressed her fingers to her temple. "Let's just say I don't marry him--assuming I believe your story." At seeing his eyes widen, she hurried and continued. "If I don't marry him, he'll marry someone else and he'll still do all those bad things."

Eli leaned in closer. "But that won't happen, Kenya. With your help, we can take Terrel out of the CEO seat and put the rightful president back in."

"Did you say the *rightful* president?"

He nodded.

"Are you referring to Terrel's father? Because if you are, he died five years ago."

"No, I'm talking about Terrel's older stepbrother, Joshua Montgomery."

"Once again, Eli, you're mistaken. Terrel doesn't have an older brother. Not any longer anyway. Joshua Montgomery died after his father passed away."

He shook his head. "Joshua Montgomery is still alive. Terrel and his evil mother, Lisa, had Joshua locked in a mental hospital the year after Adam Montgomery's death. It's true they told the press that Joshua died, but he's not dead, I can assure you of that. I can even tell you in what hospital he's being held prisoner."

She leaned toward him, narrowing her eyes. "And how do you know that?"

"Because Joshua Montgomery is my father."

She let out a small laugh and pushed her fingers through her hair, loosening the style she'd spent hours fixing it into earlier this evening. "If Joshua is in a mental hospital, when did he have time to reproduce?"

"I'm the bi-product of a nurse Joshua had an affair with." He continued, his lips drawn tight. "Although my father was falsely put in a mental hospital and kept sedated, he was still considered a lady's man."

Her laughter grew. She stood, walking to the opening of the gazebo and wrapping her hand around the column. Eli followed. All she wanted was for him to leave so this crazy alcohol-induced dream would go away.

"Oh, Eli, what an imagination you have." She shook her head. "I'm sorry, but I can't believe any of this. If you're seeking help, you've come to the wrong person."

He touched her arm and she met his gaze. In the shadows, his eyes appeared spooky, sexy, and hypnotic. With him laying on that electrifying stare, she was certain he could seduce a nun. At the moment, she wanted to be that nun just to see him try. She shook the indecent thought from her mind. What was she thinking? He had no fashion sense at all. His hair didn't even look combed. She couldn't find *that* kind of man attractive. *The alcohol was definitely working!*

"No, Kenya. I don't have the wrong person. I know you'll help me. You're the only one who can."

"Why me?"

"Because you're the closest person to Terrel."

"What about his mother?"

"Lisa is as corrupt as her son. I'm not going to ask for her help. She'll have me committed just like she had my poor father."

Kenya leaned against the gazebo frame. "Eli, I'm going to be honest with you. The truth is I don't want to help. Your story sounds great, and I'm sure my father would love to hear it and perhaps write a book out of it, but I don't have time for this nonsense. I have more important things to do."

"What's more important than trying to get my father out of the mental institution and into the CEO chair where he belongs? Terrel doesn't deserve that seat. Hell, he doesn't even deserve his inheritance."

She plopped her hands on her hips. "What makes you think that? Of course Terrel deserves it. Adam Montgomery was his father, for heaven's sake."

A grin came back to his oh-so-tempting mouth. He folded his arms across his massive chest. Hmm, what she'd give to run her hands over his muscles. She shook the thought away. *She'd have to touch him...and his clothes. Eww.*

"I hate to prove Terrel a liar, but he's not Adam's legitimate son. When Lisa married Adam twenty years ago, she had a four-year-old son from her first marriage. Lisa legally had Terrel's name changed not too long afterward, which means Terrel isn't Adam's blood son."

"Okay, that's enough." Her head pounded, the confusion overwhelming her. She placed her hands over her ears. His accusations were plaguing her own doubts about Terrel. She couldn't have that. Not when the champagne wouldn't let her think straight. "You're slandering my future husband's name and I won't stand for it." She marched down the gazebo stairs and pointed to the front of the house. "Please leave before I call security."

Eli's shoulders drooped and his sexy smile disappeared.

"Fine." He slunk down the stairs, stopping in front of her. Up this close, his spicy cologne wafted inside her head, and the incredible scent made her want to sigh in pleasure. The hairs on his goatee appeared soft, and she wanted to run her hand over his chin to see how it felt. She fisted her hands tight to hide her reaction. She'd never wanted to do this with a *bad boy* before. Why now?

"I'll leave," he said, "but I'm not giving up in my pursuit for justice." He touched her cheek. Once again, a healthy jolt of sensual power surged through her. Perhaps he was from another time. Why else would he set her body on fire this way?

"But will you do something for me?" He cocked his head. "Will you at least confront Terrel about his stepbrother and really study his reaction? Ask him about legally changing his name, and see what his answer is. Maybe then you'll believe a little of what I've said."

He leaned in closer and brushed his lips across her forehead. She held her breath. *He's going to attack me.* But when he stepped back, relief washed over her. He privileged her with his sexy smile.

"It was nice to meet you, Kenya Whitaker. I'm glad to know my first impressions of you were incorrect."

He turned to leave, but she stopped him, touching his powerfully muscular arm. "What do you mean by that?"

"I thought you would be the snobbish fiancée of the controlling Terrel Montgomery, but you're nothing like I expected." He chuckled. "In fact, I wonder even now how you and Terrel got together. I hope you don't mind me saying you deserve better. You should have a man who'll love you unconditionally, and not for the prestige your family's name will bring him."

Before she could ask him what he'd meant, Eli stepped away and into the shadows. She hesitated a moment as his comment ran through her mind. What did he mean? She rushed to where she'd seen him last and glanced around the yard. He'd disappeared. She scrunched her forehead. No, he couldn't have just vanished. Yet where was he and why couldn't she see him?

She took in a fortifying breath, moving toward the house. Tomorrow she'd realize this was all a dream. Funny, but she'd never had such weird dreams before. Definitely the champagne.

Her father would get a big kick out of this when she told him. Hopefully, Terrel would think it was just as silly, too.

Two

"Good morning, Mary Sunshine." George beamed as Kenya walked into her shop the next morning. He shook his head. "Boy, oh, boy, honey, look at you. Damn if I haven't seen anything sexier in my life." He whistled. "I've never known skin tight jeans and heels to go so well with a regular cotton white shirt and Levi jacket. If I didn't know any better, I'd think you were some biker's babe."

She groaned and held her head, trying to keep it from blasting apart from the noise. Taking cautious steps into her office, she walked behind her desk. She slumped in the chair and pushed her sunglasses back to protect her eyes.

"George? Will you cease the sexist remarks for the remainder of this afternoon? Also, will you please close the blinds? It's making my headache worse."

Her assistant laughed and did as she requested, then came up behind her and massaged her neck. "Did you tie one too many on last night?"

"You could say that," she grumbled. "Plus, my induced state gave me the weirdest dreams, and it kept my mind awake most of the night."

"Oh, I'm sorry, honey. Do you want George to fix you one of his famous Espresso's with a touch of Vodka?"

"No. I'm swearing off liquor forever." She reached up, grabbed George's hand, and moved him to where she could see him. "But you can tell me what in the hell has you so cheerful this morning."

He covered his hand over his mouth and giggled. For a gay man, he was certainly happy all the time. His forty-year-old body was as lean as most twenty-year-olds. He had a spunky personality, which contributed to his colorful taste in wild clothes, and of course, the matching glasses he had with every outfit. But, he was a brilliant assistant and wonderful friend, so she excused everything else.

He cocked his head. "Guess who popped in this morning?"

"Who?"

"Miss Tina LaRoussè." He flipped his hand through the air and lifted his nose high. "She pranced in here like she owned the place." Demonstrating, he copied Tina's little walk, even swung his arm the way Tina did.

"Are you serious?" Kenya sat up in her chair. "What did she want?"

"She didn't say for sure, but I think she wanted to take a peek at your wedding dress."

"You didn't show her, did you?"

"Do you take me for a fool? The only thing I want to show that woman is the door."

She exhaled, sinking into her chair. "Thank you. Last night she was at Lisa's party, and Lisa suggested I look at Tina's portfolio. Apparently, Tina has a killer designer wedding dress Lisa has flipped over."

"Has Lisa seen your design?"

"No, and I want to keep it that way. I don't want anyone to see it until my wedding day."

George slapped his hand on his hip. "You go, girl."

Kenya laughed. "George, have I told you lately what a great asset you are to my company?"

"Not so far today."

She leaned forward on the desk. "Well, you are. If I could give you a raise, I would."

He displayed a cheesy grin. "You just might do that anyway. After Tina left, I received five calls from women who'd been at your party last night. Honey, they loved your evening gown creation, and they all ordered one."

Kenya's smile grew along with her headache. "This is great news."

"The best."

The bells on the front door rang announcing a customer. George excused himself and hurried to greet the person.

Kenya drummed her fingers on the desktop as her thoughts moved to the comical events that had taken place last night--or more specifically, that strange dream. It had to be a dream, even though she could still smell Eli's sexy scent and remembered the tingles that had danced throughout her body. But no, it wasn't real. Why else would the man just disappear like he'd done and right before her eyes?

But he'd brought up some interesting facts about the Montgomery family; facts Terrel should have told her by now. Why hadn't her fiancé informed her of his older brother? Was he purposely hiding something from her? She should take Eli's advice and ask Terrel questions. She didn't want to act suspicious…yet she'd die from curiosity if she didn't find out what the hell was going on.

Grumbling, she picked up the phone and dialed Terrel's number. After three rings, his secretary answered. "Hello, Betty, this is Kenya. Is Terrel around?"

"No, he's held up in one of his meetings."

Kenya sighed. "Yes, I should have known."

"Is there something I can do for you?"

"Yes." She paused, debating whether or not to ask. "Betty? How long have you been Terrel's secretary?"

"I've been employed with Montgomery's Aisle for almost five years."

Kenya's heart sank. "Oh, so you didn't know his father?"

"No, I'm sorry to say I didn't get that privilege. Why?"

"Just wondering." She let out a deep sigh. "Can you have Terrel call me when he's free?"

"I sure will."

"Thanks, Betty." Kenya placed the receiver on the cradle and dropped her head in her hands. What was wrong with her? It *was* a dream...wasn't it? Eli, a dream; a figment of her imagination--and boy, what an imagination she must have because he was one good-looking man, especially since he didn't have a lick of fashion sense. But then, it was dark out and she was slightly intoxicated.

Growling, she massaged her head. Her problem was lack of affection from her fiancé. Why else would she imagine a man like Eli who was totally opposite in what she wanted in a man? She'd have to do some serious convincing so Terrel would find time for her. It had been so long. Why hadn't he touched her? Had her body suddenly repulsed him?

She hurried and called Lucinda, Lisa Montomery's housekeeper to find out if she knew Joshua. Unfortunately, Lucinda and the other servants had been hired on after Joshua and Adam's deaths.

Kenya pushed away from the desk and stood, stretching her arms above her head as she worked out last night's kinks. Taking caution, she removed her sunglasses and squinted through the slightly darkened room.

Rubbing her forehead, she walked into the bathroom to splash some water on her face, but from out in the lobby came a man's deep laughter. She froze.

It couldn't be.

She hurried toward the very sound causing tingles to dance across her skin. Stopping inside her office door, she stared at the customer her assistant helped. Standing in front of a full-length mirror with George draping different colored sample cloths over his shoulder, was none other than the man of her crazy dream.

What is he doing here? Anger welled up from the pit of her stomach, and she barely managed to bite back the frustrated scream that rose in her throat. How did he know where she worked? He must have followed her. He probably stayed outside her apartment last night and trailed her this morning.

She stood still while George fawned over the very handsome dream-like vision in her shop. Eli actually looked sexier today than he did last night. Was it because she could see him in the light? Yet Eli was dressed exactly as she remembered, except he wore a pair of out-dated sandals. She rolled her eyes. Gads, they didn't even match his clothes!

Eli laughed at George's sense of humor, which made the so-called future-man's eyes twinkle. *Sexy as hell.* She certainly didn't believe his time-travel story, but then, what was his purpose? And how did he get her father's ring? Perhaps she should find out what he really wanted.

Eli's eyes moved in the reflection of the mirror and met hers. His heated gaze traveled over the length of her. He smiled in that knee-quaking way of his. A sexual tremor ran through her and her heart skipped a beat. She cursed the strange reaction. Indigestion. It had to be indigestion.

George must have noticed Eli's distraction, because he looked over his shoulder at Kenya. Her assistant placed his hands on his hips and marched over to her, his mouth pulled in a pout.

"Why didn't you tell me your cousin was in town?"

"What?" she asked, but already knew the answer.

Eli stepped away from the mirror and came toward her. "Now George," he began, but kept his gaze on her. "I told you not to get after her." He walked up to her and stopped. His grin widened. "Hi, cuz."

She'd play along. After all, she had to find out his story. She couldn't stop the sudden tug on her lips as they lifted. "Eli."

"Now, girl." George huffed. "I want to know why you'd let your cousin walk around town looking like he'd just been dumped off the farm truck." He turned and picked at Eli's black shirt as if it were a rag. "I mean just look at him. This man should not be wearing such filth, especially since he's related to you."

She couldn't tear her gaze away from Eli's incredible emerald eyes. "Well, George, I just found out last night he was in town, which is why I told him to come to the shop today. I knew you'd be able to help him pick something out that's more presentable to wear in public."

Eli's eyes widened, and she held in her laugh. Eli glanced quickly over George's attire, and a deep blush stained the future-man's cheeks. Red was his color.

"Actually," Eli countered as he swung his gaze back to her, "I thought you could help me go shopping." He withdrew a card from his back pocket. "I have Daddy's credit card today."

She pulled a strip of material off his shoulder. The warmth from his body was still on the fabric, as was his sexy scent. "I guess I can take off a few hours to go shopping." Besides, how else was she going to get to know him?

George elbowed her in the ribs. "Now don't disappoint me, honey. You better bring him back looking like Mel Gibson."

Kenya couldn't hold back her laugh this time. "Oh, I'll try. Just let me grab my purse." She walked into her office, picked up her purse and keys, then side-by-side, she and Eli left the shop.

He didn't say a word until they reached her car, and it was just to say, "Here, let me open the door for you."

She allowed him to take her keys, and when his fingers brushed by hers, her heart fluttered again. She tried ignoring the feeling when he opened her door, and then like a gentleman, he closed it after she climbed in. She waited until he was in and had his seat belt on before speaking.

"I'm surprised to see you today."

He looked at her. "Why? I told you I wouldn't give up."

She chuckled and started the car. "I thought I had dreamed it all last night."

"Oh, really?" He leaned closer. Her gaze fell to his lips as they curled into a grin. "Is that why you called Lisa's housekeeper and asked about Adam and Joshua Montgomery in your office?"

She sucked in a quick breath. "How did you know?"

"I overheard." He reached up to his ear and took out a hearing aide. "George was talking my ear off, but I had my hearing device tuned into your office."

Her cheeks heated, so she looked away. "Okay, I'll confess, although I thought last night was a dream, you did bring up some good points that made me want to ask questions."

His finger stroked her chin, turning her face to his. Her heart seemed to jump to her throat. Damn his sexuality.

"I take it you didn't find any answers," he asked.

"No."

"Don't give up. We'll find them."

"No, *we* won't. Listen, Eli, I still don't believe you're from the future."

He shrugged. "Then who am I and how did I get your father's ring?"

"Wish I knew."

He chuckled and sat back in his seat. "For now, let's just pretend we're cousins." He gave her a wink.

Shaking her head, she put the car in drive and headed toward her destination further into the city. As she drove, her mind filled with questions that needed answering before she went completely insane. Hopefully, he would give her reassuring answers. His intoxicating presence bothered her, almost as much as her confusion.

"Eli?"

"Yes?"

"Can you kindly explain what you meant last night when you suggested Terrel was using me for the prestige my family's name will bring him?"

He chuckled. "Your father was the Senator of New York a couple of years ago."

She scowled, tightening her hands on the steering wheel. "I don't see how my father has anything to do with Terrel Montgomery. Terrel is a powerful man in his own right. Why would he need my father?"

"Because the state of New York loved your father when he was Senator. Your father has certain connections Terrel will never possess."

"It still doesn't make sense."

"Believe me, Kenya, it will in a few years when Terrel befriends some of the connections through your father, and it's through them that he gains more power."

Rolling her eyes, she concentrated on driving in silence. During the fifteen minutes to the store, Eli played with the radio stations. The constant flipping of channels grated on her nerves, but finally he settled on classic rock. He hummed along and tapped his toe. She couldn't believe how well she enjoyed his deep voice.

One thing that bothered her was the way he kept his eyes on the road...and on the other cars passing. Whenever a car would stop beside them as they waited for a traffic light, Eli would scrunch in the seat and put his hand to his face as if he didn't want anyone to look at him. Perhaps he didn't like crowds. So, instead of taking him to Montgomery Aisle, she took him to a smaller men's clothing store. One not so elaborate.

When she pulled into a parking stall and killed the engine, he leaned over and touched her arm. "Thanks."

"For what?"

"For not deserting me." He stroked her cheek. "You're an exceptional woman."

His attention dropped to her lips, and an irregular pound began in her heart. Would he kiss her? But he pulled away, opened his door and climbed out. She remained seated only until she could control her quick breaths, but soon he opened her door again.

He held out his hand for her to take, which she did. She couldn't tear her attention away from his eyes when his warm hand encompassed hers; the warmth from his body blended with hers and caused havoc to her system. Eli had literally hypnotized her.

"Tell me, do all the men from your time possess such superb manners?"

His chest shook with silent laughter. "No."

"Then why are you so different?"

"Where I come from, it's not often I see a real lady. Believe me when I say it's an honor to treat you like this." He gave her a wink. "I enjoy giving attention to such a beautiful woman."

Her cheeks tingled with a familiar burning and she looked away. "Okay, Eli, if anybody asks, you are my cousin from...from..."

"Minnesota? Just off the farm?"

He poked her in the ribs and she jumped. The mere touch of his finger sparked something incredible in her body that she didn't want to think about.

She let out a shaky laugh. "Okay, from Minnesota."

He stayed right by her side as they walked through the small store. Her elbow continued to bump into his, causing greater confusion when heat spread all over her. She didn't exactly like it--or maybe she liked it more than she should. When most of the women in the store gazed upon Eli as if he were the hunk-of-the-month, Kenya grinned. They must be looking past his outdated clothes and hideous sandals.

She was used to walking beside a good-looking man; Terrel was extremely handsome. But there was something different about Eli. He was as dark as Terrel was light--both in skin and hair color, and Eli's copper skin looked very good on him. He wasn't as tall as Terrel, but somehow because of this, she was more relaxed around him. The future-man wasn't as cocky and assured as Terrel, and Eli was more easy-going. Secretly, she wished Terrel were more like Eli.

Eli turned into a totally different man once he started trying on clothes. His zany personality came forth, and he made her laugh too many times to count, especially when he chose a style of clothing that made him look like George.

He walked out of the dressing room, swinging his hips in a feminine rhythm, then posed right in front of her with his hands at his waist. "Tell me, Kenya. Do you think George would approve?"

Laughter burst from her. "Oh, yes. You'd be George's hero for sure. Forget about Mel what's-his-name."

His smile relaxed as he touched his finger to his chin, slowly tapping as he looked over his shoulder at his side profile in the full-length mirror. "Umm, I don't know." His hands slid down the leather tight pants, bringing Kenya's attention to his very powerful legs and buttocks, not to mention the ever-present bulge behind the zipper that didn't seem to disappear.

"These pants might work, but where will I be able to wear them?" He switched his gaze back to her. "And how will I sit without them ripping my crotch and showing off my lacey thong underwear?"

Once again, she let out a bark of laughter. Without another word, he shrugged and sashayed back into the dressing room.

What was it about this man that could make her heart sing not even twelve hours after meeting him? And why couldn't Terrel make her heart leap as Eli had done? This man was still a stranger to her, yet she was more comfortable with him than her own fiancé. The new feeling scared her. Why would she feel this way about a man who was obviously insane? At least his time-travel story was.

She breathed a heavy sigh. Hopefully, she'd figure out his real story and get rid of him. She wasn't supposed to be having feelings like this. She was engaged, for heaven's sake. She must remember Terrel was real, Eli wasn't.

After another hour, Eli picked out three full outfits-- some she had to tell him to put back because they didn't match--and had the purchases charged to his credit card. *Men!* She didn't want to ask in front of the cashier, but she wondered where he'd gotten the card.

She tried to help him with his bags, but he refused. As they walked to her car, he was just enough in front of her that she could see his bulging biceps--and oh, what wonderful bunches of muscles he had. Dare she say his body looked harder than her own fiancé's?

Once again, he tried not to be noticed as he held the bags close to his face, or turned his back to the traffic. Very strange. She opened the trunk for him and he piled the bags inside. When he bent, his new pants accented his nicely shaped rump, and suddenly her palms itched to slide over his backside. When the urge threatened to get out of control, she pushed her hands into the pockets of her jeans.

He closed the trunk and stepped in front of her, draping his arms over her shoulders. "Okay, cuz, what other forms of entertainment do you have in store for me today?"

Her heart hammered. If he only knew. But no, she must not even think of such things. She was engaged to the perfect man. She just had to remember that.

Three

Kenya unlocked the door to her apartment and walked inside, Eli a close second behind her. His attention roamed around her tidy front room. He walked in further, running his fingers along the back of the sofa. "So, this is home-sweet-home, huh?"

She threw him a glare. "Eli, this is not your home, this is mine. Remember that, will you?" A slight pound started in her forehead, threatening to ruin her afternoon. She marched into the kitchen toward the medicine cupboard to get some aspirins.

This morning's shopping trip went well. Too well. Eli had been the most charming, the most fun man she'd had the pleasure to spend time with. How could she be more comfortable with him in just a few hours than the many months of being with Terrel? Of course, that could explain why she'd allowed a strange man to convince her to let him stay at her apartment. Those irresistible puppy eyes of his could melt an iceberg. They'd certainly melted her defenses.

"Which room is mine?" He followed her into the kitchen and to the window, closing the blinds.

She scowled. "The room you'll be staying in is at the end of the hallway to your left."

He flashed his wicked smile on her again before picking up his shopping bags and walking that direction. Her gaze dropped to his rear. She had the urge to reach out and grab, to glide her hands over his muscles and feel the ripple down each leg.

Cursing to herself, she yanked a cup off the shelf and filled it with water. Very cold water. She took two pills and gulped down the liquid, choking on the last swallow. She wiped the back of her hand across her mouth. *What's wrong with me? I'm acting like a teenager whose hormones are running out of control.*

"Kenya?" Eli asked from the extra bedroom.

She stepped into the hallway. "Yes?"

He walked out of the room, his shirt unbuttoned, hanging open. Dryness consumed her throat, making it impossible to swallow. She needed another drink--stronger this time.

"You sure keep an immaculate home. Everything has its place, and there's not a speck of dust anywhere."

"So."

"So doesn't that get annoying?"

She rolled her eyes. "Just about as annoying as a man who doesn't know how to groom his goatee or comb his hair."

He chuckled and ran his fingers through his long hair. "How's that?"

She shrugged.

"Do you have rules for when I'm supposed to use the bathroom?"

"Hopefully when you get the urge to go."

His grin widened. "You know what I mean."

"Well...I usually take my showers in the morning, if that's what you're referring to."

He leaned against the doorframe, folding his arms over his chest. "Do you mind if I put my toothbrush next to yours?"

Her heart lifted to her throat. She couldn't speak, let alone think. Especially when his finger lazily drew circles on his chest. The urge to add her fingers to the invisible drawing overwhelmed her. She also wouldn't mind doing a little hands-on work like a sculptor does with clay.

Dismissing the tempting thoughts, she shook her head. "Eli, you're only going to be here a week. Didn't you tell me that was how long you were going to stay?"

"Yes."

She nodded. "Good. Just don't get too comfortable."

"Okay."

His crooked grin gave away his playfulness, and damn if she didn't want to play right back. But she wouldn't. After all, he was crazy--and *she'd* soon be in a straightjacket if she kept this up.

"I need to go back to the office. Are you going to be all right?"

"Yes."

"Do you need my number at work?"

"I know how to use the phonebook."

She took in slower breaths. "Good. I'll see you later tonight."

"Have a nice day at work."

She didn't remember stepping out to her car or even driving to Terrel's office until she walked into the building. Eli was constantly on her mind and she wanted to boot him out. She blamed Terrel. It was her fiancé's fault for ignoring her. Well...she'd force him to take her into his arms and make her forget the new man in her life. It would also be reassuring if he could tell her that everything Eli said about his family was false.

Terrel stood by his secretary's desk when Kenya approached. He looked at her and smiled.

"What are you doing here?" He took a step away from Betty.

"I need to talk to you if you have a few minutes."

He glanced down at his watch. "Yes, but only a few. I have another meeting in a little while."

They walked into his room and he shut the door. His eyes scanned up and down her length, and his gaze darkened. It'd been so long since he'd looked at her this way, yet why didn't it make her heart pound the way it did when Eli looked at her?

"What's with the get-up?" He strode toward her. "I don't think I've ever seen you look so casual, yet mouth-watering desirable at the same time."

He pulled her into his arms and nibbled on her neck. She sighed and smiled. "I really need this right now."

Just as tingles began dancing across her skin, he pulled away, and they disappeared. The familiar lonely feeling returned.

"What do you need to talk to me about? Betty mentioned you'd called earlier today."

She exhaled and moved to sit on his leather-covered chair. "Yes. I had somebody come in the shop today who knew your father."

His eyes widened as he took his seat behind his desk. "Oh, really? Who?"

Her mind scrambled to think of a wealthy name. "Elijah Cavanaugh."

Terrel's brows drew together. "I don't think I've heard of him."

She shrugged. "Probably not. He said he's been out of the country for a few years. I guess he knew your father and your brother quite well."

"How did he know to look you up?"

Her mind scrambled again. Thankfully, she was better prepared than she'd been this morning when Eli made her forget things. "He saw our engagement announcement in the paper, and since he'd passed by my shop a time or two, he decided to come in and make my acquaintance." She waited for his reaction, but his face remained impassive.

"How nice. Did you invite him to the wedding?"

"Of course." She leaned forward on Terrel's desk, resting her elbows on the smooth wood. "But he said something that made me curious."

"What'd he say?"

"He mentioned you were not Adam Montgomery's biological son. Is this true?"

Her heart hammered as she waited for his reaction. Terrel didn't seem the least bit surprised. Once again, he kept an all-to-familiar business expression.

"Yes. Most everybody knows my mother married Adam when I was four years old. A year and a half later, Adam decided to adopt me, so my last name was changed."

She chuckled and shook her head. "I was shocked to hear him say that because you hadn't mentioned it before."

He shrugged. "I'm a Montgomery now. In my mind, I've always been a Montgomery. My life began the day my mother married Adam."

She smiled. "I wish I'd known Adam. He sounds like such a remarkable man."

"He was."

"What was Joshua like?"

This time, Terrel's expression did change. Hard lines crossed his face, his brown eyes turned dark. Obviously, this topic wasn't welcome. She squirmed in her chair, awaiting his response.

"Joshua and Adam were exactly opposite. Even now, I wondered if Joshua had been a legitimate son. I was more like Adam than Joshua."

"I'm sorry. I didn't mean to upset you."

He flipped his hand through the air and relaxed in his chair. "But it doesn't matter now. Joshua's death was a relief to both my mother and me. We didn't know what would have happened to Montgomery's Aisle if Joshua had taken over."

"I hope you don't mind me asking, but what was wrong with Joshua?"

"He was crazy. Loony. Not to mention a very wicked man. In fact, I think it was Joshua who'd given Adam the heart-attack that finally killed him."

She gasped. "Why, what happened?"

"Adam found out about Joshua's gambling habits. That wasn't too bad, but the next day Adam discovered another one of Joshua's bad vices." He paused, but only for a moment. "Joshua was heavily into cocaine, and he was depleting his inheritance."

"Are you serious?"

"Very. Mother knew about it, but she kept it from Adam in fear of what the news would do to his bad heart. Adam confronted Joshua, and Joshua laughingly admitted to his drug problem. Right then, Adam had an attack. The next day, he died."

A sob tore loose from her throat, and she covered her mouth with her hand. "Oh, I'm so sorry."

He scrubbed his hand around his neck. "You didn't know. Right after the funeral, Joshua's habit got out of control and so mother had him put in a drug rehabilitation clinic. Joshua escaped and came home. While we were at work, Joshua had a little party in the kitchen and overdosed."

She reached across the table and touched Terrel's hand. "I'm sorry to make you talk about it. I'll never bring it up again."

He turned his hand over and clasped her fingers. "You didn't know, but the memories are so painful I'd rather forget."

She nodded. Now she couldn't wait to get home and kick that lying so-called *future-man* out of her house.

~ * ~

Kenya stepped into her apartment and slammed the door. All the curtains had been pulled closed on the windows, only a few lights were on in the front room.

She stood in the hallway, listening for Eli's movement. A heavenly aroma wafted from the kitchen and pots clanked together. After throwing her keys and purse on the small table, she marched into the kitchen--and stopped dead in her tracks. He stood by the stove, stirring a wooden spoon around inside a pan. She sucked in a quick breath. *My kitchen's dirty!* But when she studied him more, that thought vanished.

From his appearance, he looked as if he'd just taken a shower. His wet hair swept away from his face and hung down his neck. Although he wore a new pair of jeans and a shirt--that actually matched--and his feet were bare, once again. He looked so damn cozy standing in her kitchen...so damn cozy she wanted to cuddle him next to her. She should be cuddling him right out of her apartment!

He turned toward her and her gaze dropped. His opened shirt showed the ripples of muscles on his hard chest and stomach. His skin looked naturally golden; touched by the sun, and not a hair was visible.

Her mouth grew cotton dry and she wished to hell that he didn't look so incredibly sexy right now. She forced her gaze to meet his eyes, reminding herself how angry she'd been. He smiled, and her traitorous heart started to melt. *No. Can't let that happen!*

"Hi," he said. "I hope you like Fettuccine Alfredo and chicken."

Her heart slipped another notch. *He cooks, too?*

She shook her head, trying to focus on her anger, but he dipped the spoon in the saucepan and brought it to her. Up this close, his spicy cologne nearly made her knees buckle.

"Here, taste this and tell me what you think."

Hypnotized, she kept her eyes on his and obediently opened her mouth. When he slipped the warm spoon inside and the cream coated her lips and tongue, her heart took on a different rhythm. Her body turned gooey and moist, and it had nothing to do with the temperature in the room. The thermostat in her body grew steadily. Taking it slow, he pulled the spoon out, and with his finger, he wiped away a spot on her lips where the sauce had remained. He slipped his finger inside his mouth and she tingled.

"Well? What do you think?" His voice was lower than it had been a moment ago.

I think I'd like to taste you, too. After that thought, her mind went blank from everything else but him. Things she shouldn't be thinking about clouded her mind. She breathed in his aroused musky scent. Hot sensations escalated through her body, touching and awakening secret areas that had never experienced such desire.

"I...I..." She mumbled like a fool, but was unable to correct the mistake.

He grinned, damn him. Setting the spoon down on the stove counter, he moved toward her. Her wobbly legs retreated, but they only succeeded in backing her up against a wall. Now he had her pinned. *I'm in big trouble.*

He pressed his hard body to hers. It was all she could do not to moan aloud from the intense pleasure it brought. When he brushed his fingers so very gently up her neck and face and threaded them through her hair, she closed her eyes, unable to watch his heated green eyes any longer.

"Kenya," he whispered huskily. "God help me, but I want to touch you when you look at me like that."

Stay angry! She brought up her shaky hands and pushed on his chest, intending to stop him. But once his hot muscles flexed beneath his tight skin, all thoughts of stopping him fled. She wanted to run her hands all over his bare chest then search for other parts of his body she could make bare.

"I've wanted to touch you since last night." He bent his head and placed his mouth to the curve of her neck. A moan broke from her throat.

"You smell wonderful," he muttered.

So do you.

The tip of his hot tongue stroked her skin, and she released a deeper moan.

"And you taste good, too."

She had to stop him. She had to stop herself, yet her voice wouldn't work and her body ignored her. Once he gathered her in his arms, she was lost for sure. He kissed her neck then nibbled and sucked, thrilling her completely. Her body melted against his, and she was totally in his control. She clung to the edge of his shirt for support and closed her eyes.

One of his hands slid down her back and cupped her buttocks, pushing her into his hips. When his hard arousal straining through his jeans met with her, another sexual ripple shot through her. He lifted her leg and hooked it over his hip, allowing her to feel more of his heat.

His hand slid up her waist to her breast and her eyes flew open, but she had no intention of stopping him. His eyes were a deeper shade of green, and an intense emotion etched across the very handsome features softening in his eyes.

He flicked his thumb over her tightened nipple. "Kenya, you take my breath away."

She knew exactly what he meant, because for some inane reason, she found it hard to breathe. She licked her dry lips. "Eli–"

He bumped her with his hips again, his hardness separated from her body by a mere piece of cloth. Heat shot through her again. She wanted him...now. She lifted her pelvis and rubbed him back. If he didn't take her right this minute...

The shrilling ring from the phone in the kitchen erased from her mind what she'd been wanting. When the second ring sounded, it had pulled her completely out of her hypnotized state.

She dropped her leg and pushed away from him. Disappointment flooded through her, creating loneliness. She quickly moved over to the phone.

"Hello?" Her voice sounded much too deep to be normal.

"Kenya?"

Inwardly she groaned. "Yes, Dad, it's me."

Out of the corner of her eye, Eli turned off the stove and left the kitchen. She released a ragged sigh. Thank heaven's she'd gotten out of that scrape, but what would happen if he convinced her to continue this later? Would she want to experience the thrill he gave her again?

She leaned her forehead against the wall for support, but her legs still quivered. She wobbled to the kitchen chair and sat. Her breasts ached, and between her legs throbbed, reminding her of what she could have had.

"How did Lisa's party go last night? Anything exciting happen?" her dad asked.

That's an understatement. "No, in fact, I couldn't wait to get home. You know how fake people can be."

"Yes, dear, I do know. But your dress must have been a hit. Your mother talked to a few ladies who'd attended the party and they all said you looked beautiful."

She smiled. "Thanks, Dad. You know, this morning when I arrived to work, George told me that we'd sold five more dresses."

He laughed. "That's my girl. You've certainly made me proud."

"Dad?" she asked, quickly changing the subject. Suddenly, Eli's remark about her father's connections disturbed her. "Can I ask you a serious question?"

"Sure, honey."

"Do you like Terrel?"

He laughed. "Of course I like Terrel. He's a very successful man that will provide a good life for my daughter. What's not to like?"

"Do you think he's marrying me because of...well...because of the ties our family has with New York City?"

Her father paused, and the lengthy silence bothered her. After a few awkward moments, he spoke. "I was never totally satisfied with any of your boyfriends, mainly because I wondered if they just wanted you because of our family name. When I first met Terrel, I wondered the same thing, but he seems like a man who's got his head on straight. He treats you well, gives you anything you want, and he hasn't once asked me for money or my influence."

"Do you think he will?"

"Kenya, honey, why do you ask? Are you having second thoughts?"

She let out a deep sigh. "Sometimes I think I am, but then it's just because I'm getting cold feet. I think Terrel is a great guy, and on a few occasions I find myself questioning my love for him, but all in all, I think he loves me, and he wants to provide for me."

"I think so, too. But honey, does he love you the way you want to be loved?"

She squeezed her eyes shut and rubbed her forehead. This was something she didn't want to answer. Terrel wasn't exactly gifted in the lovey-dovey side of their romance. Not like Eli.

She cursed under her breath. *Why did I think of that?*

"Dad, I really appreciate your help."

"Well, I love you, Kenya, and if you don't feel right about marrying Terrel, your mother and I will understand. I'd hate to see you make the biggest mistake of your life by marrying the wrong man."

"Thanks, Dad. I needed to hear that."

When she hung up the phone, peacefulness settled in her heart. She still didn't know exactly how to handle the situation with Eli, but at least she wasn't as angry as she'd been when she first entered her apartment.

Four

Eli paced the floor in his room, cursing the untimely phone call. He hadn't planned on being so hot for Kenya when he first set out on his mission. He'd seen her before at a distance and thought she was a very beautiful woman, but she belonged to Terrel. Yet now...now he didn't want her to belong to Terrel. That evil man--who had the audacity to call himself a Montgomery--didn't deserve a precious, delicate flower like Kenya.

He stopped at the window and parted the blinds a little, overlooking the street that crossed in front of the apartment building. Taking deep breaths, he calmed his anger. So far, so good. Yet time was running out, and he couldn't get distracted from his goal. The week would soon be at an end, and before next Saturday, he had to stop Kenya from marrying Terrel. At the same time, he had to encourage her to find a way to release the rightful President of Montgomery Aisle from the mental hospital.

He ran his fingers through his hair and sighed. Could he possibly get everything accomplished in such a short time? He had to. His life--his very existence--depended on it. And he couldn't get caught. He had the distinct feeling someone had followed him. If they found him, they'd take him back. That couldn't happen until after he brought Terrel down.

From out in the other room, Kenya's voice echoed in the kitchen as she said goodbye to her father. He hesitated in going out to talk to her. She'd be upset from what had just transpired between them. He couldn't let her hate him. His whole plan would be ruined.

"Eli?" she called.

With a heavy sigh, he walked into the front room where she waited for him, arms folded across her chest and her lips tight.

"Yes?" He took hesitant steps toward her.

"We need to have a little talk."

"Okay." He sat on the sofa.

She remained where she was by the small liquor bar in the corner of the room. "I talked with Terrel today."

He lifted his brow. Why wasn't she going to yell at him for kissing her? "And what did he say?"

"You mean you don't know?"

He shrugged. "Apparently not. I don't know what lies he's been telling lately."

"Well, let's just say he painted a different picture of Joshua Montgomery than you did."

He creased his forehead. "Of course he did. Terrel has never liked Joshua because of the closeness Joshua and his father shared."

She shook her head. "See, there again, Terrel tells a different story."

He relaxed back in the cushions, crossing one leg over the other and stretching his arm over the back of the couch. "Oh, really? What exactly did he say?"

"Only the truth."

"Maybe Terrel's truth."

"The truth is the truth."

"And I guess you're going to believe him over me?"

"Of course. Terrel is my fiancé and you're still a stranger to me." She tucked a lock of her chestnut hair behind her ear.

He stared at her while he wracked his brain with ways to convince her. But she wasn't going to believe a stranger. This was only a temporary snag in his plan, but one he'd figure a way out of soon.

He scrubbed his hand over his goatee. "Okay, let me think of someone you can talk to who knew Joshua when Adam was alive. Maybe a servant?"

She shook her head. "I've already tried that. Apparently, Lisa dismissed Adam's servants right after his death."

"I'm sure they're around New York somewhere."

She huffed. "You're bound and determined to make a liar out of my fiancé, aren't you?"

He jumped up. Taking three long strides, he stood in front of her. Color disappeared from her face, her eyes widening. Damn. He didn't want to frighten her. Just the opposite.

He inhaled slowly, cooling his fury. "Kenya." He caressed her cheek, loving the softness of her smooth skin. "I'm sorry you think the worst in me, but I must admit, I'm trying to prove your fiancé is a liar. I hate to point out the fact that I know him better than you, but I do. Terrel isn't going to show you his bad side because he needs you, or more specifically, he needs your family's influence."

Her chest rose and fell with her quick breaths. Did it stem from her fright or his closeness?

"Give me one more day, please?" He ran the pad of his thumb over her bottom lip. "I'll locate one of Joshua's servants and you can ask them."

She licked her lips. "Eli, I don't know anymore."

"Just one more day, please?" He leaned forward and kissed her neck, just under her ear. Her erratic pulse quickened, as did his heartbeat. Damn, this was exciting, but he didn't want to push her. Now was not the time to continue this.

"One more day and that's all," she said in a shaky voice.

Although he wanted to take her in his arms and smother her with kisses, he regained control over his desires and pulled back. Her eyes had been closed and her lips slightly parted. And, when her lids fluttered open, her eyes were dark with passion.

He stayed close, not really wanting to break the heat sparking between them right now. The longer he watched her face, the more he wanted to kiss her, especially when her attention dropped to his lips. How could he stop himself now? Not when the curious look of interest was evident in her eyes.

He stroked the pad of his thumb across her bottom lip again. "Kenya, do you know how irresistible you are?"

He pressed his lips to hers, and she let out a soft moan. Her hands moved up his chest and linked around his neck. Her body relaxed fully against him. He groaned from excitement. This was easier than he'd thought.

He cradled her perfect body in his arms as his mouth slid across her, nipping and pecking gently, then when her lips opened, he dipped his tongue inside to caress with hers. She kissed as good as she looked--wonderful and heavenly.

He had to keep the kiss simple, but the way she hungrily kissed him drove him crazy, and he wanted to do more. He moved his hands over her back, then down to cup her bottom, pulling her hips into his. She fit perfectly against his growing arousal. He growled and turned the kiss wild, slanting his mouth over hers to deepen the kiss with his tongue.

Quickly, she broke away. "We can't do this." She bumped him aside and walked to the kitchen.

He followed, hoping to do a little more convincing. She stood by the stove dishing up the dinner he'd cooked. Anger lines weren't marking her face as they were earlier. Instead, doubt lingered in the eyes that tried to avoid him. He could tell. And he wouldn't give up.

~ * ~

Kenya stared at her plate of food, moving around the noodles with her fork. She had eaten a few bites, but her nervous stomach wouldn't allow much more, especially when she thought about what she and Eli could have done.

Was she stupid? Why was she so eager to give herself to a total stranger? She couldn't be that sexually frustrated could she? Thanks to Terrel's unwillingness to please her, she already knew the answer. Yet, she couldn't let that rule her thoughts. Lately, the more she considered marrying him, the more frightened she became--and that was before Eli had entered her life.

Still, Eli was unfamiliar to her, and she continued to suspect he was a few cans short of a six-pack. Something about him seemed weird, out of place, but she couldn't identify what it was. Besides, he was all wrong for her...the exact opposite of what she wanted in a man.

The awkward silence at the table kept her from raising her gaze to look at him. She didn't want his hypnotic green eyes to spin her sexual drive out of control again. She didn't want to get to the point where she'd push everything off the table, grab and pin him down, and make wild, passionate love to him. Although the idea had always been a fantasy of hers, it was something she couldn't do with a man she barely knew.

Across the table, Eli shifted his chair, but she kept her attention focused on her plate. Even when he cleared his throat, she wouldn't look at him.

"Kenya? Earlier, we got side tracked from our conversation, and I'd like to talk about it."

Her heart dropped. Did he want to discuss what had almost happened between them?

"Will you please tell me what Terrel had to say about his stepbrother Joshua?"

She released a sigh, then glanced up at him. *Big mistake.* She quickly dropped her attention to her plate. Why did he have to be so damn gorgeous? Why were his eyes so incredibly dreamy, his lips pouty, begging to be kissed? And why was she forgetting that he was so opposite of what she liked in a man?

Food caught in her dry throat, so she finished swallowing. She took a drink to moisten it. "Terrel said that Joshua was a wicked man. He said Joshua was the reason Adam had a heart attack."

When Eli's fork dropped on his plate, she looked up. Anger lines creased on his forehead, and he kept his lips tight.

She continued, "Terrel said Joshua was out of control with his cocaine and gambling habits. When Adam found out about them, Joshua laughed in his face. Terrel said that was when Adam had his heart attack."

He curled his hands into fists and his knuckles turned white. "What did Terrel say about how Joshua died?"

"Terrel said Lisa put Joshua into a clinic to get help for his problem, but Joshua escaped and returned home. That afternoon while Terrel and his mother were at the office, Joshua had his own little drug party and overdosed."

Eli rested his elbows on the table as his head sank into his large hands. His breathing turned heavy as if trying to calm himself.

"Kenya?" he mumbled. "Will you hate me if I can prove Terrel wrong?"

She set down her fork and leaned back in her chair. "How can you?"

He took in a deep breath then straightened, meeting her eyes. "If I remember correctly, my father told me about a disturbing article written in the newspaper around that time. The article was about the Montgomery family secrets." His hard jaw relaxed. "Actually, the article talked more about Terrel than it did Joshua. I remember my father telling me how upset it made Lisa."

A small throb began to build in her head. "What did it say?"

He shook his head. "I think I'll take you to the library tomorrow and we'll look up the article in the archives together." He pushed away from the table and stood.

"Eli." Her voice rose. "Tell me what the article said."

He took a few steps toward the hallway, then stopped, glancing over his shoulder. "Let's wait and see what we find out tomorrow."

Five

Another sleepless night had passed and Kenya was sure if she had any more of these, the bags underneath her eyes would stay permanently. She took a cool shower hoping to bring down the swelling, but even after all the make-up she applied she still looked hung over.

She dressed in a simple pair of gray trousers, a white shirt that showed a little of her tummy, then accented her attire with gray and white striped suspenders. This outfit wasn't one she'd designed, but because it wasn't a popular fashion, people tended to think her creative mind was at work again.

She left her hair down, not even bothering to curl it. Lately, she'd been too tired even to get dressed in the morning. She left the apartment with Eli at ten o'clock, the time she knew the library would open.

Eli wore another pair of new jeans and a green polo shirt. At least he dressed a little better than when she'd first met him. Right now he looked good enough to eat, so she tried not to stare directly into his smoldering eyes. She should have let him buy those ugly, outdated outfits yesterday. Maybe she wouldn't think this way about him. It must be Cupid's fault. Obviously, he'd hit her with a crazy arrow.

Thankfully, Eli didn't talk about their passionate moment last night. Hopefully he never would. During the night as she tossed and turned, she realized how wrong it was to let him pin her against the wall with his hard body and kiss her neck. She wasn't an animal. Yet, she'd acted like one. From now on, she had to remain in control of her body. Just because she had doubts about her wedding didn't mean she could jump in the sack with the next available guy.

Only a handful of people were at the library this early, so an employee showed them into a private room to look through the archives. They each sat at a different computer and scanned through all the articles written the months following Adam Montgomery's death.

The first page about the Montgomery family was about Adam's life. Kenya scanned across the full screen, fascinated with the kind of life he'd led. The article honored him, and the black and white photo slightly resembled Eli with the square jaw of authority, especially, the bedroom eyes and knee-buckling smile. Sexiness must run in the family.

She skipped over a few more pages, and then moved on to another week. After a couple of minutes, Eli sat up straight beside her at his computer. She glanced his way. His eyes narrowed; his mouth drooped in a frown.

She touched his arm. "What is it?"

"It's an article about Adam Montgomery's funeral."

She slid her chair next to his and leaned in to read the newspaper clipping.

"I know you can't see the picture very well, but that man right there," he said, pointing to a broad figure that stood beside the casket in the photo, "is Joshua Montgomery." He zoomed in on the picture, but its image was too blurred to see.

"Terrel is easy to recognize," she added.

"Yes. Terrel always liked to stand out."

She chuckled. "He hasn't changed much in five years."

His manly scent of spice stirred feelings inside of her again, so she scooted back to her own computer. Silence lagged as she and Eli concentrated on searching through the articles.

Suddenly, across the top of the screen in a large print was Terrel Montgomery's name. It nearly jumped out of the screen and slapped her across the face. Her hand froze on the mouse, her body stiffening. The caption read; *Terrel Montgomery arrested for possession of cocaine.* She forced herself to read on, her heart hammering against her ribs.

Late Tuesday night, Terrel Montgomery, son of the deceased multi-billionaire Adam Montgomery, was arrested at his home. Ten ounces of cocaine were found in the Montgomery mansion, and all five people in the house were arrested with possession of a narcotic drug. Terrel Montgomery denied charges, but the drug test administered by New York City Police proved he was indeed, under the influence.

"Oh, God," she mumbled. Her heart plummeted, the blood in her head going along with it. A sharp pain constricted her chest, making her breath come in shallow gasps. Eli moved beside her, leaning in to read the article. He took hold of her cold hand and squeezed.

"I'm sorry, Kenya." His fingers stroked her knuckles.

She continued to read in silence.

The eldest son of Adam Montgomery, Joshua, commented about his reckless brother. He promised to

*have Terrel put in a facility that would help him with
the problem. Joshua promised his brother would not
manage the family business until Terrel was clean.
Lisa Montgomery remains inside the Montgomery
mansion refusing to comment.*

Kenya wasn't aware of her tears until Eli's finger
touched her cheek, wiping them away. She pulled her stare
off the computer screen and looked at him. "You must
think I'm a fool."

"You're not a fool. You trusted Terrel. It's not your
fault he lied to you."

She squeezed her eyes closed and took deep breaths.
"It's amazing," she said, looking back at Eli, "that he
would tell me such an outlandish lie when he knows I could
discover the truth."

"He's not thinking about that. He believes he has
control over you, and in doing so, he knows you'll trust his
word on anything."

She chuckled. "It's true. All this time I've never had
any reason to doubt him." She shrugged. "If not for you, I
would have never come here."

He slipped his arm around her shoulders and kissed her
forehead. "Why don't you go home? I'm going to try and
find some of Adam's old servants."

She rested her head on his shoulder and released a soft
moan. Eli was so comfortable to lean against, and yet so
strong. "I don't know if I want to hear anymore. If Terrel
has lied about this, what else has he lied about?"

"That's what we need to find out." He lifted her face to his. "And we need to find a way to get Joshua out of the mental hospital."

She nodded. "Okay."

"Will you help me?"

"Yes."

He smiled and kissed her forehead again before pulling away. She leaned on him for support as they walked back to the car. Although her body cried out for rest, her mind wouldn't sleep until the truth came out. And that scared her to death.

~ * ~

Kenya lay curled in the same position for several hours. She tried closing her eyes, but the bold letters of the article that proved Terrel's lies ran through her mind. Yet, staring at the wall wasn't doing her any good either. She finally pulled herself out of bed and stretched the stiffness out of her arms and legs.

Eli hadn't returned, and her soul cried out for his company. Funny she'd feel this way after only a few days. How did she become involved so quickly? The answer lay deep in her heart. She must break off her relationship with Terrel. Lately she hadn't been very happy, and she'd been finding fault with him. Was there any goodness in him at all, or had he been lying to her all this time?

She shouldn't keep stringing him along. Tomorrow. She'd talk to him tomorrow and explain she didn't love him any longer.

The ringing of the telephone jarred her to awareness and she hurried to pick it up. "Hello?"

"Kenya? Hi, this is Lucinda."

She snapped to attention. "Hi. How are you?"

"Fine." She paused and cleared her throat. "I am calling because I found some pictures you might like to see."

"Really? What pictures?"

"They are from Terrel's childhood."

Kenya clutched the phone. "Are they any with his brother Joshua?"

"Sí."

Her heart beat with renewed life. "Oh, you're the greatest. When can I see them?"

"I have this afternoon off. Would you like me to bring them over to your place?"

"Yes, please."

"I will be there in a few minutes."

"Lucinda, you, umm, didn't tell Lisa did you?"

"Of course not. Besides, Señora Montgomery has not been around the house lately."

"Oh, Lucinda, please don't let Lisa know. I think she'd get upset."

The housekeeper chuckled. "I stumbled across them in the back of one of her walk-in closets. I knew you would like to see them."

Kenya laughed. "You're a treasure."

"And do not forget it."

Kenya waited for Lisa's maid to arrive, pacing the front room floor like a caged animal. It seemed like the minutes passed by slower than the hours. Finally, there was a knock and she bolted to the door, twisting her ankle on the way.

Gritting her teeth against the sharp pain, she opened the door and let Lucinda in. The older, rotund woman with white stripes in her black hair was the friendliest woman Kenya knew. Lucinda would give the shirt off her back if it meant helping someone in need. After giving her a hug, Kenya ushered her into the front room and sat beside her on the sofa.

"I found three boxes full of pictures hidden way back in one of Señora Montgomery's closets." Lucinda pulled out a large manila envelope. "I do not know why she would have shoved them behind everything unless she is still mourning her husband and Joshua's death."

Kenya kept herself from grabbing the pictures out of Lucinda's hands, but waited until her friend handed them to her. The first bunch of pictures was of Terrel in his younger years. He was a cute boy, so blond he looked almost white, but the slightly older boy in the photo caught her attention.

"Who's this?"

Lucinda smiled. "I believe that is Joshua. He looks so much like his father. Sí?"

Kenya's heart softened when she looked at the dark haired boy with the brilliant smile, and as she continued flipping through the pictures, her heart melted even more. By the time she held the photos of Joshua as a man, she was at a loss for words. He was absolutely the most handsome man she'd ever seen. Now she knew where Eli inherited his good looks.

Joshua was leaner than Terrel, and in most of the pictures, he was the one smiling. Terrel held a scowl.

"I wonder why Terrel didn't like to smile."

"I do not know." Lucinda shrugged. "Right after I started working for Señora Montgomery, I could not help but think what a happy person Terrel was. At first, it bothered me a little because he was not mourning his father and brother like I thought he should, but then I realized he mourned in a different way. Terrel had to be outgoing and happy. He was the new president of a major department store. He had to act the part." She shook her head. "Poor boy. He could not express his loss for his father the way he had wanted."

Lucinda gave Kenya a hug. "You have been good for Terrel. Since he started dating you, he has been a different person. He has been more self-assured; he thinks about the company more, and how he can expand his wealth. To me, that is a good sign. It says he is thinking about his future, and the future of his posterity. I am assuming you plan on having children with him?"

The subject of children turned Kenya's stomach. If what Eli said were right about Terrel, her fiancé wouldn't make a very good father.

She forced herself to smile. "I do want children." *But not with Terrel.*

Lucinda patted Kenya's knee, then stood. "I hope those pictures helped."

"Yes, they really did. Terrel has been so closed mouth about his past, and especially about his older brother. I'm happy you shared these with me."

Kenya gave Lucinda another hug before the housekeeper left. Thankfully, the pictures helped put a face to the man Eli kept talking about, and if Joshua Montgomery was truly alive, it was her duty to help free him.

Six

After a full day's search, Eli's temper was ready to snap. He'd tracked down five of the nine servants who'd been in Adam's employ, only to find those five had left the country unexpectedly right after they were laid off, or they had died from unnatural causes. The information left a bitter taste in his mouth. Terrel and Lisa had to be behind it.

The end of the day approached quicker than he'd expected, leaving him no choice but look for the other four servants tomorrow. Hopefully, they would have a different fate since leaving the Montgomery household.

On the subway ride back to Kenya's apartment, he kept a sharp watch for anybody suspicious that might be watching him in a peculiar way. During this time, the image of Kenya's face kept disrupting his thoughts. This morning all he wanted to do was hold her in his arms and comfort her, yet he'd also wanted to find Terrel and beat some sense into him. That man was so damn sure of himself he never thought she would find out about his past.

Eli smiled as his hopes escalated. Perhaps he'd stopped the wedding after all?

He hated to see Kenya so upset. He didn't like her frown, and he didn't like the lines of stress marking her flawless face. His gut wrenched. He also couldn't stand seeing her broken heart reflected in her amazing blue eyes.

Of course, Terrel and Lisa were in the business of ruining people's lives, which was why Eli had to stop them.

He balled his hands at his side when he thought about all the injustice those two people had created. He was lucky to be able to come back and attempt to correct the wrong that had been made, but when he thought about leaving in a few more days, a wrenching pain began in the pit of his stomach and made his chest hollow. How he'd fallen head-over-heels so quickly for that woman, he didn't know. But she'd formed a place in his heart, a place he rather enjoyed having there. When he made her smile, it brightened his day, and when he made her laugh, it was like angels singing from heaven. How could he live without that? He couldn't. But he just might have to, and the thought tore him apart.

He stepped off the subway and headed slowly toward Kenya's house. Through the busy streets, he kept searching for anything suspicious. He didn't trust anybody, except Kenya, and it worried him somebody would eventually try to stop him from completing his mission.

After stopping by a drug store to get a box of condoms...just in case...Eli hurried toward Kenya's apartment. He knocked on the door before opening it. "Kenya, it's me." He stepped inside and closed the door.

"I'm in the kitchen," she answered.

He grinned. The kitchen was where they'd started things last night. Would tonight be a repeat? Would tonight be the night he could show her how he felt? Because of the uncertainty Terrel placed on Eli's life, he didn't know what his future would hold, and he wanted to be with Kenya just once before he had to return.

He set the small plastic bag on the end table and followed the scent of food into the kitchen. Kenya sat at the table reading the newspaper as she ate her dinner. He glanced at the large flat box beside her and laughed.

"Pizza?"

She shrugged. "I didn't feel like cooking."

"You're just so perfect in every way, I didn't think you'd be the type to like pizza." He walked to the table and plopped down on a chair, lifting the lid to the pizza box. "Sausage and mushroom. My favorite."

Her eyes widened. "Are you serious?"

"Yes. Why? Don't you think they have pizza in the future?"

She shook her head. "I...I just can't believe we have the same taste in food. Terrel absolutely abhors eating this."

Eli rolled his eyes. "Goes to show you how much Terrel knows." He picked up a slice and sank his teeth into the gooey cheese and sighed. "Terrel is definitely missing out on the finer foods in life," he mumbled with a full mouth.

"Guess what I did today?" she asked.

He shook his head, continuing to consume another bite.

"Lisa's housekeeper, Lucinda, found some old photos of Terrel and his brother when they were growing up, and she brought them over for me to look at."

Eli met her stare, but said nothing.

"For some inane reason, Lisa had hidden all the pictures in boxes and stuffed them in the back of her closets."

"Well? What did you think when you saw them?" he muttered in between chews.

She tilted her head, her eyes narrowing on him. "I think you resemble your father and grandfather quite a bit."

He smiled. "Thank you. I take that as a compliment."

"I also noticed Joshua smiled a lot more than Terrel."

He swallowed before talking this time. "Of course. Terrel was extremely jealous of Joshua. Lisa wanted her son to have everything, but Adam knew who the rightful heir was. Although Adam loved his stepson, Adam could never love him as he loved his own flesh and blood. Terrel couldn't stand that, which made Terrel one very unhappy child."

"Did your father ever like Terrel?"

He nodded. "My father told me stories of when he and Terrel were younger. He enjoyed having a younger brother to play with. It wasn't until they were older when he noticed the selfish change in his stepbrother. Terrel was always trying to get him in trouble, and when his plans failed, it made Terrel even angrier. That's why I think Terrel had him locked up in an asylum." He hesitated, scratching his head. "I just wonder how he was able to buy people to lie for him. Most people liked and trusted Joshua more than Terrel, so I wonder where Terrel found the people to do his bidding."

"I think that will be hard to prove."

"Yes, but we must in order to get my father released."

She leaned forward, crossing her arms on the table. "So, what did you do today?"

He blew out a frustrated breath. "Not what I'd planned, that's for sure."

"What happened in your search?"

"You wouldn't believe it. I didn't."

"What?"

"I found five of the nine servants, but I didn't get to talk to one."

Her perfectly shaped brows drew together. "And why not?"

"Because they were either dead or had moved out of the country."

Her eyes widened. "You've got to be kidding."

"I wish I were."

"That's too coincidental."

"You're not telling me anything new."

She pushed away from the table and picked up her empty plate. As she walked past him to the sink, he couldn't keep his attention off her cute little derriere. The exposed skin around her waist made his fingers itch to touch her softness, to let his hands roam underneath her shirt. She looked so damn sexy right now. Hell, she always looked sexy.

Suddenly, his appetite changed and the pizza no longer interested him. What interested him more was using those thin shields of rubber that were still in the box in the other room; and using every last package before he had to go back in a couple of days.

As she rinsed her plate at the sink, he pushed away from the table and moved to her, stopping mere inches in back of her. Kenya's body stilled, as did her breathing. He touched her wavy, chestnut hair, stroking his hand down the length, leaving it on the small of her back where her hair ended.

"I missed you today," he mumbled as his other hand caressed her arm.

She shivered. "Eli, I...we...we shouldn't do this."

"Do what? We're not doing anything." He slid his hand from her back and around her waist, pulling her body against him.

"No, but if you keep this up, we'll probably be doing something soon."

He found her fingers with his other hand and linked them. "And the idea doesn't tempt you?" He brought her hand to his mouth and kissed her knuckles.

"It's not that."

"Then what is it?" He circled his other hand around her waist and on her tight stomach where the skin showed.

"This is wrong," she answered deeply.

He moved his hand underneath her shirt. Her body remained still until he cupped her breast, then she melted against him. His other hand released her fingers in order to hold her up.

He squeezed her breast lightly, her nipple hardening beneath her bra. "This doesn't feel wrong to me."

She let out a small gasp. "You're missing the point."

He lightly pinched her nipple. "No, the point is right here, and I don't plan on missing it tonight."

Her hand came up to her breast, but she didn't pull it away. Just the opposite. She helped him to squeeze her again.

"Oh, Kenya," he muttered as he kissed her hair. "I wanted to do this to you last night."

"Me, too."

"You're perfect for my hands and mouth." He brushed his fingers over her nipple.

A cute little gasp came from her throat and she let her head fall back to rest on his shoulder.

"I think you feel wonderful, too." She snuggled her backside against his growing arousal.

A deep groan tore from his throat as he slid his hand down the front of her body to the junction of her legs and pushed his fingers against the heat forming in her pants. While one of her hands helped him play with her breasts, her other hand held his fingers against her. The thrill was too much, and he wanted more. He nibbled on her ear and she shivered again.

"Kenya, is your bed bigger than mine?"

"Yes."

"I want to take you there."

"Yes."

She swung around in his arms and kissed his mouth hard. He met her demanding kiss as he lifted her and carried her to her bedroom, grabbing the small plastic bag on the way. A lamp beside her bed was on, so he didn't bother with more lights. He set her on the bed, and quickly ripped off his shirt. Before he could get to his pants, her hands were there, helping.

Within seconds, she'd removed his jeans then yanked on the elastic of his boxer shorts. He stopped her hands before they came off.

"Whoa, slow down, my sweet. We've got all night."

Her attention was pulled to the mark on his upper left thigh. She ran her finger over it. "What's this?"

"A birthmark."

"Looks good on you."

He grinned and pulled her up. "I want to see if your birthday suit looks good on you, too."

She remained still and let him remove her clothes. He took his time, enjoying seeing each section of her body exposed. When she stood in front of him wearing nothing but her white laced panties and matching bra, his hunger grew.

He cupped her perfect breasts and she helped him take off her bra. He stroked her nipples and loved the way they hardened, which in turn made his arousal heavy. When she stepped back and lay on the bed, he followed. As he lay beside her, she placed his hands on her breasts. He cupped them, readying them for his mouth.

"You're perfect," he mumbled before bending his head and sucking a point inside his mouth.

She moaned and arched, giving him more. He swirled his tongue around the beaded texture, then sucked harder. She cried out, but held his head to her.

He moved on top, pressing his stiffness between her legs. With his aide, she removed his boxer shorts before he latched his mouth back to her breast.

She wiggled beneath him, turning him on that much more. He tore his mouth away from her breasts and trailed his kisses down her stomach to her white panties. He breathed against the very part he couldn't wait to devour, and she squirmed. She moved her hand near his mouth, touching herself over her panties. He nipped at her finger then sucked it into his mouth. When she pulled it out, she slid her finger underneath the silky material.

He latched his teeth on the edge and pulled them down her slender legs. He couldn't believe how incredibly sexy she was--and to think she was all his.

He kissed her stomach again then over one hip. Trailing his fingers near hers, he let her take them and lead them to the spot he couldn't wait to touch again. She pushed his fingers inside her and groaned. He added another finger then slid them in and out of her wetness.

She cried out, tossing her head on the pillow. He withdrew just enough to stick his fingers in her again, stroking her.

"Oh, Eli."

Laying her head back on the bed, she closed her eyes. God, she was beautiful, and so damn sexy.

Soon she was writhing on the bed, her hips bucking wildly. He couldn't take any more pleasurable torture. He had to be inside her. Now. He jumped off the bed to retrieve the condom and placed it over his swollen length.

Her gaze remained on him, and she welcomed him back on top of her with open arms. When he slid inside of her wet body, he groaned. He moved his hips with hers, and the rhythm began to build again. He bent his head and captured her breast as he pushed himself inside. She wrapped her legs around his waist, making him go deeper.

Soon, she cried out and repeated his name. He, too, rejoiced in the erotic feeling of joining with her. It surprised him how well they fit together, but then, he'd felt that way about her since their first meeting.

It wasn't long before he lost control. With one last push, he released himself, finally able to reach that heavenly place. The place he wanted Kenya to take him to again. She'd made him feel things he'd only dreamt of feeling. She made him laugh and sing, want to hold her in his arms and never let go.

They crawled under the sheets and he gathered her back in his arms. She snuggled against him and within minutes, she was asleep. This would be the first night in many that he'd be able to sleep comfortably. He only hoped this week could go on forever.

~ * ~

Kenya lazily extended her arms over her head and smiled, knowing her grin stretched from ear-to-ear. With a sigh, she snuggled back into the mattress, pulling the blankets over her naked chest. Eli had climbed out of bed an hour ago, kissing her forehead before leaving the room. She'd been too tired to make him stay. After all, they'd made love four more times during the night. His passionate lovemaking had tuckered her right out.

Perhaps Cupid knew what he was doing after all. A giggle bubbled up from her throat. Eli definitely knew how to make her body come alive. He knew what buttons to push, and what spots to lick. *Damn, he was good!* Even now, her body tingled from remembrance, and she wanted more.

She yawned and stretched a final time before climbing out of bed and padding to the bathroom to take a shower. Work had suffered because of her new houseguest, and she really needed to get back to her shop. George was probably livid by now.

When the hot water sprayed on her body, she closed her eyes and relaxed to the pounding of the massage dial on the showerhead. Although she was eager to return to work, she knew Eli would be on her mind all day. How could he not? He'd set her body on fire and left her breathless. Her fiancé had never done that.

Terrel.

She sighed heavily and leaned her head against the wall. What was she going to do about Terrel? Over the past few months, her love for him had evaporated, but she'd refused to believe it was happening. Apparently, her heart had known she didn't love him any longer. She wouldn't have been so willing to give herself to another man any other way. She'd betrayed Terrel's trust...but hadn't he been lying to her since she'd met him?

Now she had to find a way to tell him the wedding was off. Yet should she wait? If Eli needed more information on Terrel, she might be the only way he could get it.

When an idea sprang to mind, she straightened and opened her eyes. Terrel might have something in his office that would be beneficial to Eli's father's case. Only she could get it for him. So far, Eli had proved he was the man telling the truth. Not Terrel. If Eli was also correct in thinking Terrel was corrupt, she couldn't stand aside and not help. If Joshua Montgomery was the rightful heir to Montgomery Aisle, she had to do something to get him out of the mental hospital.

She hurried with her shower and quickly dressed in a pair of tan slacks and a coffee colored long-sleeved blouse. While buttoning up the front with one hand, she flipped through her day planner with the other. Had she written anything about Terrel's agenda?

"Damn." She slammed the book closed. She hadn't. She hurried over to the phone and called his secretary. After a short chat with Betty, Kenya grinned, her mind turning a million times over. She should sneak into his office while he was at one of his meetings. Her heart hammered from the mere thought. She'd never done anything devious in her life. Could she actually do it?

She walked into the bathroom to style her hair. As she used the blow dryer, she mapped out the plan in her mind.

She'd wait until Betty went to lunch--usually around noon. The first place Kenya would look in Terrel's office would be his important files. He usually had them under lock and key, but she knew where he kept the extra keys.

What was she searching for? Invoices? Bills? Something that showed he was paying the institution where Joshua stayed. But where was it? She'd forgotten to ask Eli that minor detail. In fact, she hadn't asked Eli a lot of things. Funny she'd taken his word so easily about being a future-man.

She laughed and turned off the blow dryer. Did she really believe he was from the future? Deep down inside she didn't, yet how else would he know everything he'd proved to her yesterday? How else would he know the future if he hadn't been there? She'd read her father's time-travel book right after it was published. His book did make sense--if time travel were really possible.

She let out a frustrated breath and shook her head. Time-travel was too damn mind-boggling.

It only took her a few minutes to apply her make-up. Pulling a brush through her hair only took a moment, too. Once again, she didn't do anything fancy to it. Didn't have time. Or was it because Eli liked it down?

Eli.

She smiled again. There was no way she'd be able to take the giddiness out of her. For the next few days, she'd live life to the fullest, and if that meant enjoying a sexual relationship with a very handsome and sexy man, then she'd do it. For several years now, she'd lived by her day planner. Everything she did had a perfect schedule. Now, she wanted to do things by the seat of her pants as if tomorrow were her last day.

Her smile gradually weakened. Within a few days, Eli would be gone. He'd go back to wherever he'd been. A pain shot through her heart. It hadn't taken him long to come into her heart. Could she live without him? Did she have a choice?

Seven

The lights were out. *Good sign.*

On shaky legs, Kenya crept toward Terrel's office, listening for any indication she might have company. She'd tried to come this afternoon, but some of the managers were in Terrel's office for a meeting, which ruined her plans. The lobby remained silent, so she continued her pursuit.

She reached the door to Terrel's office and stopped. Placing her ear against the door, she listened for any sign of movement. Nothing. She released a sigh.

When she pulled her keys out of her purse, her hand shook as she tried to slide the silver key into the hole. She cursed her unsteady body. If she didn't know better, she'd think the wild hammering of her heart could be heard three floors away.

Taking control, she unlocked the door and walked inside. She closed the door, trying not to make a sound. Afraid turning on the light would only draw attention; she pulled a mini key-chain flashlight out of her purse and clicked it on. In daylight, the office was familiar, but in the dark was a different story.

On tiptoes, she crept over to his file cabinet. Reaching behind, she felt for the extra set of keys. When her fingers brushed across them, she sighed.

So far, so good.

This lock was harder to open, mainly because her hands were shaking worse than before. *Calm down, Kenya.* She took a deep breath and tried again. This time the key slid in and unlocked the cabinet.

What was she doing? It was one thing to distrust Terrel, but another to actually sneak around in his office to collect information for the man she was beginning to fall in love with.

She shook her head. This wasn't like her at all. What had Eli done to her heart to make her act completely different and risk jail time?

But, she must. An inner force guided her, making her feel more alive than ever before. The newfound feeling regenerated her, revived her--and scared the hell out of her. Would she get caught and handcuffed? Her business would certainly suffer. Of course, she could always design new prison jumpsuits.

She groaned and rubbed her forehead.

Holding the small flashlight between her teeth, she flipped through the files in the first drawer. Nothing out of the ordinary, so she moved to the next one down. Once again, she came up empty. The third drawer held nothing exciting, so she moved to the fourth. This drawer was harder to pull out, and she realized something was stuck. She yanked harder, and when the drawer gave way she nearly fell back. This particular drawer was only half-filled with files and the other half-stacked with Newsweek Magazines.

In a different drawer, she flipped through the files and came across the name of a hospital. *St. Benedict's.* Could this be where they held Joshua prisoner? Her heart leaped with hope.

Because of her shaky hands, it was hard to read the label, and now as her teeth chattered, the flashlight slipped. She took it out of her mouth and focused on the file as she pulled it out and opened it. Invoices. She glanced over at the figure column. One hundred thousand dollars? She raised her eyebrows in suspicion as she turned over the invoices. They dated back for five years.

Five years.

This had to be what she was looking for.

A noise from out in the lobby stopped her. She froze, except for her heart beating out of control. Somebody was here. She was going to get caught. Prison--and orange jumpsuits were just around the corner.

She closed the file and slipped it in her jacket, pushing the drawer closed with her foot as gently as she could. She turned off the flashlight then searched the darkness for someplace to hide. The only place was underneath Terrel's desk. She was too far away to hide in his adjoining bathroom.

Without another thought, she fell to her knees and scooted under his desk. A stream of light from the lobby came through, the door slowly opening. Someone wearing a pair of black shoes stood just outside the office. She held her breath, praying whoever it was couldn't know she was there.

The feet came closer to the desk.

"Kenya, are you here? It's me, Eli."

She sighed with relief and crawled out. "Good hell, Eli. You scared me to death."

He chuckled as he grasped her hand and pulled her to her feet. "I hadn't planned on you being here."

She propped her hands on her hips. "I have more right to be here than you. And what if Terrel saw you? You know how much you resemble your father."

"Yes, I know, but--"

"There are no buts. You should have stayed home."

He circled his arms around her and pulled her against his chest. A grin stole across his face. "Thank you for caring. And thank you for being on the same brain-waves." He shrugged. "I had no idea you'd search through his office, too."

She rested her face on his chest. "I want to help your father. I'm beginning to realize exactly what type of person Terrel is, and he's not the kind of person that should be running a multi-million dollar company."

"No, he's not." He kissed the top of her head. "Did you find anything?"

She looked up at him. "Yes. It's under my jacket. Let's hurry and get home and I'll show you what I found."

She pulled away and turned toward the door, but he grabbed her arm to stop her. "Wait, Kenya. Do you have something that Terrel might miss if it's gone?"

"I don't know."

"What do you have?"

"A file."

He pulled her to the copy machine against the far wall. "Let's make copies. I don't want to alert Terrel just in case he finds the folder missing."

She exhaled a rush of air. "I never thought about that." She handed over the manila folder.

"Why don't you stand by the door and be our lookout, and I'll make the copies."

Although it seemed forever, while her heart beat a million miles a minute, Eli finally finished and they were able to walk out of the office.

Once inside the car, he grabbed her hand and squeezed. "You'll never guess who I talked to today."

"Who?"

"I found Adam and Joshua's driver. Lamont Waters."

She gasped and took a quick glance his way. "And he's still alive?"

"He's been at a retirement home for five years. Apparently, Lamont was the one who drove Joshua to the mental hospital. Afterwards, Terrel and Lisa gave Lamont a choice. He could either die a slow, painful death, or be holed away for the rest of his life in an old folks home, as long as he forgot everything that happened."

She cringed. "Poor man."

He held up a min-tape recorder. "And it's all right here on tape."

"Thank God. This will really help when we try to prove your father's mental stability."

He squeezed her hand again. "Thanks for believing in me. I don't know how to repay you for your kindness."

Emotion tugged at her heart. *Repay me?* He could stay by her side...forever. But if he was really a future-man--and she was beginning to think he was because he knew about Terrels' dealings--that could never happen.

~ * ~

"I want to visit your father."

Eli smiled, his heart jumping to his throat. He reached across the table and took hold of Kenya's hands. Since they'd returned, they'd been at the kitchen table discussing what they found in Terrel's office.

"You will, eventually."

"I know, but I want to do it now."

He shook his head. "What are you going to say to him? Are you going to tell him you're helping his son?" He chuckled. "He doesn't know he has a son yet."

"No, of course I won't tell him that. I thought about telling him I know he was put into the hospital under false pretenses, and I'm going to try to release him."

He squeezed her hands. "That's a good idea, but I don't know if you'll be able to make it past the doctor. His particular doctor is being paid quite nicely to keep Joshua inside. Doctor Goodwin isn't going to just let anyone in to see him."

She shrugged. "There's got to be a way. Maybe I could go when the doctor leaves to return home."

"Only if you have a way to talk the nurses into letting you in." He tightened his hold on her hand. "And remember, my father isn't listed under Joshua Montgomery."

"He's not?"

"No. Terrel made sure every little thing was covered so people wouldn't recognize him."

"Then what's his name?"

"He's still Joshua, but they used Smith for his last name."

She scrunched her nose. "Smith? That's a regular name, for heaven's sake."

"Exactly. Harder to track that way."

She frowned and slumped her shoulders. "You're not doing a great job of encouraging me, you know."

He laughed, pulled away from the table, and stood. Keeping her hands in his, he lifted her up with him. After wrapping his arms around her waist, he fit her body against his. "There are other ways to encourage you, my dear."

She smiled and stroked his goatee. "I just want to help you out any way I can before you leave." The smile disappeared; even the sparkle left her eyes. "Which reminds me...when are you supposed to leave?"

"I'll be gone tomorrow morning."

She frowned. "Before Valentine's Day?"

"Yes." He sighed. "I don't want to leave yet, but I have to."

She nodded. "Then we have a few more things to do before you leave."

"Like what?"

"Like contacting my father."

He narrowed his eyes. "Why?"

"Because my father will know what we need to do to get Doctor Goodwin checked out. Apparently he's not a very good physician, and the mental hospital needs to know this."

"This is true." He dropped his hands to her buttocks and squeezed. A small groan tore from her throat, making his libido kick in a notch higher. "Then let's hurry and get a hold of him. There's something I want to do, and I don't know how much longer I can wait."

She tilted her head. "Hmmm…wonder what that is?"

Bending his head, he pressed his lips to her neck. His tongue flickered against the sensitive spot, and she giggled.

"I want to do naughty things to you," he muttered. "I'd like to give you a Valentine's Day gift early."

She pulled away and walked to the wall where her keys hung. "That will have to wait until after I talk to my father. It won't take long, I promise."

He frowned, folding his arms over his chest and leaning against the wall. "I'm holding you to that promise, because if you're not back here within an hour, I'm coming after you. And I don't think your father will like the way I touch his little girl in front of him."

She laughed and blew him a kiss, then hurried out of the room.

His heart tightened. How could he walk out of her life tomorrow? In the past week, she'd found a place in his heart, and he didn't want to let it go. Since meeting her, life had more meaning, and to think that might be taken away nearly stopped his heart from beating--for she had somehow become his life.

But, he had no other choice. He had to return.

~ * ~

Kenya didn't want to explain to her father about Eli, so she made it sound like she had come across some information that involved Terrel and his stepbrother, Joshua. Her father was understanding and said he'd get to work on it right away. He knew a few members of the state's medical board, and he'd have Doctor Goodwin's history researched thoroughly. She hesitated in telling him about her suspicions with Terrel and his previous drug usage, but her father could tell something was bothering her, so she confessed her feelings.

She cried on his shoulder for a while, but he promised not to say anything until she could tell Terrel himself. Her father mentioned he had connections with the Feds, and he could get a tail put on Terrel if she thought he was still doing drugs. She told him no--at least not now.

On the way home, the tight knot around her heart had disappeared. Ever since she'd doubted her feelings for Terrel, she'd been getting headaches. Now the stress had been relieved. She'd made the right decision.

Eli greeted her at the door when she walked in. She didn't have to say a word. Neither did he. They fell into each other's arms as if kismet controlled everything.

When his mouth captured hers, all problems ceased to exist. Tonight all that mattered was pleasing him...and receiving pleasure from him.

Their lovemaking grew by the second, her heart expanding along with it. No doubt lingered in her mind any more. She loved him. There was so much emotion each time he kissed her and touched her that she wanted to cry with happiness.

When they were finished, she slumped against him in pure, heavenly exhaustion. Together their breaths slowed and soon returned to a normal rhythm. He kissed the side of her head and wrapped his arms around her tightly.

"That was the best I've ever had," he whispered.

She grinned. "Me, too."

"Nothing will ever compare to this feeling I'm experiencing right now."

She lifted her head and met his gaze. "I know."

"Kenya, in such a short time, you've created a permanent place in my heart."

Tears filled her eyes. "Once again, I feel the same." She pushed his long hair out of his face, realizing that she didn't care how shaggy and unkempt it was. He was still the most handsome man she'd ever known and ever loved. "I know I shouldn't be feeling this so soon, but I think...I think I'm in love with you."

"God, Kenya--" He cupped her face and brought it down to his as his mouth captured hers.

He didn't kiss her passionately as they had before, but more meaningfully. Love burst in her chest, and tears fell from her eyes. She broke the kiss and held him tight.

Why did the most wonderful man in the world come into her life for so short a time?

Eight

When Kenya awoke the next morning, Eli was gone. Even his belongings were missing. How could she go on without him? Knowing she would never see him again broke her down, and she sobbed into her pillow. Her heavy chest and throbbing head made it so she couldn't go to work.

The day passed slowly, and the night was just as bad. Memories from when they'd made love in this very bed came tumbling back, and the pain of missing him filled her greater than before. Although she didn't think she had tears left to shed, she cried a bucket-full.

The next morning she forced herself to go to work, even with puffy eyes. Today was Valentine's Day, and it was nothing to celebrate.

When she entered through the front door, George's eyes widened, his mouth gaping. "Good Lord, woman. What's wrong?"

She opened up and told him everything--even about Eli being from the future, and especially about Terrel. George remained supportive and encouraged her to continue in her pursuit in helping Joshua out.

After a long day at work, she closed the shop and returned home. Loneliness overwhelmed her. She couldn't stay in this apartment one minute longer without going crazy.

Her gaze fell on the stack of papers she and Eli had copied from Terrel's secret folder.

Joshua Smith.

Yes, she could go see him. The mental institution was only an hour's drive away, so she still had time.

She ran in to fix her hair and make-up, then hurried out to the car. Excitement made her heart leap and gave her a brighter outlook. She tried to tell herself she didn't want to see Joshua just because Eli resembled him...but wasn't that the main reason for her enthusiasm?

No. Joshua was a completely different person. He wasn't Eli.

Although...what if he was just as charming as his son? She grinned. Eli certainly took the prize for sweeping her off her feet in such a short amount of time. Eli had even mentioned his father had been a sweet-talker in his younger years, which were really these years in her time.

Moisture gathered in her palms the closer she came to the hospital. Joshua Smith. She had to remember this was the name they listed him under.

When she parked her car and walked through the front doors, her legs shook. Even her knees knocked together. She wrung her hands against her stomach and held her shoulders straight as she made her way to the receptionist desk.

An older, silver-haired woman looked up from the book she was reading and smiled.

"Hello," Kenya greeted. "I hope visiting hours are not over. I've traveled an hour to see someone."

The other woman shook her head. "There's still another hour to go before we close the doors."

Kenya sighed, placing her hand on her chest. "Good."

"Who is it you're here to see?"

"Joshua Smith."

The lady's white bushy eyebrows drew together, and she opened the patient logbook and thumbed through it. "Really? Joshua usually doesn't get visitors."

Kenya's heartbeat hammered against her ribs, the beat pounding through her head just as fast. "Why?"

The woman met her stare. "I don't know. I thought he didn't have any family." She smiled. "But I guess I was wrong. You are family, aren't you?"

Kenya tried not to let out a relived sigh. "Yes. I'm his first cousin on his mother's side, Kenya Whitaker."

The other woman snapped the book closed and stood. "Then I'm certain Joshua will be thrilled to see someone." She walked behind the desk. "Like I said, he hasn't had any visitors for as long as I can remember."

Kenya held her shaky hands together and followed the nurse down the hall. The older woman withdrew a set of rings and inserted one in the keyhole of a door, then opened it. The large room looked to be a game room of sorts. She arched a brow. *Probably where the patients spend most of their time.* Five or so patients dressed in the hospital's light gray colors were scattered in the room, and people dressed in street clothes sat beside them. If she could get Joshua in a corner, they could speak in private.

Her heart quickened. What could she say? She couldn't tell him about Eli. She chuckled. Joshua would think *she* had escaped from a mental hospital.

The nurse stopped at a table and motioned to the chair. "Have a seat, and I will go get him."

She nodded and sat, clamping her hands between her knees. Damn her nerves.

She glanced at the others. It was easy to identify the patients. Even if they hadn't been wearing their gray, scrub-like clothes, the expressions on their faces were absent as they stared into space. A few played with checker pieces on the tables, or continually shook dice in a cup. Her heart went out to these poor, unfortunate souls.

The squeaky hinges of the door drew her attention to the nurse coming through. Shuffling behind her came a tall man with very short, black hair. His head lowered as his eyes aimed toward his bare feet. His hands clasped together in back of him. Her heart leapt to her throat. Even from over here, she recognized the resemblances he had with Eli. Of course, they were father and son. Why wouldn't they look alike?

He didn't meet her gaze even when the older woman led him to the chair across from Kenya and he sat.

"Joshua," the nurse said, touching his shoulder. "This is your cousin, Kenya Whitaker." She looked at Kenya and nodded.

Kenya cleared her throat. "Joshua, it's good to see you again."

The man across from her kept his chin to his chest and didn't say a word. *Was* this man insane? Eli seemed to think differently. Of course, after having this kind of treatment for five years, any sane person would go crazy.

"Ma'am," the nurse said. "If you need anything, there are several guards around the room who will be ready to assist."

Kenya took another glance. Why hadn't she noticed them before? Four men stood around the room, each one at an exit, and a few others wandered through the room. She gritted her teeth. She wouldn't have any chance to talk to him in private.

After the nurse left, an awkward silence came between Kenya and Joshua while she struggled to find the right words. During this time, she studied him. Handsome, just like his son, he had muscles that bulged underneath his hospital attire. His hair was just as dark but much shorter, and she assumed they'd have the same color of eyes--if he'd just look at her. Instead of the shaggy, but sexy, goatee Eli had, Joshua was clean-shaven which emphasized his square jaw.

Yes. It was easy to see where Eli had received his rugged good looks.

A guard dressed in a black and gold uniform walked by, peering at her through narrowed eyes. She smiled and nodded, hoping to appear unaffected. When the man turned his back on her, she looked at Joshua. What could she say? She had to say something.

She took a deep breath to begin, but didn't get the chance.

"You're not my cousin."

Joshua's voice was deeper than she'd expected and reminded her of Eli's sexy tone. He lifted his gaze and met hers. Her heart flipped. Heaven help her, Joshua had Eli's intoxicating green eyes.

He took a quick glance at the guard then looked back at her. He placed his clasped hands on the table and leaned closer. "I don't know you."

She smiled and resisted the urge to reach out and touch his hands. *He's not Eli.* "I know. I had to say I was family or they wouldn't let me see you."

He nodded. "Do you know who I am?"

"Yes. You're Joshua Montgomery," she whispered. "Son of Adam Montgomery, former President of Montgomery Aisle."

His eyes misted over, and her heart tugged with emotion.

"Be careful not to say that too loud." His voice was low, also. "They might want to put you in here for being crazy."

"You're not crazy." She followed her instinct and touched his hands. In one smooth movement, his fingers gripped with hers. Once again, her heartbeat pounded lively, quickening her breath.

"How do you know?" he asked.

No way could she tell him about Eli. "Let's just say I know someone who convinced me of your innocence."

The guard walked back their way, and Joshua lowered his head again. She continued to hold his hand, even used her other hand to stroke his arm, trying to look like the grieving relative.

"...And my mom and dad say hi. Remember Cousin Billy?" She raised her voice for the guard's affect. "He'll be getting married next month. I feel sorry for his wife, though. Billy eats like a pig and probably out-weighs one, too."

Joshua's mouth quirked at the corners, a dimple flashed in his chin. How adorable.

The guard walked by, and Joshua met her gaze. His eyes sparkled, just as sexy as his son's had done. "Are you purposely trying to make me laugh?"

She shrugged. "I had to say something in front of that guard so he doesn't think we're being secretive." She tilted her head. "Why? Don't you laugh in here?"

"Rarely." He glanced around the room. "What's there to laugh at?"

Once again, emotion suffocated her. No matter what, she must get him released.

"Joshua, I have people looking into your case--"

"Don't," he said roughly. "Terrel will do something awful to you just like he did to me and all my father's servants. You shouldn't put yourself in harm's way for a man you have never met before."

She smiled. "But I feel as if I know you really well." She squeezed his hands. "My father will help protect me if it comes down to needing it."

His forehead creased. "Why are you doing this?"

"Because...I love the person who told me about you, and I want to get you out of here."

The guard came their way again, so she quickly changed the subject and lifted her voice. "...And Cousin Jill, well, she broke her arm the other day. She's been interested in body-building and looking like Popeye, so she challenged a man three-times her size and lost." She shook her head. "Poor, foolish idiot."

This time she noticed the guard hide a grin as he walked by. Once he passed, she looked back at Joshua. His smile had widened, as had the dimple in his chin.

"Would you quit?" he asked.

She chuckled. "Sorry. I like to make jokes when I'm nervous."

"Why are you nervous?"

"Because I don't want anything to go wrong. I want to be able to get you out and have everything fall right into place."

He shook his head. "If you know Terrel at all, you know it won't work like that."

"I can dream, can't I?"

His thumb stroked over her knuckles, and the gentleness of his action caused tingles to shoot up her arm. *Good grief.* What's wrong with her? Why was she getting these feelings from Joshua? She shook the crazy thoughts from her mind. This was Eli's father, for hell's sake. Yet, he was the same age and looked almost as Eli had. Could be why Joshua left her breathless.

She pulled her hand away and tucked it in her lap. "I came here today to get to know you, and to tell you what I'm doing."

"How will you keep all of this from Terrel?"

She shrugged. "Eventually he'll find out, but I hope by that time, it'll be too late. My father knows a few people on the Medical Board of Directors who will look into Doctor Goodwin's past. We know Terrel is paying him to keep you here, but there's got to be a reason the doctor is willing to jeopardize his practice."

He nodded. "You're right. But how will your father accomplish this?"

"He was the former senator of New York. He has connections and can help us."

"Have your father check out a couple of names. They're connected to Terrel one way or another."

"Who are they?"

"Thomas Pett and Lance Monroe."

"I will, I promise."

Joshua swiped his fingers through his hair. In the back of her memory, she could see Eli doing this very thing. Why did she have to compare the two?

He shook his head. "I don't know how I became so lucky all of a sudden. You're a walking dream, Miss Kenya Whitaker...it is Miss, isn't it?"

"Yes, I'm single." As soon as she breaks off her engagement to Terrel, anyway.

Joshua smiled again, and her heart jumped.

When the guard walked by again, Kenya pushed away from the desk. "Of course I'll come see you again, Joshua. Is tomorrow all right?"

He raised his gaze, his deep green eyes penetrating into hers, and she almost melted. He nodded.

It wasn't until the older nurse touched her elbow she realized the woman had walked behind her. "Ms. Whitaker, I must say what a remarkable difference you've made. Why, Joshua rarely smiles and he never speaks."

Kenya let her grin widen as she continued to gaze into his warm eyes. "Good, because this man needs to smile a lot more."

The nurse moved around Kenya, helped Joshua up, then led him back out of the game room. He didn't look over his shoulder at her, but she didn't mind. She partook of the magnificently built man as he left the room, wishing he were Eli instead.

Nine

The next time she visited Joshua, she stayed a little longer. They could not go outside the game room, so they strolled around the mostly empty space. She couldn't stop comparing him to his son, especially when she realized Joshua was as tall.

It was nearly impossible not to look at him and see Eli, but sometimes she didn't see the future-man. Joshua acted more reserved, and didn't have the nutty humor his son had. Of course, being cooped up in a mental ward for five years, she didn't blame him for not being as spontaneous.

Although she could visit, there was still a guard or a nurse looming near, which meant they couldn't talk serious for very long.

After their little stroll around the room, they sat at a table, and set up the checkers game. She teased him about how she was going to whip his butt, and it took him a few minutes, but he soon returned her taunt. She loved to make him grin just to see the adorable dimple on his chin. Whether Eli had a dimple there, she didn't know because of his goatee. But it didn't matter. This was the very thing that helped her separate the two men. Too bad it didn't work all the time.

"Kenya," Joshua whispered. "Has your father found out anything about Doctor Goodwin yet?"

"No. Why?"

"Because he's been acting different lately."

She arched her brows. "What's he doing?"

"He's treating me differently. He hasn't really talked to me for a few months anyway, but suddenly he thinks he needs to do more tests on me. He hinted around about my visitor last night, but he never really said anything."

She sucked in a quick breath. "Is he here now?"

"No. He leaves to go home around five o'clock, unless he decided to stay to check things out."

Fear lodged in her chest and her hands turned cold. "Do you think he stayed after today?"

"No, but I'm sure once he learns of your visit today, he just might stick around tomorrow."

She fumbled with the game pieces. "Then, perhaps I shouldn't come tomorrow."

He grasped her hand and squeezed. "I don't want you to get hurt, but it makes my day when you come."

She gave him a shaky smile. "It makes my day to see you, too."

Pulling her hand away, she concentrated on the checkers again. Once they were all set up, she lifted her gaze. His eyes met hers, and the tender emotion in his green stare nearly shattered her.

"Kenya, can I ask you a personal question?"

She shrugged. "Depends how personal it is."

He chuckled. "Will you tell me how you know so much about my family? About me?"

As much as she wanted to tell him all about his wonderful son, the fact still remained--Eli hadn't even been born yet. How could she talk about a man from the future? But she didn't want to tell him about Terrel either. There was no other choice. Joshua would eventually find out, and she wanted to be the person to tell him.

She nodded and licked her lips. His attention dropped to her mouth, the color of his eyes darkening. Her heart thumped crazily. There was another similarity between him and his son. They could both make her quiver by one look of their passionate gaze.

"Well, I was engaged to Terrel."

His smile disappeared and his jaw hardened. "Really?"

"Yes. I didn't know what a terrible person he was at that time." She picked up a checker piece and rolled it between her finger and thumb. "Since then, I've discovered his deception." She met his gaze. "He not only lied to me, but to others, and he ruined the life of one terrific man."

The anger lines in his face quickly disappeared, and a smile touched his mouth. "I guess I can be happy you finally saw the light."

She nodded. "I was finally *shown* the light."

"So, are you ever going to tell me who it was that led you in my direction?"

"Not yet. Maybe someday."

He chuckled. "If you keep that up, *you'll* be the one driving me insane."

She laughed with him.

When the guard came back, they were playing checkers and not talking about anything personal. She found Joshua as delightful as his son, but thankfully, he wasn't as flirtatious. She didn't know what her reaction would be if Joshua did start charming her as his son had done. Already, she had a soft spot in her heart for Joshua. But was it only because he was helpless and needed her assistance? Or was it because of what Eli meant to her?

She rubbed her forehead. Everything was so very confusing, especially her feelings. She could never have Eli. He was in a different time. What about Joshua? Could she ever have feelings for him like she had for Eli?

Most importantly--would it be right if she did?

Perhaps Eli's purpose for coming into her life was to lead her to Joshua. But, if that were so, why did he make her fall in love with him? Why did he make incredible love to her--something she would never forget?

Unless he didn't know what his true purpose of coming would be... She rubbed her forehead again, the headache she thought had disappeared was returning. She needed to get rid of this extra stress in her life.

"Are you all right?" Joshua asked.

She smiled at him. "Yes. I'm just developing a headache."

He slipped his hand over the top of hers, his thumb gently stroking her skin. "You don't need to stay and keep me company. I'll be all right."

"Nonsense. I enjoy being with you."

He squeezed her hand. "And I enjoy being with you."

She sighed heavily. "I was just thinking of everything ahead of us--everything that has to be accomplished before we can get you out of here."

"I wish I could help you. Unfortunately, everyone in this facility thinks I'm crazy. Doctor Goodwin is the only person who knows the truth."

Once again, his eyes misted over and heaviness gathered in her chest. "Joshua, we *will* get you out of here. Soon."

He nodded and rubbed his eyes. When he met her gaze again, he smiled. "Is it too soon to tell you I think I'm falling in love with you?"

Humor laced the tone of his voice and, although heat rushed to her cheeks, she laughed. "I think you're getting that emotion confused with gratitude."

"Maybe...maybe not."

He winked, and she cursed herself for thinking of Eli in that instant.

~ * ~

The next morning, Kenya opened her front door to find her father standing there, his face void of color and worry etched in his eyes.

"We need to talk." He pushed past her and walked into the apartment.

She closed the door and met him in the living room. "What's wrong, Dad?"

"I don't want you going near Terrel ever again. Is that clear?"

Suffocation tightened her chest. "Why? What did you find out?"

"My FBI friends are still checking things out, but if it's as bad as it looks, Terrel isn't a very good person at all. He just might have connections to the Mafia."

Her heart lodged in her throat. She held onto the corner of the wall to keep from collapsing to the floor. "Are you serious?"

"It's looking that way. Remember those names you gave me the other day? Thomas Pett and Lance Monroe?"

She nodded.

"This morning, I received a call from my friend and he told me to warn you. Pett and Monroe are linked to the Mafia. If Terrel connects with them, shit could hit the fan when his illegal operations are revealed. The FBI will not only arrest him, but others linked to him."

She covered her face with her hands. "I can't believe this is happening."

"It is."

"Does Terrel know he's being investigated?"

"Not yet. But he will soon." He wrapped his arms around her. "So please be careful."

"I will, I promise." She paused, then asked, "What about Doctor Goodwin?"

"He's also being investigated. I think he'll be losing his job here shortly, poor bastard."

"Why did he put his job on the line for Terrel?"

He patted her cheek. "Are you sure you want to know?"

"I think I already do."

"Doctor Goodwin is a cocaine addict. Terrel is his supplier."

She shook her head. "Figured."

"Kenya, honey, I've decided to hire a bodyguard for you. I don't trust Terrel."

"Do you really think he's going to hurt me?"

"I don't know, and I'm not going to find out." He motioned his head toward her front window. "Outside in an unmarked vehicle is a man I've hired to protect you."

"Do you think all of this is necessary?"

"Do this for your old man. Once this is all taken care of with Terrel, I'll let Shane go, but for now Shane is here to protect you."

He kissed the top her head, turned, and left. She let out a ragged sigh and leaned her forehead against the cold wall. What had she done in her life to become involved with such a man as Terrel Montgomery? Had they met by chance, or had he sought her out because of her father? It didn't matter any longer. She must break it off with him immediately.

With a bodyguard around, how could she do it?

There was only one way. She had to try to lose her bodyguard. Somehow, she had to give him the slip--just long enough to talk with Terrel anyway.

With her heart beating like an Indian drum, she hurried and readied herself for the day, preparing to tackle the *Terrel* problem. It had to be done today, no matter how frightened she was of telling him.

She called George at the office to let him know she'd be coming in later. Thankfully, her friend understood. When she hung up the phone, her hand shook. She clasped it with her other and held it to her jumping stomach. She closed her eyes and breathed slow and deep, fighting for control.

This must be done. Today.

She called the cab company and gave them an address one block away from her house. She slipped out of the window of her bedroom and fell into the bushes. Cursing, she jumped up and wiped the small branches off her clothes.

She peeked around the corner of the house and, thankfully, Shane still sat in the white Ford Taurus, acting as if he were reading the newspaper.

So far, so good.

It didn't take long for the cab to pick her up. She gave the cabbie directions and told him to drive slowly. Peeking over her shoulder every other mile, she checked to see if Shane was following. Once again, she was in luck.

They arrived at the Montgomery Mansion within twenty minutes. She paid the cabbie, climbed out, and walked up to the front door on shaky legs. Within seconds, the butler came to the door.

"I need to speak with Terrel. Is he here?"

"Yes. I'll let him know you're here."

With a ragged sigh, she wandered into the parlor and to the liquor bar. She should pour herself a good amount of whiskey, but decided against it. She needed a level head right now, and although the alcohol would calm her nerves, she needed to think clearly.

The tile outside the parlor thudded from someone's shoes, and she turned just in time to see Terrel strolling through the double doors. Wearing a three-piece, pinstriped gray suit, he looked as if he were on his way to work...*or running for President of the United States*. He smiled as he walked up to her and wrapped her in his arms. Hard to believe she preferred the gruffy look of Eli compared to Terrel's perfect appearance.

"It's about time you came out of your hole." He kissed her lips, but she turned her head.

"What do you mean by that?" she asked.

"You've been holed up in your apartment for the past several days. Have you been sick?"

How does he know I've been in my apartment? "Uh, yes, I was having my migraines again."

"You're feeling better, I hope."

"Yes." She stepped away from him and over to his sofa. "Terrel, I think we need to talk about the wedding."

He lowered to the sofa, pulling her with him. "All right, honey-bear."

She cringed, hating when he called her that name.

"What is it you need to talk about? Aren't the plans going on schedule? Are you having a problem with the wedding planner? Do you need me to fire anybody?" He chuckled.

She rolled her eyes. He was so full of himself, thinking he had to do everything for her. She cocked her head to the side. "Actually, there is someone you could fire for me."

His brows rose. "Really? Who is that?"

Here was her chance--she had to take it. "My fiancé."

It only took a second before he laughed out loud. He took her hand and stroked it. "Oh, honey-bear, I know I haven't been very attentive lately, but the company has picked up business and we're getting ready--"

"I don't care about how inattentive you've been lately, Terrel." She took a deep breath. "The reason I'm here is to...to...to cancel our engagement. To stop everything."

The laugh lines around his eyes and mouth disappeared, his brown eyes turning icy. "This is a little sudden. Are you getting cold feet perhaps?"

She moved to the window. Pulling back the white lace curtains, she gazed out to the green lawn and manicured hedges. She'd always thought this was a beautiful home. If it weren't for Lisa and Terrel living here...but then Joshua would take over his house once he got out of the hospital.

She cleared her throat. "At first I thought I was getting cold feet, but the more I pondered about it, the more I realized--" She looked back at him. "I realized I didn't really love you." She shrugged. "I don't believe I was in love with you before."

A nerve on his cheek jumped, and his hands balled into fists but his expression remained calm. Too bad she couldn't feel that emotion right now. Her heart was leaping so frantically, she thought she might have a heart attack.

Finally, after several earth-shattering silent minutes passed, he sat back on the sofa and rubbed his chin. "What made you decide this?"

She sighed heavily. "Oh, Terrel. Everything made me decide that. I'd been having really bad headaches, and I knew I wasn't happy. I don't like the way you belittle me, and I especially don't like the way you never put me first in your life. All you and your mother wanted to do was control me, and I can't have that kind of marriage."

He stood and walked over to her, his gaze burning right through her. "So, there's no other man in your life that helped you come to this decision?"

Her heart jumped to her throat. She hoped he didn't know about Eli. "No, Terrel."

He nodded and folded his arms, wearing that all-too-familiar cocky, smug expression. "My brother Joshua didn't sway you at all, huh?"

She sucked in a quick breath, and the blood drained from her face. Her tight throat made it impossible to swallow, so she gritted her teeth and held onto the edge of the window. "Joshua?" She shouldn't have said anything, because she knew the quiver in her voice would tell him the true story.

It had. He arched a condemning eyebrow. "Yes, Joshua. You know, my brother."

"The brother that died right after your father did?"

He reached out and took a lock of her hair, rubbing it through his finger and thumb. She tried not to flinch, but her body stiffened automatically.

"You know Joshua isn't dead."

She tried to steady her quick breaths. "Terrel? What are you saying?"

He narrowed his eyes on her. "Doctor Goodwin recognized you from our engagement photo. He thought I might like to know my future wife is visiting my loony brother."

She slapped his hand away from her hair and scowled. "If anyone is loony, it's you, Terrel. You know as well as I do Joshua isn't crazy." She shook her head. "I can't believe what a greedy son-of-a-bitch you really are. All of this because you had to be the president of your stepfather's company. All of this because you couldn't stand to be second best."

He released a growl before his claw-like fingers bit into her shoulders. He shook her. "Don't *ever* talk to me like that. I deserve more respect."

She wanted to spit in his face, but refrained for now. "You deserve every terrible thing you've done to your brother...and more. You're the one who needs to be locked away from the rest of the world."

His mouth twisted in an evil smile as he pulled her body against his, crushing her with his steel-like arms as they wrapped around her. He placed a not-so-tender kiss on her mouth and she squirmed.

"Oh, why, why did you have to find out?" he mumbled, pulling away just enough to glare into her eyes. "You know I can't have you running around telling everyone about my brother. Soon, the right people will start asking questions and all hell will break loose." He paused, his jaw hardening. "And I can't have that, can I?"

Her blood turned to ice. Was he threatening her? She held her breath, afraid to make any movement at all.

"I guess I could just kill my brother." He shrugged. "It's either you or him, and he'll be easier to kill." He tilted his head and gave her a look of sympathy. "Of course, if you go blabbing your mouth about what I've done, you may end up like Joshua." He ran his knuckles down her cheek to her neck. "And I'd hate to think of you locked away in a mental institution for the rest of your life."

She shook her head. "You can't kill Joshua. I won't let you."

Where that came from, she had no clue. Terrel frightened her out of her wits, so to challenge him to his face...that was suicide.

He widened his eyes. "You won't let me?" he mocked. "And what are you going to do to stop me?"

She bit her tongue. She'd said too much as it was. There was no way she could tell him about how she'd involved her father already. Why in the hell had she ditched her bodyguard? He could be here with her right now prying her ex-fiancé off her. Inwardly, she groaned. She'd dug herself in a hole now.

"Oh, let me guess who'll try and stop me. Dear ole Daddy?" He chuckled. "Honey-bear, there's nothing your father can do that I can't undo. I have connections beyond your imagination. I have half of the police force in my back pocket."

She cringed. "What are you going to do with me?" she asked, her voice quivering.

He sighed. "I don't know. I haven't figured that out yet. But I can't keep you here, especially today." He yanked her arm and pulled her toward the door. "Besides, once the police realize you're missing, this is the first place they'll look."

Her heart dropped to the floor her feet where shuffling on. "Missing? I'm going to be missing?"

"For now, until I figure out what to do with you."

She couldn't let him do this to her--yet, as he pushed her out the front door to his car, she couldn't think of how to stop him. He was bigger, stronger, and definitely, more commanding than her.

"Get in," he growled.

She turned and planted her hands on her hips. "Terrel, leave me the hell alone. I'm tired of being pushed around by you."

He pressed her against her car, his body blocking any escape she could have. "Listen, my dear honey-bear. There's a gun in the pocket of my suit jacket. Don't make me get it out."

She bit back the sob threatening to leave her throat. What had she done? Why didn't she listen to her father and stay away from Terrel?

"Why...why are you carrying a gun?" she whispered.

"I'm heading to one of my top priority meetings." He grinned. "Now get in the car like a good girl. I would hate to be forceful out here in public." He stroked his knuckles down her cheek. "And I'd hate to bruise your pretty face."

Although he'd already injured her heart, she didn't want him bruising her face, too. She gave him a nod, as shaky as it was, and climbed in the car.

Ten

After she parked the car in the driveway of a house she'd never been to, Terrel pushed her out and toward the front door. Although this subdivision didn't have the grand mansions as where Terrel lived, they were almost as ritzy.

Who could possible live here? Weren't all his friends wealthy and snobby like him and Lisa? She dared not ask about the occupancy--not yet.

He reached in his pocket again and moved the bulky object against the material. "Ring the doorbell."

A gray-haired woman wearing a maid's apron answered the door. She smiled at Terrel. "Hello, Mr. Montgomery."

Kenya threw a glare over her shoulder at him. Whoever lived here knew Terrel quite well.

"I need to speak with Tina."

A woman? How interesting.

The minute they stepped into the house, Kenya had a sinking feeling she knew who this Tina was.

After the maid left, she whispered to him, "What are the chances we're at Tina LaRousse's house?"

He raised his eyebrows. "Good guess. What gave it away?"

She cocked her head. "How close are you and Tina?" She paused, then continued, "You can be honest with me for once. After all, we're not getting married, and I already hate you."

He chuckled. "Tina and I have been lovers for quite some time."

She nodded. "If I would have married you, would she have continued to be your mistress?"

"Yes, until I became bored anyway."

His answer was like a slap in the face. It shouldn't bother her, but the sting of rejection was like pouring salt on an open wound. Her chest ached and she cursed her reaction. "Why didn't you just ask *her* to marry you?"

He shook his head. "Tina didn't have the right connections."

"My father," she muttered. Eli had been right.

Tina came skipping down the stairs in a T-shirt and regular blue jeans until she noticed Kenya. The woman stopped on the steps. Automatically, her genuine smile turned fake.

"What a pleasant surprise to have the future Mr. and Mrs. Montgomery grace my home."

"Tina love," Terrell said. "No need for pleasantries. This isn't a friendly visit."

The other woman's forehead creased as she continued down the stairs. "Oh?"

Terrel gripped Kenya's arm and pushed her forward a couple of steps. "I need a place to hide her. She knows about Joshua."

Tina's eyes widened and Kenya was sure hers did also. Tina LaRousse knew about Joshua and was actually going along with it? What was the real story to all of this?

The other woman huffed and folded her arms across her chest. "Why here?"

"Because I can't keep her at my house. That's the first place the cops will look."

Tina walked up and stood in front of her. Kenya wanted to claw her face, but retracted her nails. She'd save that privilege and effort for Terrel.

"What are you going to do with her?" Tina asked.

He glanced at Kenya, his gaze sweeping over her body in one quick motion. "I'm thinking about holding her for ransom. What do you think?"

Kenya threw Terrel a glare. "Will you two quit acting like I'm not standing here listening to every word you're saying?"

Tina let out a throaty laugh. "Oh, you're so brave, darling." She ran her long, manicured nail over Kenya's cheek. Kenya grimaced and pulled away. Bile rose to her throat, and she wanted to spit it at the other woman. Soon she'd get her chance, but now wasn't the time.

Terrel glanced at his watch. "I've got a meeting in a half hour. Let's lock her in the attic."

Tina swiveled around so fast her fake blond hair flipped over her shoulder. She hurried up the stairs, Terrel pushing Kenya ahead of him as they followed.

Kenya pictured the attic to be dark and musty, even littered with cobwebs, but once she entered, she realized it looked like any normal room--except with a lower ceiling. There were only a few pieces of furniture in the room; a bed against the wall with pillow and blankets, a dresser, and a single chair near the small diamond-shaped window.

Terrel pushed her on the bed as Tina ran to take some rope out of one of the drawers. The woman brought it over to Terrel. Yanking her hands in front of her, he began tying her.

The ropes burned her wrists and she whimpered. "Not so tight."

He glared at her. "You'll be fine."

She cocked her head. "I take it you've done this before. Why else would there be a rope nearby?" She glanced around the room again. "And why is the room so clean for an attic?"

Tina laughed and jabbed Terrel in the sides with her finger. "She's smarter than you thought, isn't she?"

After tying Kenya's feet, he cupped her face and brought his mouth down hard upon hers. She struggled but he kept her head still. Thankfully, he didn't try to stick his tongue in her mouth or she would have bitten it off.

When he pulled away, he wore a satisfied grin. "If you're a good girl, we won't have to hurt you."

"Go to hell," she spat.

He laughed and Tina joined in with him. Taking Tina in his arms, he brought his face down to hers and shared a passionate kiss. Kenya's stomach churned. He then broke away and took Tina by the hand as they walked out of the room together, shutting, and locking the door behind them.

Just outside the door, she could still hear them talking. She stood and hopped as quietly as she could to the door, then pressed her ear against the solid oak. Terrel's calm and steady voice came through very clear. She could also hear Tina's raised and panic-stricken tone.

"Terrel, you can't leave her here," Tina whined. "Especially tonight."

"It'll be all right, Tina. Kenya is a timid woman. She won't make a sound."

"I know, but with her here, I won't be able to concentrate. Tonight is my big shipment, and I want to make sure everything is in order."

Kenya scrunched her forehead. *Big shipment?* Her fashion designs probably. But then, what did Terrel have to do with that?

"Tina, my dear, Pett and Monroe are professionals. They'll know how to handle things if something goes wrong," Terrel said.

Tina gasped. "You think something will go wrong?"

Terrel chuckled. "No, but I've dealt with them many times, and I trust them completely. Kenya won't mess things up. She's not that kind of woman."

An ache grew in her chest and she wobbled back to the bed. *Drug trafficking.* That could be the only thing Terrel could have going down tonight. Why else would he talk about Pett and Monroe? Although she wanted to do something to ruin their plans, she couldn't because of her present situation. If only she could get to the phone. If only she could get out of these ropes.

She yanked her wrists against the knots, but they only pinched her skin more. She sobbed and sank to the bed. As she relaxed, her whole body shook with the nerves she'd been trying to hold in, and with it a fresh new batch of tears poured down her cheeks.

Where was Eli when she needed him the most?

~ * ~

Joshua sat in his cell and waited on his lumpy bed. As each minute passed, his heart descended lower. Kenya should have been here by now. His chest tightened. What if Terrel knew? What if Doctor Goodwin suspected he was being investigated? No, if that were the case, Joshua would have been heavily drugged and beaten. Just like all the times before.

He growled and ran his fingers through his short hair. What if Kenya was in danger and needed him? Could he do anything about it?

Cussing under his breath, he pushed himself off the worn mattress and paced the floor in his small room. Something was wrong. Anxiety of the unknown ran through his bones, and the chills of trepidation coursing over his body confirmed his suspicions. Since Kenya wasn't here, she must be in danger.

He walked to the door and banged on the thick steel designed to keep him inside. This wasn't a mental ward--it was a prison. Through the barred window, he peered down the corridor. "Hello? Anybody there?"

He banged again, but still no answer.

"Damn." He slumped his head against the cool steel, but that didn't help in simmering his temper.

He squeezed his eyes closed. *Hold on, Kenya. I'm coming as soon as I can find a way to get out of here.*

The squeaky hinges of the entrance to the bedrooms echoed through the hall. The soft pad of nurse's shoes overrode the beat of his heart. "Hello," he called again, searching the narrow path.

When the nurse stopped in front of his door, he sighed. Thank God it was Carrie--the only nurse he trusted in this hellhole. After a year of being placed in this facility, he'd made friends with the cute, young nurse. Thankfully, he still had retained his charm, because he got her to believe his innocence. Unfortunately, nobody else would. If it weren't for Carrie, he wouldn't have been able to do what he'd accomplished so far.

"Hi, Joshua. You have a visitor again this evening."

He widened his eyes, the tightness in his chest beginning to disappear. "I do?"

"Yes." She unlocked the door.

He stepped out and wanted to heave a sigh of relief but held it inside for now. "Is it my cousin, Kenya?"

She shook her head. "No. There's an older Hispanic woman and a middle-aged man."

Panic settled back in his heart. He didn't recognize her brief description. Hurrying his steps to get to them, Carrie almost had to run beside him to catch up. When she unlocked the door going into the game room, and he noticed the man, his heart clenched. George, Kenya's assistant and Terrel's housekeeper, Lucinda.

What are they doing here? Will they recognize me?

This really wasn't the time he wanted the truth to come out, but he didn't have a choice in the matter. Then it struck him and he caught his breath. *Kenya.* Something was definitely wrong.

Deciding not to act insane in front of the hospital faculty this time, he rushed over to Lucinda. Tears swam in her eyes and she bit her knuckles. Her gaze swept over him and little by little color left her face.

"Ay, Díos mío," she muttered. "Estas vivo!"

Joshua touched her shoulder. "Yes, I'm alive." He glanced at Kenya's assistant. "George, what's happened?"

The man sucked in his breath. "You know me?"

"Yes."

A sob tore from George's throat. He covered his hand over his mouth and shook his head. Joshua didn't have time for this. He needed answers now.

"What's happened to Kenya?"

All at once, Lucinda began mumbling, some words in English some in Spanish, and George blubbered like a fool, making it almost impossible to follow the conversation either of them were having.

He held up his hand. "Please slow down. I don't understand."

Lucinda wiped her wet eyes. "It is Kenya. Mr. Montgomery has taken her."

For a quick second, all energy left him, and he swayed. Grabbing the back of the nearest chair for support, he breathed slow, trying to regain control. He squeezed his eyes closed and scrambled for an idea. But in the end, there was only one thing to do to save Kenya.

He needed to escape...again.

He looked back at Lucinda. "Do you know where he's taken her?"

"Sí."

"Will you take me there?"

Her eyes widened. "But Señor, you are in here."

He fisted his hands. "Not for long."

George reached out and grabbed his arm, stopping him. "Wait."

"What?"

"Are you...Eli?"

Joshua nodded. "How did you know?"

George wiped his wet eyes. "Joshua didn't know Kenya well enough to care for her this much. Eli did." He withdrew a silk blue handkerchief and dabbed his nose. "I can tell you really love her."

"I do. And I'll do anything to protect her." Joshua turned and hurried toward the nurse, Carrie. The closer he came, the wider her eyes opened. Before he could say anything, she held up her hands and shook her head.

"No, Joshua," she whispered. "I know what you're going to ask, and the answer is no. I'll lose my job this time. Dr. Goodwin is back from vacation and he'll know. I'm surprised they didn't find out about this last time."

He grasped her hands. "Dr. Goodwin may not work here much longer. Kenya's father is having the *good doctor* checked into. I have a feeling he'll be staying in his own padded room for a while."

She bit her bottom lip and glanced around the room. "But Joshua, look at those guards over there. They will stop me--us. They are three times stronger than we are." She shook her head. "This time it won't work, I just know it."

He surveyed the room. There had to be something they could do. Suddenly, an idea popped into his head and he swung his gaze back to Carrie. "Fake a heart attack."

She arched a brow. "Excuse me?"

"You heard me. Clutch your chest and fall to the floor. Pretend you're having problems breathing."

"Are you serious?"

"Yes. Do it, but give me the keys to the front door first."

Her hand opened and closed over the large set of silver keys, her eyebrows drawing together.

"Carrie, you know I'm not crazy. I've done nothing wrong. In a few short weeks all of this will be in the open." He touched her shoulder. "I won't let you lose your job. Once I take over as the president of Montgomery Aisle, I'll have control again, and I'll be in the position to help you better." He squeezed his hand over her shoulder. "Please believe me."

Slowly she brought the keys to him and dropped them in his hand. "You know I've never believed you were crazy."

He smiled. "Thanks."

She nodded. "Now go save the woman you love."

Joshua moved away and motioned his head for Lucinda and George to follow. They took slow steps toward the exit. Joshua kept his eyes on the nearest guard, praying Carrie's little scene would work.

Within minutes Carrie's cry echoed through the room, then came a loud gasp for air. A strong clunk made the floor shake briefly as she fell. Just as he'd hoped, all the guards ran to her. He didn't waste any time in hurrying to the door and slipping the key inside. George and Lucinda watched for any signs of trouble, ready to warn him, but so far, there weren't any.

When they reached outside, they all made a mad dash to George's car. "Let me drive," Joshua shouted.

George didn't question, but threw the keys to him.

Once they were all inside and buckled, Joshua stomped on the gas pedal, squealing tires as he drove them out of there. All the way out of the parking lot, Lucinda and George kept their gazes out of the windows as they watched for guards. It was as if luck were on his side, because they made it to the freeway without any problems.

After a while passed of nothing but silence, George leaned forward from the back seat and looked at Joshua through the mirror. "Why didn't you tell Kenya?"

Joshua glanced at the assistant then moved his attention back to the road. "You mean tell Kenya that Joshua and Eli are the same person?"

"Yes."

He sighed heavily, inwardly cursing. It had been haunting him for a few days now. How could he explain things to her if he couldn't understand them himself?

"Because I never thought things would get this far." He shook his head. "During the five years I've been locked away, I've tried many times to escape. Each time my attempts were unsuccessful. Nobody believed who I was, and if they did, they believed Terrel's story, not mine. Terrel found out about my escapes and had Dr. Goodwin torture me." He shuddered, not wanting to remember the kind of punishments that man had put him through. "Anyway, one day I found a book in the institution's library. It was the story Kenya's father wrote. That was when the idea of *future-man* struck me. If Kenya thought I was a man from the future, maybe, just maybe, it might work. She wouldn't think I was a man who'd escaped the mental hospital like everyone else had thought."

He paused and chuckled. "Maybe I am crazy." He glanced in the mirror at George's wide eyes. "Do you think she'll hate me when I tell her the truth?"

George shrugged. "Eli swept her off her feet like no other man had done. She was deeply saddened when Eli left because she didn't think your love was meant to be. Maybe she'll be thrilled to see you again, and maybe she'll hate you when she realizes you've tricked her."

Joshua gritted his teeth. "But I didn't mean to trick her," he bit out. "I was desperate to find someone to help me. I didn't want to go back to that prison and be tortured again."

George patted his shoulder. "I'm sure everything will work out with you and Kenya."

He smiled, but not fully. "Thanks, George. You're a good friend to Kenya."

Lucinda directed him to the house she'd driven by when following Terrel. As they passed and she pointed it out, he sucked in a quick breath. "Lucinda? Do you know who lives there?"

"No. I saw Señor Montgomery take Kenya away, so I followed. Do you know who lives here?"

"Tina LaRousse."

Both Lucinda and George gasped simultaneously. Anger lines popped in George's forehead. "Why, that little tramp. I wonder why Terrel is dealing with the likes of her?"

Joshua chuckled. "Little Miss Tina LaRousse was one of Terrel's early drug friends. Before my father died, Tina and a handful of others like her would party with Terrel all the time. That was before she became big in the fashion world, of course."

George huffed. "Did you know Tina ships some of her designs to California and Hawaii?" He leaned back in the seat and folded his arms. "I still can't understand why they think her designs are better than Kenya's."

"I can." Joshua met the other man's gaze through the rearview mirror again. "Because of Terrel's drug trafficking business, that's why. I bet you a million dollars she sews the bags of cocaine in the hems of her dresses."

George gasped and covered his mouth. "Holy shit!" he muttered.

Joshua chuckled and nodded. "Shit--exactly."

He drove to the end of the block and stopped. Resting his wrists on the steering wheel, he took a deep breath. "Now...what are we going to do?"

George puffed out his chest. "Give me two minutes alone with that LaRousse, and I'll take care of her."

Joshua held back a laugh. By the heat sparking in the assistant's eyes, Joshua had no doubt the man would carry through with his threat.

From the passenger's seat, Lucinda released a shriek and pointed out the window. "Look, there's Miss LaRousse now."

He swiveled his head and looked behind him toward her house. Tina, dressed in regular blue jeans tight enough to have been painted on, and a pink belly-shirt, strutted out to her car and climbed in. While she backed out of the driveway, Joshua's smile widened.

Perfect timing!

~ * ~

When the door closed downstairs, Kenya sighed in relief. At least no harm would come to her while Tina was out of the house. And Terrel was probably in some ridiculous meeting trying to figure out a way to blackmail someone--maybe even her or her father. She rolled her eyes. He'd always been selfish and devious. Why hadn't she seen that before now?

She sat upright on the bed and struggled with the ropes on her wrists, but Terrel had fastened them too tightly. Her skin burned from the effort it took to release them, yet she hadn't been able to budge them an inch.

Fresh tears gathered in her eyes, and she bit her bottom lip to keep from crying aloud. Terrel had been correct when he'd called her weak. Not only physical, but lately she'd been an emotional mess. She'd never liked arguing, and she'd been foolish enough to let Terrel walk all over her.

She gritted her teeth. But no longer. If she ever got out of here alive, she'd make sure Terrel was put behind bars where he belonged.

The sound of a downstairs door opening snapped her out of her thoughts. Her heart sank. Tina must be back. But when her name was called by a familiar voice, her heart leapt to life.

"I'm up here."

"Kenya?" The tone grew louder.

"Up in the attic," she screamed.

"I'm coming, Kenya."

She shook her head, trying to clear it out. Why did it sound like Eli? Couldn't be.

Heavy footsteps boomed on the stairs and she jumped to a standing position. "I'm here," she called out.

The doorknob rattled as someone shook it. "Kenya, are you in there?"

It *was* Eli!

Eleven

Kenya's heart bounced with excitement and she hopped to the door. "Eli, is that you?"

There was a pause on the other side for a brief moment, then came his voice again. "No, it's me, Joshua."

She gasped. "Joshua? How did you get out?"

"There's no time for questions. George and Lucinda are with me. We need to get out of here before Tina returns."

"The door's locked. You'll have to break it down."

"Then step away from the door."

The door rattled as he bumped into it, but it remained closed. Another set of footsteps sounded on the stairs. A familiar voice joined Joshua's.

"Let me help you with that door."

She smiled. *George.*

After three more bangs, the door busted open. George frowned while he rubbed his shoulder, but Joshua stepped into the room, still in the clothes the institution provided for him. And barefoot. For a brief second, she remembered this was how Eli looked when she first saw him, except he wore black instead of the gray Joshua had on.

She smiled through her tears. "You don't know how happy I am to see you."

Joshua took her in his arms and hugged her tight, kissing her forehead. "Not as happy as I am." He pulled away and struggled with the ropes at her wrists. George knelt in front of her and worked loose the ones at her ankles.

"How did you know where to find me?"

Joshua grinned. "Lucinda. She saw Terrel take you away, so she followed him."

She sighed heavily. "Thank God for that woman."

Once they removed the ropes, she wrapped her arms around Joshua and embraced him, laying her head against his chest. The rhythm of his heart beat as fast as hers. She smiled, finally feeling a little comfort from the day's strenuous activities. She didn't want to analyze why she felt so safe with him. Not now. She'd deal with her confusion later.

He kissed her head again. "As much as I'd like to do nothing but stand here and hold you, we'd better get out of here."

She looked up at him. *Why did he say that?* Perhaps Joshua did have strong feelings for her. Once again, she pushed away the confusion.

"I think Terrel has a shipment of drugs going out tonight. Because Tina is involved, it might have something to do with her designs."

"I'm sure it does."

"But we need to catch them in the act. That will get Terrel put away for good."

He smiled and stroked her cheek. Warmth spread throughout her, awakening tingles only Eli had stirred. Although confusing, she didn't try to push the emotions aside. She cuddled her face against his hand. Very nice.

"But we don't know where it'll happen," he said.

"We do now," Lucinda said.

All heads turned toward the housekeeper's voice at the bottom of the stairs...and next to her stood Tina. The Hispanic woman had a clump of Tina's hair in her fist, the other hand grasped Tina's arm. The once very beautiful designer now whimpered and crumpled her face in pain, resembling an old hag perfectly.

George gasped and flew down the stairs to help hold the struggling woman.

Joshua left Kenya's side and took slow steps down the stairs toward Tina. He shook his head. "Why did I ever believe you'd change?"

Tina glared at him. "My, my, look who escaped the nut house."

"I finally found people to believe my story." He shrugged. "Guess you and your druggie lover are going down."

She snickered. "Don't count on it, Joshua. Terrel has connections you'll never have as president of Montgomery Aisle."

"I don't want those kinds of connections, thank you very much." He stopped in front of her and folded his arms. "Besides, once we catch Terrel and put him away, then where will you be?" He shook his head. "What will happen to your designing business then?"

She scowled, her eyes turning darker as she glared at him. "Nothing will happen to me, Joshua, because you can't prove a thing."

Kenya hurried down the stairs and stood next to Joshua. "I bet if we had her warehouse searched this very night, the police would find some incriminating evidence."

Tina's eyes widened and her face lost color. Kenya grinned. "I think we've hit the nail on the head, don't you agree, Joshua?"

He chuckled. "Yes I do." He glanced at George. "You and Lucinda take her into the other room and watch her closely. I'm going to see if I can find some clothes to change into." He picked at his hospital garb. "I think people might get the wrong impression if I go around wearing this."

Joshua looked back at Tina. "Does Terrel still keep some of his clothes in your room?"

The other woman pursed her lips and held up her chin in defiance.

He grabbed Kenya's hand. "Come with me."

She hesitated. Did he want her to help him undress? Heat flared to her cheeks from the indecent thought. She shook her head. "I'd rather not."

"Please. I need to talk to you...in private."

Reluctantly, she allowed him to lead her back upstairs. He opened every door until he found Tina's room. Just as Joshua had suggested, some of Terrel's clothes were sharing Tina's closet.

"Thankfully, Terrel and I are about the same size," he said, grabbing a T-shirt and pair of jeans.

She reached down and pulled out some athletic shoes. "Do you think you can squeeze into these?"

"I'm going to have to try. It's better than going barefoot."

After digging through Tina's dresser drawers, she found some of Terrel's socks and brought them to him. He sat on the edge of the bed and undressed. For some reason, he didn't seem at all embarrassed about taking off his clothes in front of her. And for some reason, she didn't mind him doing it.

When his shirt came off, she held her breath, knowing she'd let out a pleasurable sigh. She bunched her hands into fists and folded her arms to keep from touching the many muscles decorating his beautiful body. He pulled on the shirt, and she almost groaned in disappointment.

As he yanked down his pants, a mark on this upper left thigh caught her attention. Eli had a mark just like this one...

She gasped and covered her mouth. Eli's image flashed through her mind--looking remarkably like Joshua's naked body. Every muscle was shaped the same, every hair, every dent...everything.

He met her gaze and gave her a tender smile. "You know?"

Her heart beat quickly, a knot rose to her throat. "You're...Eli."

He nodded. "I was hoping to tell you before you figured it out."

She took a tentative step toward him. Reaching out, she brushed her fingers lightly against his hair. Lastly, she stroked his clean-shaven chin. "You cut your hair and shaved your goatee?"

"Yes."

"How...how did you get out of the hospital?" Her voice quivered.

"One of the nurses believed me. She knew I had to leave in order to find someone out in the real world to help me. Every year for the past five years, I've escaped, which is the time Doctor Goodwin goes on vacation. But I've never found anyone to help me...until you."

"You...kept going back?" she asked with a shaky voice.

"I had to. Every time I escaped, Terrel found me and took me back. For several months after that I was kept heavily drugged. And that's not including the torture Dr. Goodwin put me through for escaping. I couldn't give up, though. I had to find someone to help me. This time I went back because I was worried that Terrel would discover I'd talked to you and I didn't want him to hurt you." He shrugged. "Guess I was wrong, huh?"

She threaded her fingers through her hair, lifting the bulk off her shoulders. Her fingers squeezed her head, hoping the growing pound would subside. "But...this can't be. What about my father's ring? How did you get his ring if you're not from the future?"

"The book I read of your father's...he has a picture of himself on the back. He's wearing a ring. I thought if I had a ring made just like his, and I could come up with a time-travel story, you might believe me."

He hurried and slipped on his pants, zipped them and stood. "I wanted you to think my mission was a life-altering situation, because in reality, it is. Now, you know what a terrible person Terrel has been and that I need to regain my position in my father's company. If nobody stops Terrel, he'll only get worse, and you know it."

It was as if strong fingers were clutching her chest, the pain in her heart was unreal, making it hard to catch her breath. She wanted to scream at him, she wanted to claw at his face in anger. Yet...he was right.

He grasped her hand. "Kenya, everything I said to you during our time together was true, except about coming from the future. My feelings for you are real. I'm deeply in love with you."

She yanked her hand away. Tears filled her eyes and streamed down her cheeks. "Not now, Eli...or is it Joshua?"

He frowned. "Joshua."

"Please give me time to think about this." She sniffed. "I feel like...like...a fool. Like I was the victim of a cruel joke."

He shook his head. "I didn't mean for it to be like that. I've tried to convince people of Terrel's plan many times since being locked in St. Benedicts, but nobody believed me. Everyone thought I was some escaped lunatic." He swallowed as his eyes misted over. "You were the first person to take a chance on me."

A sob rose to her throat, but she held it back. She mustn't cry in front of him. A part of her wanted to hate him, but another part of her wanted to wrap her arms around him and love him for the rest of her life.

She moved to the door. "Hurry and dress. I'll meet you downstairs. I'm going to call my father and have him arrange for the police to meet us at Tina's warehouse."

He nodded. "Okay."

~ * ~

Joshua's heart broke a little more every time he looked at Kenya. Her eyes were red and puffy as if she'd been crying, but in front of him, she just displayed a frown upon her lovely face. They drove in silence to Tina's warehouse. Well...not exactly silence because in the back seat Tina kept making threats, and George keep telling her to shut her trap.

Tina never told them what they needed to know, but her panicked actions spoke the truth. The annoyed woman glared at Joshua through the rearview mirror. "You guys are going to lose, you know. They're expecting me to be there, and if I'm not there, nothing will happen."

Joshua clenched his teeth and glanced at Kenya. She snapped her gaze from the side window back to him. Worry etched her brow and her mouth pulled lower in a frown. She nibbled on her bottom lip--a nervous reaction he loved watching.

She glanced in the back at Tina, turned back, and pulled down the visor. Kenya peered in the mirror attached and ran her fingers through her hair, lifting the mass off her neck and twisting it a bun. Scrunching her nose, she shrugged.

"I think I have an idea," she whispered.

"What?"

"I could dress like Tina," she continued in a soft voice. "She's about my size. We both have a thin face. And if I wear my hair up and put some kind of hat over it, they may never know we have different hair color."

He raised his eyebrows. Taking a quick peek in the rearview mirror at the angry bee in the back, he looked back at Kenya. "No. I won't let you do this."

She cocked her head. "You won't *let* me? I don't think you have any right to tell me that."

His fingers tightened around the steering wheel. "Kenya, I'm only saying that because I don't want you to get hurt. The people we'll be dealing with are dangerous. They carry guns on a daily basis and they won't hesitate to use them."

She folded her arms and stared straight out the window. "Do you have a better suggestion?"

Inwardly, he groaned. He didn't. In fact, if he weren't so worried about her safety, he'd have commended her on a great idea. But the truth was--she could get hurt, and he didn't want to put her in that situation.

"Well, do you?" Her voice rose as she glared at him.

"No."

"So? Do you think I could pull it off?"

He took his eyes off the road for a moment to glance at her. "Yes, I think you can do it."

The streetlight turned red, so he stopped the car. She placed her hand on his arm. When he met her eyes, she smiled. "Remember, my father and his FBI friends will be there helping."

He nodded. "I'm just worried about you. I couldn't bear if anything bad happened to you." His voice strained with emotion and he cleared it.

"We're not going to let Terrel win."

A tug pulled on the corner of his mouth and he grinned. "Good."

When the light turned green, he continued heading for Tina's warehouse. A block away, Kenya pointed to the car by the gas station. "There's Dad. Pull over."

Joshua and Kenya met her father and two of his FBI friends who were with him. Thankfully, the men were dressed in everyday clothes. The agent in charge carried himself well. Straight shoulders, an in-control lift to his chin, gave Joshua confidence that things would work out. She told them what they'd already suspected, and then explained to them about her plan.

"No." The blond agent folded his arms. "I won't have you putting your life at risk. We have agents--"

"But do your agents resemble Tina LaRousse? Do they know the fashion world like I do?"

By the way his lips tightened, she knew she'd made her point. "Besides, I trust all of you to protect me. I believe this will work, but only if I go in as Tina."

The tall, blond agent nodded. "There are undercover agents posted all around the warehouse. I discovered two have already been working undercover as dealers for a few months now. If everything goes our way, we should be making several arrests tonight."

The short, rotund agent nodded. "If you see something that's not right, get the hell out of there. No heroics on this one."

"All right," Kenya said.

Joshua breathed a little easier. Kenya stood beside him and he squeezed her hand. She presented him with a hesitant smile, and his heart leapt. At least she wasn't throwing daggers at him.

She glanced at her father and the agents then rested her warm gaze back on Joshua. "Well, I better get dressed." She looked down at her clothes. "There's no way Tina would be caught dead wearing this."

Kenya's father hugged her and kissed her cheek. "Don't forget to wear the bullet-proof vest."

"Okay."

Once Kenya's father and the FBI agents walked toward the car to talk to Tina, Joshua took her in his arms. She stiffened for only a brief moment, but when she locked gazes with him, her body relaxed.

"I'll be watching every move you make," he told her. "I won't let Terrel hurt you again."

She gave him a tender smile. "Thank you for not talking me out of doing this. Terrel would have."

He chuckled. "I wanted to, God knows I don't want you hurt, but it's a brilliant idea."

She laughed. "Yes it is."

He picked up her hand and kissed her palm. "I want you to know how proud I am of you...and I also want you to know how much I care about you."

She arched a brow. "You mentioned before you were deeply in love with me."

He nodded.

"That's not a lie?"

"You're looking in my eyes now. What do you think?"

Her smile relaxed, and a hint of a twinkle flashed in her eyes. "I think you're either heavily sedated...or you're deeply in love with me."

He laughed and hugged her tighter. "I'm intoxicated all right. Cupid's arrow must have a different potion in it."

She pushed him back, moving her head so he wouldn't kiss her. "Joshua. Don't think I've forgiven you yet. I'm still wounded from your deception."

He frowned. "I'm sorry. I'll give you more time then."

His hands moved down her arms, and he linked his fingers with hers. "Come on; let's get you looking like Tina LaRousse."

Twelve

"Ugh!" Kenya grimaced in the mirror as she stared back at her reflection. She and Tina LaRousse definitely had different tastes. Why, she wouldn't be caught dead wearing this...yet that might be what happened if things didn't go as planned tonight.

She bit her bottom lip and ran her hand over the frilly dandelion blouse and white skirt. The floppy white sunhat complimented the outfit--so Tina probably thought since this was one of the designs in the designer's warehouse. She, Joshua, and the FBI arrived at the warehouse early to get everything ready for the meeting. Thanks to the way they interrogated Tina, she spilled like a broken damn, telling them everything that would happen tonight.

She took a deep breath then released it slowly. As long as she didn't stand too close to Terrel, she might be able to pull it off. White netting hung on the front of the sunhat, helping to shield her face, but if Terrel came too close, he'd be able to tell her true identity even if she sprayed the horrendous scent on her body that Tina liked to call perfume.

Footsteps echoed on the wooden floor mere seconds before a knock came upon the door.

"Enter, if you dare," she said.

Through the reflection, the door opened. Joshua poked his head inside the room. "How are things coming?"

She flipped the veil over the top part of her face and turned to give him a full effect of the costume. "Well, what do you think? Will I pass?"

He scrunched his face and shook his head. "That's awful."

"Yes, and to think Tina wore something like this at my engagement party." She stuck out her tongue. "Sad, isn't it?"

"And women actually buy that crap from her."

She shook her head. "I bet only older women with no taste buy this."

He walked further inside and stood in front of her. Lifting the hat from her head, he touched the hair she'd wound so tight to try to conceal. "I like it better long."

"So do I."

His knuckles brushed her jaw before he bent and placed his lips on hers. The kiss was soft, and tender. He sucked her bottom lip and tingles shot through her body. *Blast it all.* He was doing it again, and she cursed her weak body for letting him. She broke the kiss before the heat spiraling through her body became greater.

"Are you ready for this?" he asked.

"I have to be. There's no turning back now. If Tina doesn't show for this meeting, then everything will go wrong."

"I agree." He took her hands in a loose hold. "I'm going to be up in the rafters. Agent O'Donnell's men will be scattered about the warehouse hiding. All they need is for you to show them the drugs and for them to turn over the money to you."

She nodded. "Sounds easy, huh?"

"No. But I think you can pull it off."

His warm green eyes melted her, just as they had always done. When he was Eli, she couldn't get enough of his hypnotic gaze, and as Joshua, she loved the way they sparkled when he smiled. It still didn't seem real. This whole story still confused her. A small part of her heart argued with her brain to forgive him for being so distrustful with her. Seeing him actually care for her, and watching the pain in his eyes when he'd thought she hated him...that was her undoing. Why couldn't she resist this man? And why couldn't she stay angry? She did love him, whether Eli or Joshua, he was the man she wanted to be with...forever.

She took a deep breath. "Wish me luck."

"Good luck," he said before gathering her in his arms for another kiss.

She stiffened her body, but as soon as his lips touched hers, a sigh escaped her throat. Wrapping her arms around his neck, she settled her body against his. She'd always thought they fit together since the first time he held her. So perfect...so made for each other.

Someone cleared their throat--and it wasn't her or Joshua. She pulled away and swung her head toward the sound. Federal Agent O'Donnell stood in the doorway with his arms folded over his chest. A cheesy grin stretched across his mouth.

"Excuse me for interrupting, but it's time to get in our places."

Joshua nodded, kissed her one more time, and left the room with the agent. Even though her heart quickened from their brief, but passionate moment, it also dropped with each step Joshua took out of the office. Would she see him again after this was over? Would they both live through it?

She ground her teeth and fisted her hands. Yes. She would *not* allow Terrel to win. Not this time.

Turning back to the full-length mirror, she focused on her attire once again. *Disgusting.* But she did have to admit she looked like Tina. She snickered and placed the hat back on her head, adjusting the netting over her eyes.

As the minutes ticked down to show time, she paced Tina's office. Wringing her hands against her stomach, she prayed everything go her way. She prayed the agents would catch the bad guys, and that she and Joshua would return home safe and sound.

But unlike Eli, Joshua had a home. He wouldn't be staying with her. Her nervous heart sank a little deeper. He would move back into the Montgomery Estate and take over as president of Montgomery Aisle. And she would continue to be the struggling designer.

Would he still want her after this?

He'd told her he loved her deeply, but was he just saying that because of everything she'd gone through to help him? She squeezed her eyes closed. *Hope not.*

Voices carrying from out in the warehouse snapped her out of her thoughts. Taking a deep breath, she lifted her chin and sashayed out of the room, trying to imitate Tina's walk.

Along with Terrel, two men sauntered toward the rack of evening gowns Tina had designed. Terrel chatted with the men, motioning his hand in the direction of the dresses. The two men in suits wore stern expressions, while Terrel's eyes appeared a little too far gone to be his regular self. Inwardly, she sighed. Looks as if he may have been snorting some of his own *happy dust* tonight.

Terrel glanced up at her and acknowledged her with a nod. The other men looked her way and stopped. Her heart slammed against her ribcage. Did they know she wasn't Tina?

She cleared her throat again. "Good evening, gentlemen." She poured on the sweetness in the same French accent Tina used. "I see Terrel has shown you my dresses."

The shorter men out of the two nodded. "Tell me more about your design, Miss LaRousse."

She stepped over to the rack of dresses and proceeded to tell how she designed the dress, what specific material she used and why. Lastly, she added the part they wanted to hear--the large seams along the hem--large enough to hold bags of cocaine.

Although she focused on the two men, she did glance at Terrel every so often. His grin widened the more she talked. He didn't suspect at all. If he did, he'd be wearing a scowl and have a gun to her head.

Ease seeped through her stiff body, relaxing her if only just a tiny bit.

~ * ~

Joshua had never loved any woman more, or had been more proud. Kenya pulled off a fine acting job. In fact, if he hadn't known who she was, he would have guessed her to be Tina.

What a special woman, and to think she was all his. He'd never dreamed this moment would happen. After five long years, his hopes faded. Kenya not only lifted his heart but made him believe in angels. She risked her life to save his. What better way to show her love? He would do all he could to make sure nothing happened to her. He intended to keep her by his side forever.

Holding onto a steel beam on the ceiling, he watched the woman he loved, and the man he loathed. Joshua's future was within grasp, and he couldn't let his stepbrother take it away from him again. Those five years were too long.

Across the room, he glimpsed an elbow of one of the agents. After surveying the floor more, he picked out a few more. Right now, swarms of more agents and police were surrounding the building. Terrel definitely wouldn't get away this time.

So far, everything had gone according to plan. After Kenya explained about her evening gowns, the two dealers inspected the dress, especially the hem. Terrel stood back with his arms crossed, his focus on the gowns instead of Kenya. There were only a couple of times the man tried to stand by Kenya, but she discreetly moved away as she pretended to be into the discussion about Tina's designs.

One of the men carrying a briefcase reached in his pocket, withdrew a small packet of white powder, and handed it to Kenya. She knelt in front of a gown, withdrew a needle, and began to unpick the hem. Within seconds, she demonstrated how to hide the drugs in the dress.

Emotion grew inside Joshua's chest. She gave him so much of herself, not only with her love, but with her actions. Never had a woman affected him this way. He swallowed the lump in his throat. God, he loved her so much. He couldn't let anything happen to her.

The moment he waited for all evening finally arrived. The two men with briefcases stood and gave Kenya a nod, smiling from ear to ear. She led them to the table she'd already set up for their deal. Chilling in a bucket of ice was a bottle of champagne, and beside it sat four empty goblets. She motioned for Terrel to do the honors. He took the bottle, popped the cork while the men laid their briefcases on the table, and snapped them open displaying the bundles of money.

That was it. The signal.

Just like ants raiding a picnic, the agents ran out from their hiding spots, their guns raised and pointing at the dealers. "FBI--don't move."

Terrel grabbed Kenya around the neck, withdrawing his gun from his pocket at the same time.

Joshua's heart froze, his breathing stilled. Sweat coated his forehead as the scene unfolded. The agents yelled at Terrel to drop the gun, but the crazy man screamed at them to back away. He pulled Kenya backward toward one of the exits. She gripped his arm and struggled, fighting his control.

Joshua needed to do something. Anything. And sitting upon a beam like a damn cuckoo-bird wasn't his idea of a hero.

Terrel stepped closer his way. They were almost underneath him. Just as they neared, Kenya raised her gaze and met Joshua's. She nodded before bringing her foot down upon Terrel's instep. She lowered her elbow and plowed it into the other man's groin.

Doubling over, Terrel lost his grip on Kenya and she backed away. Terrel raised the gun toward her.

Shouting Kenya's name in panic, Joshua jumped from the rafters. Mere moments before he landed on Terrel, a gunshot rang through the air. Everything around him turned black.

Thirteen

Kenya's head hit the floor, ringing filling her ears. Shouts lifted all around her--the explosion of a gun being fired.

She rubbed her throbbing temple and glanced to where she'd pulled away from Terrel. The son-of-a-bitch was lying on the floor with Joshua on top of him. Both men were still as the scent of gunpowder hung thick through the air.

A spot of red caught her eye seeping from the back of Joshua's shoulder. Her heart dropped, but she found the strength to scream. "Joshua!" She scrambled on her hands and knees to him. Three other agents rushed to his side and turned him over. He lay still. Too damn still. Blood oozed from a ripped hole in his shirt near the shoulder.

"Oh, God, no," she sobbed, pushing people aside on her way to him.

Beside her, an agent touched her shoulder. "I don't think the bullet hit any major arteries. I think he'll be all right if we can stop the flow of blood. We've called for an ambulance."

Kenya maneuvered her body beside his, gently laying his head on her lap, using the palms of her hands to put pressure on the wound. Her chest tightened and threatened to close. A large knot formed in her throat, and she couldn't swallow. Tears blurred her vision and dripped down her cheeks. *What have I done?*

She traced the pallor of his lips, his skin color matching dangerously close.

"Hold on, my love. You'll be fine." Her voice cracked.

Squeezing her eyes closed, she cursed her rotten timing. Why hadn't he jumped later? Why had Terrel pulled the trigger at that exact moment? She bent her head over Joshua and pulled him close. A cry broke from her chest, followed by more.

"Hold on. Don't leave me."

Her body shook with sobs, an indescribable ache growing everywhere inside her. It hurt with every breath she took. Opening her eyes, she focused on him lying so still. So pale. She traced her finger along his cheek to his chin. A fresh dam of tears broke free. "I love you."

From outside, sirens roared through the night. Help was on the way. Soon.

"You bitch."

Terrel's voice grated on her nerves, and she glanced over his shoulder. Two agents handcuffed him and read him his rights. Her ex-fiancé glared at her as he struggled.

"What in the hell are you doing looking like Tina? And why are you here with *him*?" He looked at the men beside him. "Joshua is the one you want." Terrel motioned his head toward her. "He's the one who killed Adam Montgomery. He's the one who escaped a mental hospital."

O'Donnell yanked Terrel to his feet. "Shut up. I'm getting sick of your lies."

Kenya didn't watch Terrel being dragged out to the police car; instead, she looked back at Joshua. She swallowed. "Hold on, my darling. You're going to be all right."

The crowd around them parted, and two paramedics hurried to Kenya's side. It took every effort she had to pull away from him, but she allowed the paramedics to do their job. Before too long they had an IV in his arm and were strapping him to the gurney.

A warm hand curved around her elbow and she turned her head. Her father stood beside her, tears in his eyes. His smile wavered as he looked at Joshua. "He'll be just fine."

Kenya nodded. "I know. It's just hard to see him like that. He's waited so long to escape the mental ward and to have it end like this..." Her voice broke again.

Her father gathered her in his arms and she rested her head on his chest. "Come on. Let's follow them to the hospital."

~ * ~

"I have done nothing but mess things up today." Kenya took in a deep breath and rubbed her forehead. A strong disinfectant scent stung her nose. Although the waiting room was filled, and chattering swarmed all around her, she had her mine on one thing and one thing only. "Because of my stubbornness, Joshua was shot."

Her father grasped her shoulders and turned her to face him. "And because of you, Terrel and Lisa Montgomery are in jail, not to mention that hussy, Tina."

"I know, but I still wish I could have done something to keep Terrel from shooting Joshua." Tears filled her eyes.

He squeezed her shoulders. "Then you would have been shot instead. Joshua will be fine. I know it."

The door to the waiting room opened and an older man in a professional white jacket walked in. He smiled at Kenya. "Joshua is awake. He's asking for you."

She held in a sob of joy as she rushed to his room. As she entered, she slowed her pace, but her heartbeat kept the quick rhythm. His eyes were closed when she stepped to the bed, but as soon as she touched his warm hand, he looked at her.

"Hello, handsome."

He smiled. "Are you okay?"

"Yes." She squeezed his arm. "You were the only one to take a bullet."

"Terrel?" His voice came out rusty and he cleared his throat.

"He's in jail, along with his mother."

"Tina, too?"

"Of course. Although, I think they'll go a little easier on her because she cooperated."

He rolled his head on the pillow and looked at her again. "I couldn't have done any of this without you."

A tear slid down her cheek. "Yes, you could have."

"No. The reason I couldn't accomplish anything these past five years is because you were not by my side." He slid his hand over, linking his fingers with hers. "I love you more than you could ever know."

The tightness in her heart made her breathless as love blossomed inside her. The anger she'd felt for his deception had disappeared when she thought she'd lost him. More tears streamed down her face and she leaned forward to briefly kiss his lips. "I love you, too."

He smiled. "Promise?"

"Promise." She hiccupped a laugh. "I still don't understand it all. It's crazy to think I could love you so quickly."

He nodded. "Yes, love is crazy, all right. I fell hard and fast for you, too. I think it's because we've wasted five years of being apart. Although I didn't know you back then, I believe we would have met eventually." He licked his lips. "Kenya, you're my soul mate, and I don't want to live my life without you."

She shook her head. "You won't." She leaned up and kissed him again, this time it lasted longer. When she pulled away, she smiled. "I can't wait until you get out of this hospital."

He chuckled. "You and me both. I'm sick to death of hospitals."

"And I can't wait to get you naked and in my bed."

His brows shot up and down as a grin stretched across his face. "Um...that sounds tempting."

"You don't think I'm crazy for wanting to jump your bones as soon as you're out?"

"No, because I'm as crazy as you for thinking the very same thing."

She laughed. "I think Cupid is the one who was crazy, but for once, he did something right in my life." She cuddled beside him on the bed, laying her head on his chest.

He stroked her hair. "The only thing I know is I'd better be completely healed by the time we get home."

"Why?" she mumbled against his chest.

"Because I have a feeling you're going to keep me extremely active."

She chuckled. "You're damn right!" She lifted her head. "All that and more."

Dang Crooked Arrow

Liz Hunter

Champagne Books
Calgary, AB Canada

In high school, a guidance counselor told Liz that the desire to be a writer was unrealistic. Years later, homebound during a five day blizzard with a brown paper sack full of romance novels, Ms. Hunter soon realized that part of her fascination with these romances stemmed from her dormant desire to write.

Liz's first book, a romantic suspense called *Beyond the Shadow*, was published in 2001, followed by *Plain Jane's Tight End*, and *A Precious Gift*. A member of Romance Writers of America, Wisconsin RWA, The Golden Network, EPIC, Jewels of the Quill and Diva's All Stars, she places highly in most contests she enters, and her stories consistently garner four and five star reviews. Ms. Hunter hails from Madison, Wisconsin, where she lives with her husband, teenaged daughter, four Zebra finches, three cats, two fish tanks, and a hamster named Chewy.

Books by Liz Hunter

A Precious Gift
Footloose
Mistletoe Magic

Don't miss any of our special offers. Write to us at #35069-4604 37 St SW, Calgary AB Canada T3E 7C7 or visit us online at www.champagnebooks.com to sign up for our quarterly newsletter.

One

"Promise you'll act civilized," Satara Avery, Tara for short, counseled her nephew and three nieces as she closed the van door. Last week's two inch snowfall lay in dirty piles at curbs and in medians

"It's just a flower shop," Kevin, the eldest at six years old, replied. "It's not like we're in church or something."

"It's brand new and upscale, and I really don't want us to get kicked out. I'll make it fast. Tiffany, remembered you promised me. You'll keep your clothes on, right?"

The two-year old smiled sweetly. "Okay."

"Kimmy, Erica, please keep an eye on her."

Kevin demonstrated his good manners by holding the door open for the adult and three young girls.

They all stopped to inhale the flower scents inside the shop. "Oh, it smells just like bubble bath," Kimmy said.

"Smells like roses," Erica corrected her.

"You're both right," Tara said to keep the peace.

Whatever the exact smell, it was heady, as was the décor. Elegant marble statues and stands holding various sized pots greeted Tara and the four children. Peace lilies and vases of roses predominated. Healthy vines, potted plants and colorful flowers of many varieties tempted the senses with their colors and aroma. Tara realized the walls were painted in a garden scene, tricking the eye into thinking the shop was considerably larger than actual.

Two year old Tiffany offered Tara a single rose.

"Tiffany, honey, you can't pick the flowers. They're decorations for the shop. You have to buy anything you want, and that you can afford. Let me help you put it back.

Try to keep your hands to yourself. Please? If you're all good, I'll take you out for a treat later."

"Okay."

By then, the other three children had already separated. "Come back here, all of you. You promised to stay close by and behave."

Tara felt like a heel, being so strict with the kids. The children were good, they really were. It was just difficult to keep all four occupied for very long, say more than thirty seconds at a time.

A young woman greeted them. "Hi! How can I help you?" Her name tag read 'Lindsey.'

Kevin materialized at Tara's side and spoke up. "We want to order flowers for our fathers for Valentine's Day."

"You mean your mothers," the clerk corrected.

"No, I mean our fathers. They never get flowers. We decided to surprise our dads."

The clerk frowned. "Isn't that what Fathers Day is for?"

"Hardly," Kevin argued. "When was the last time you sent your father flowers on Father's Day? More likely, you sent a shirt or a mug or a tie."

"You're right," the clerk admitted, frowning. "How old are you?"

"I'm six and I have an IQ of 168."

"Stop bragging," Tara whispered to the boy and cleared her throat. "Can we have the flowers delivered to a cruise ship in the Caribbean?"

Lindsey's mouth dropped open. "I haven't the slightest idea. I'm new here. So is the shop, actually. We opened yesterday." They all followed her to the counter. "Do you have the information--the port and name of the cruise ship?"

Tara dug in her hand bag for the itinerary. The three girls had wandered back to Tara's side by now. "Why don't you guys go memorize the names of all the plants while we do the paperwork and I pay for it?"

"Can we each get a plant?" Erica asked.

"Sure... as long as they're small ones...and don't pick anything up! They're heavier than they look."

From the gleam in her eye, the four year old already had something in mind. The foursome tore off to pick their favorites.

"No running! Kevin, you're in charge. Make sure the girls behave."

The clerk checked some sort of listing in a plastic sleeve. Probably directions to the computerized cash register, Tara thought suspiciously.

"It may take me a few minutes to figure this out, and the manager is out of the shop picking up an order of roses. Do you have some other shopping to do?"

"Not really. This is our outing for the day." She'd found that one errand a day with the children worked better than grouping several in the same day. Though the kids were well-behaved, they had a finite amount of patience. So did Tara.

The shop door opened, activating a wind chime to announce a new arrival. "Oh, here's the owner now," the clerk said. "She'll be able to help."

Lindsey soon explained the problem and the owner instructed her how to handle the order.

"Congratulations on your opening," Tara said. "You have a beautiful shop. It smells as good as it looks. Good luck to you!"

"Well, thank you." The door opened, setting off the chimes again, and the owner turned to see who entered. "Be still, my heart," she whispered. "Do you see what just walked in the door? Adonis, every woman's dream come true...and I saw him first. He's mine."

Tara laughed heartedly until she looked at the newcomer. One glance left her speechless. Tall and well-built, hair spiked up in the current style, his bright blue eyes caught hers before moving on to the florist's gaze.

Tara felt bereft, briefly, before reminding herself that she wasn't his type. He was obviously into feminine, fawning women while she was self-sufficient, unimpressed with looks or hooks. She doubted that the shop owner was the type of woman who relied on a man's largess, either, but she didn't mind pretending. Just with his brief glance, he'd identified Tara as being too independent for her own good, and someone who didn't offer pretense.

His smile encompassed all three of the women, though, and Tara suspected hers was not the only heart of the three that went pitter-patter. What woman between nine and ninety could resist his charms?

"How do you do," the owner said, offering her hand. "I'm Glenna Evans. How may I help you?"

Gee, Glenna didn't introduce herself to me, nor did she offer a handshake, Tara thought. She suspected the owner's offer included more than flowers. The man smiled widely, displaying gleaming white teeth against his tanned complexion. Either he was just off the plane from a month in the tropics or he owed his tan to an artificial bulb.

"Harrison Howard, Harry for short," he said, offering his hand.

How many people shook hands with a shop owner? Honestly, he was too transparent. All he wanted was to get into Glenna's--

Tara's thought ended abruptly when he extended his hand to her in greeting, and for a few awkward moments, she couldn't remember her name. "Satara Avery," she finally responded.

"Satara? Are you aware that your namesake was the Anglo Saxon goddess of spring, fertility and the rising sun?"

She laughed. "I definitely don't fit that image. As a matter of fact, I seldom use my full name. Please call me Tara." Why would he have the need to call her anything at all? He was a virtual stranger and after a few minutes they'd never set eyes on one another again! Customers or not, the shop owner resisted being left out. She cleared her throat and repeated her original offer. "How may I help you?"

"I need to order some flowers, red roses for Valentine's Day. I assume you deliver."

"Of course. No charge. If you'll just give us a few minutes, we'll finish Ms. Avery's order. Unfortunately, the shop has a single cash register. Lindsey?" Glenna addressed the younger girl. "Are you about finished with Ms. Avery's order?"

"Almost. I'll need your credit card, Ms. Avery."

"Don't forget the kids are choosing plants for themselves, in addition to the roses for their fathers," Tara said.

"I'll go see how they're doing," Lindsey offered.

The shop owner looked torn, as if afraid the newcomer might become impatient and leave, versus anxious to make more of his acquaintance. Apparently the latter won out. "Where are you from. Harry?"

"Indianapolis."

How could anyone he make the name of a city sound sexy, Tara wondered?

"What brings you to Chicago?" Glenna persisted.

"Business. I sell medical equipment over a two state area. Will this take a long time? I'd hoped to get on the road before traffic got too heavy."

"Perhaps I could begin handwriting the order? Do you have the name and address where the roses are to be delivered?"

"Actually, I need twelve dozen roses."

"There's twelve in a dozen," both the shop owner and Tara said simultaneously.

"I'm aware of that. I have twelve separate names and addresses for delivery."

"Oh, I'm so sorry. I thought you meant a dozen red roses to a single address. I'll have to charge extra to deliver a single rose to twelve separate addresses."

"No, you were right the first time. I want to send a dozen roses to a dozen women, all separate addresses."

Tara smiled knowingly. She'd pegged him as a Lothario at first glance. Glenna's eyes sparkled with dollar signs. "Oh, my," she said. "That's a huge order. Are you sure?"

He laughed. "I'm sure. Are you able to handle an order that big?"

"Of course. It's still several days until Valentine's Day, so even if I have to deliver to all twelve addresses from here, I can order more roses."

He shook his head. "The ladies are scattered across two states."

Tara stared at him for a long minute. "I know this is inexcusably rude of me, but I have to ask, do you really have that many girlfriends?"

"As a matter of fact, yes."

Her mouth dropped open. "How do you mange a dozen women at once? Are you Mormon? Or do you have a harem or something?"

He smiled, sending a glow through her, and she wished she could find a batch of one-liners to keep him smiling indefinitely.

"Hey, I like that idea," he said. "But, no. No harem. No orgies. My love life is very organized and civilized. You see, as I said, I sell medical equipment and have a territory covering two states. I make my rounds at quarterly intervals, so I have all the major areas or accounts on three month call-backs."

"Let me guess," Glenna said. "You have a girl in every port."

"Exactly." He beamed. "One week in each area every quarter, one female the object of my attention for that week, and that location."

"And they don't mind the other eleven weeks you're gone?" Tara said incredulously.

"Not one bit. I'm very attentive to them while I'm there."

"I'm surprised you have time to sell your product in between...rotations." Tara grunted, ruining the seriousness of the situation.

"Every one of them has clout with purchasing."

"Oh my goodness, do you realize you're prostituting yourself? Are you sure it's legitimate to conduct business in this manner?"

"I've never had a complaint." His comment suggested a double entendre.

What an over-sexed, full of himself jerk. "Excuse me. I need to round up the little ones." She left Lover Boy in the shop owner's capable hands. Talk about a double entendre, she chuckled to herself.

She found the kids with the young clerk Lindsey, explaining the care and feeding of their chosen plants. She excused herself to fetch a cart to transport their selections.

Kevin, typically, had chosen a spider plant, and with his genius IQ, Tara could envision him majoring in a scientific field eventually, possibly some Arachnid-related-ology.

His sister Erica, the healer, had an Aloe plant, of course, and their cousin, Kimmy the peacemaker, picked a Peace Lily bigger than she could carry. Kim's little sister, Tiffany, clung to a Norfolk Island Pine, also too big for her to carry. Tara could see the little tike as a wanderer since she was prone to wander away all too often, so her choice also fit the type.

"You all did a wonderful job picking your first plants."

"I'm afraid they're a bit expensive," the clerk said. "I tried to steer them to the ivy and greenery."

"Not a problem," Tara assured her. "It's worth every penny. They'll have many years of learning responsibility taking care of their new 'pets.'"

"Will that do it for today then? You don't want a plant of your own?"

"Not today, thanks. We'll stop by for fertilizer and whatever another day. I think Casanova is getting restless. Time we check out."

Tara followed the clerk with the cart to the register. The four kids got sidetracked, gazing through the window into the hothouse area where the fresh cut flowers were kept. That should keep them busy for another short while, Tara thought. She'd learned by experience that the last few minutes waiting at checkout was always the killer as far as their patience was concerned. Once they were done shopping, they were immediately ready to move on. Waiting at checkout? B-O-R-I-N-G.

The shop owner and her other customer, Harrison Howard--Harry-for-short, had edged away from the counter and were laughing and flirting. Harry-for-short noticed Tara signing the computerized credit card and sauntered over to stand beside her, Glenna-the-shopkeeper nearly pinned to his side.

"Where'd the children go?" Glenna asked.

One glance toward the hothouse and Tara groaned. "Oh Lord, it looks like they're playing Loves Me, Loves Me Not with your daisies."

Glancing at Tara's total on the computer screen, Glenna glanced at Harry, probably gauging his patience, and apparently decided that she could afford to write the destruction of the daisies off. "Don't worry about it. A dozen daisies won't break me."

Suddenly the lighting changed and an eerie atmosphere transformed the shop to twilight background. Tara heard raucous laughter and loud voices. "What's happening?"

"It sounds like a drunken brawl," Harrison Howard said.

"I'm not drunk! I'll prove it to ya, jus watch."

"It's okay, really."

"Watch Bunny."

"Ouch!" Tara said.

"Ouch!" Harry-for-short said.

"Dang Crooked Arrow!"

Tara rubbed her left shoulder.

Harry rubbed his right arm.

Their glances met and held. Plump little red hearts floated before Tara's eyes. Was this love?

Two

"Mommy, Mommy," little Tiffany cried, running across the flower shop. "Did you see them? Did you see them?"

"Did I see whom?"

"Easter Bunny and Cupid!" Kevin interjected.

Tara gave a doubtful glance at him, then knelt down to be on the two-year-old child's level. "Oh, honey, remember we talked about this, about not making things up?" She couldn't come right out and tell the children that the Easter Bunny and Cupid didn't exist. It was like walking a tightrope with no net.

"But we did see them! They were right over there on the wall."

"We did, we did!" the three other children confirmed.

Tara looked at the wall, thinking they might have seen posters on the wall, but there weren't any.

It surprised her that Kevin participated in the protest. He was old enough and smart enough to know better.

Tara had no answer for the children. Something had happened. She recalled that eerie light and the raucous laughter, and her arm still stung. She looked over her shoulder to Harry, and her heart quickened at the soft look in his eyes.

"Something weird happened," he confirmed, offering a hand to help her up off her knees. His touch was warm and strong, gentle and kind.

She thought she'd die if he ever let go of her hand.

Tiffany started crying.

"Oh, sweetheart," Tara said, gently wrestling her hand from Harry's grasp. "It's nothing to cry about."

"Yes it is. I couldn't help it. I peed my pants."

Tara couldn't resist laughing. Just what she needed, getting hot over a self-professed Lothario, a total stranger, temporarily responsible for the well-being of four children aged two to six... and cleaning up their messes. She pictured herself riding into the sunset with him, not necessarily on a mustang, rather 'in' a Mustang. She shook off the image, knowing that she'd flipped out.

She was too realistic a person to believe in love at first sight, too independent to follow any man into the sunset. Love didn't strike unannounced, unprepared. Love took it's time finding the perfect mate.

"Kevin, would you please get the carry-all out of the van?" She didn't dare call it a diaper bag, Tiffany would go into hysterics. "Can you do that safely, Kevin?"

"Would you like me to help him?" Harry offered.

"No!" Kevin protested. "I can do it myself."

"Thanks, Mr.--" Tara couldn't call the 'Man of her Wildest Fantasies' Mr. Howard. "Thanks, Harry. It's kind of you to offer, but Kevin is very responsible for his age. I know he can handle it or I wouldn't have asked."

The boy accepted the keys Tara handed over and left.

All this time the shop owner, Glenna, had waited patiently. She took advantage of the short lull to catch Harry's eye. "Do you have that list of women?"

To Tara, the message came across as a pointed reminder of Harry's fickle love life. She knew darn well that Glenna intended it as such. Tara could have kicked herself for her whimsical thoughts.

He dug his wallet out of his back pants' pocket and retrieved a folded sheet of paper. He seemed to hesitate before handing it over to the shop owner. "I have the list on CD, but I wasn't sure you could import the addresses to your shop's program."

"I should check into that, though it's rare to get a dozen orders at once."

"Do I get a discount for volume?"

"Sorry, but no." She smiled to take away the sting.

Kevin returned in short order. "Don't even ask"

Tara read his mind. "You remembered to lock the van."

He gave her a proud smile. When she looked at Harry, he was smiling, too.

"I'll be right back," she announced in general, but with Harry in mind. She didn't want to miss him if he finished his order before she changed Tiffany.

"I'll show you where the bathroom is," the clerk offered.

"Thanks, Lindsey. Erica, Kimmy, please pick up the mess in the hothouse. Kevin, you can help, too. Maybe Lindsey will lend you a dustpan and broom."

"Sure thing," Lindsey said.

"But I want to check out this computer," Kevin protested.

"You have one at home," Erica said. "They're all the same."

Kimmy the peacemaker spoke up. "Actually, they're not."

Tara hurried away before the fur started to fly between the threesome.

Her biggest fear was that Harry would be finished with his order and long gone by the time she changed Tiffany. Naturally they'd missed their after-school-snack. Only Kevin and Kim were in school, both one grade ahead of their age level. Erica was in preschool mornings only, and Tiffany home all day, Tara had planned to have their snack after the stop at the florist. Unfortunately, they'd been much longer than she'd anticipated, and the kids simply got grumpy, even sometimes unruly, when they missed their snack. Now Tiffany was whiny and uncooperative while Tara attempted to change her niece's panties.

"Honey, the sooner we finish, the sooner you get a snack. Remember the juicy oranges we got at the grocery store this morning?"

"Want candy."

"Candy isn't good for you. Maybe I have raisins in my purse."

"Don't want raisins."

"Okay, I'll give them to Kevin. He's always hungry."

"No! Tiffy raisins!"

"Tiffany, stop jiggling so I can get you changed." Tara dug through her purse, finally locating the little red box, and ripped the top off. "Here."

"Don't want raisins." Tiffany threw the box. The treat scattered across the tile floor. "I want my daddy."

Tara wanted to swat the kid for her bratty behavior, but she realized the child was overtired and overly hungry. She might also be coming down with the virus Kimmy had a few days ago. Tara gathered the raisins up and threw the box in the trash. She hoped she got them all so the next customer wouldn't mistake a raisin for a bug.

Finally finished with the chore of changing the two-year-old, Tara scooped her up in her arms and carried her out of the bathroom. Tiffany cuddled her head into the crook of Tara's neck. She'd be asleep in minutes. Tara peered around the corner, afraid Harry would have left already, and her heart jumped when she saw him still at the register. She ducked her head so he wouldn't know she cared.

Harry spotted them the instant Tara came through the hallway. A big grin lit his gorgeous face. For Tara, the sun came out on this cloudy day.

Glenna noticed, and she shot mental darts at Tara.

Shaking her head and wondering if she could offer an apology, Tara called the children to her side. "Ready to go?"

"I'll help you out," Lindsey offered.

"No need," Harry said. "I'll help."

"But we're not finished," Glenna protested.

"I'll be back in a few minutes."

So he plans to string both of us along, Tara thought.

He looked directly at Tara. "I need to wait around to finish the orders so I can pay for them."

Sun broke out of the clouds, lightening her mood, providing hope that this connection with the stranger was not only real, but mutual.

~ * ~

Harry offered to help Kevin load the four sizable plants in the back of the van while Tara belted the girls into their seats. Money apparently wasn't an issue, Harry decided, since she drove a new and very expensive model. Once they were finished and Kevin climbed into the vehicle, Harry shut the door and cornered Tara between the side of the van and his body. Her eyes widened in reaction to his touch.

"How come you're not in the Caribbean with your husband?"

"How'd you know about the Caribbean?"

"You don't wear a wedding ring, so I asked Glenna. All she knew was that you sent flowers to the kids' fathers in the Caribbean."

"You cared enough to ask about my marital status?" A pleased little smile touched her lips briefly. "I'm not married."

"Have dinner with me."

"I'll never find a sitter on such short notice."

"Won't you even try?"

"I know for sure that there's a play at the high school and everyone in the neighborhood will be there, either as a cast member or to see the performance. It's sold-out."

He leaned closer making sure she could feel his heat. She wore a subtle come-hither scent that intoxicated his senses. "I'm supposed to go back to Indianapolis for the weekend."

"Tomorrow already?"

"Tonight. That's my home base," he told her. "I always go home for the weekend."

"Oh, yeah. I remember you mentioning that to Glenna. Are you married? I mean, I know you have all these girls on the string, but do you also have a wife and kids back home?"

He shook his head emphatically. "Never been married. I doubt I ever will."

"But it'll be three months before you come back to this area..."

"I could make an exception in your case." He leaned down and caught her earlobe between his teeth, touching his warm tongue to her cold skin. Her eyelids slipped closed and he knew he was getting to her.

She jumped away. "Don't, Harry. The kids might see you. Go back to your harem. I'm not interested."

"I shouldn't have told you."

"Yes, you shouldn't have. If I found out you lied, I'd be even madder. I might have been tempted otherwise, but I could never live like that, seeing someone for a week four times a year. I'd never share a man with even one other woman, let along eleven."

"You've never tried it."

Briefly, she looked at him as if he tempted her. "Oh, but you don't have any vacancies, based on the Valentine's Day orders."

"Give me some time. I can juggle things around. Just come to dinner with me right now. We need to get to know each other first, to see if we even fit." She shook her head, and he leaned against her. "Feel what you do to me." He captured her hand and showed her exactly how much he wanted her. "How can you doubt my feelings?"

She removed her hand the instant he let her and he gave an inward sigh. So she was playing coy. One thing about a woman with four children, she must know her way around a bed. She'd surely thaw for him in good time.

None of his dozen regulars had kids. He shouldn't even consider involving himself with someone like her. He was used to his women's total attention during whatever week they were together. Hell, other couples with kids dated. That's what baby-sitters were for. Yet he played devil's advocate. "What if we just walk away and forget we ever met? I think I'll feel lost if I never see you again."

She pushed him away. "You can't have it both ways with me." Inside the van the kids were getting impatient, stamping their feet on the floor and whining for her to hurry up. Much longer and Kevin would surely come to her rescue. "I have to go."

"You can't just walk away now that we've found each other. Just have dinner with me."

"We've been through this. I don't have a sitter."

"Then bring the kids." He watched her pretty green eyes widen in surprise.

"You're not serious." She stared at him, her mouth open in obvious shock.

He was in shock himself for making the offer. What had taken possession of his faculties? "I am. Totally. I think there must be something wrong with me."

That brought a smile to her face.

She wasn't beautiful, not in the Hollywood sense, but pretty in a wholesome way. Blonde highlights lightened her dark, chin-length hair. Even though she wore a coat, it was of fine leather and he could tell that she was slender but not curvy. She had the body of a gymnast, fit and muscular...athletic. The thought triggered a smile. He'd like to see the athletics they would do together in bed.

"I'll go sign for the credit card charges and be right back. Give me the keys so I know you won't sneak away."

"I won't sneak away."

He was halfway to the shop's door when she called out to him. "Harry? We can't go to dinner."

His heart sank. "Why not?"

"It's only three-thirty."

"Well, shit," he said under his breath. Out loud, he told her, "We'll go to a movie instead."

By the time he returned, she came up with another excuse. "I'm afraid the plants will freeze. They're so healthy and gorgeous; I'd hate to chance it."

"How far away do you live?"

"Five minutes, maybe."

"I'll follow you."

She hesitated and briefly he thought she might refuse to allow him to know her home address. He could be another Ted Bundy for all she knew, but he put on his most winning smile to convince her he meant no harm.

She led him to a high-priced subdivision just east of the shopping plaza, and when she first pulled into the driveway of a huge brick two story, he was sure she must be just turning around. To his surprise, the double garage door opened and she pulled the van inside. He parked his Audi A8 n the middle of the drive and turned the ignition off. A separate garage door gave access to a third stall. He stepped inside before the door slid shut. Once inside the garage, he saw a new BMW parked in the next stall. A sleek power boat occupied the third space. As comfortable as she seemed with the finer things in life, he marveled that she wasn't impressed with his $100,000 car.

He helped her wrestle the plants into the laundry room. A young St. Bernard greeted them with lots of tail wagging.

"What's your name, Buddy?"

"Baraboo," Tara said in a deep voice, as if the dog were answering.

"That's different."

"Yeah, it's a town in Wisconsin," Tara said. "We were all up in the Dells a couple summers ago, and the kids spotted that name and teased each other nonstop. Bar-a-BOO! So when the pup came along last summer, they all had the perfect name."

Harry looked around, glancing into the huge kitchen. "Nice place," he commented, hoping she'd offer to show him around.

She didn't. "Thanks. The plants will be fine here for now until I decide where to put them. Probably the sun porch."

"You sure you can lift them?" His question gave him the excuse to study her figure, though she still wore the leather coat. His perusal made her aware of him, though, and that had been his intent.

She stiffened. "We better go if we want to catch the four o'clock show. I already told the kids on the way home, so we can't back out... just in case you changed your mind."

"I haven't changed my mind. Should I just leave my car here and ride with you in the van?"

She stared at him for an instant and then shook her head. "You can follow me."

She didn't trust him totally, he figured, or she would have handed over the keys, but trust would come in time. All the way to the movie theater, he obsessed about her, or more accurately, about her sexual delights. He couldn't wait to get her into bed. With that gymnast's figure, she'd surely be...active in certain sports.

Why did she appeal to him so forcefully? She wasn't drop-dead gorgeous like Phyllis. She wasn't outgoing like Bobbie, or outrageous like Sybil. He never complicated his affairs with children or conscience or scruples. He lived from day to day, taking one thing at a time. No complications. No rules.

She must live with somebody already in that big house. Otherwise why the BMW and the boat? She couldn't afford that size place with the kids all on her own. All the clues warned him to stay away, that she was sure to ruin his lifestyle. His present life was perfect. Keeping a dozen women happy enabled his need for diversity. She must be getting hoards of alimony and child support.

Three

Harry surprised Tara by adjusting to a family outing, even though he wasn't a family man. He bought popcorn and soda for all six of them and let the children choose the movie, a rollicking adventure with lots of laughs. Instead of having the two adults at opposite ends with the four children in between, as she suggested, Harry maneuvered the two adults into the middle with two children on opposite ends. He had the two older kids, Kevin and Kim, while Tiffany and Erica sat on the far side of Tara.

Not that Tara could concentrate on the children or the movie, even thought she tried to watch the movie. Her whole attention was centered on the hunk of man next to her. Every time she snuck a look at him, he was watching her. He couldn't have seen enough of the action to know the basic plot. If the kids weren't around, he probably would have tried something, but he seemed content with holding her hand.

Before long, Tiffany crawled into Tara's lap and fell asleep. Tara worried again that she might be coming down with something. Guilt crept up on her. She should have refused Harry's offer of a movie, but she couldn't say no. She had an irresistible compulsion to be with him, despite the fact that she didn't respect his lifestyle or values.

With Tiffany in her lap, she couldn't handle her container of popcorn. Erica had moved over next to Tara once Tiffany fell asleep in Tara's lap. Her popcorn sat on the floor under her seat, but when she tried to grab it, the container tipped over, spilling the contents. The tsk of her tongue caught Harry's attention.

Instead of offering his container, he picked out a few fat kernels and fed her, the tips of his fingers lingering on her lips. She touched her tongue to her lips, knowing he watched her every move. Her mouth was so dry with thirst for him, she could barely swallow. He offered more popcorn, but the next time she swallowed, he slipped his buttery finger in her mouth and stroked her tongue to clean the butter off. She automatically sucked his finger.

Twice he adjusted his seat and 'accidentally' rubbed his leg against hers. Both times, butterflies took wing inside her. She wished she could invite him over to her apartment after the movie, instead of her brother's house with the kids. She knew she was moving too fast in falling for him, but he was the most exciting, most desirable man she'd ever met. He was the 'once in a lifetime lover' every woman dreams of. Judging by his interest, the feeling was mutual. She wished for magic to catch him, now and forever, all the while she chided herself for her folly.

Unable to concentrate on the movie any longer, she faced him, determined to tell him to quit playing around, but he grabbed her hand and brought it to his mouth. He licked her fingers, and slowly and thoroughly sucked her middle finger. Her bones melted at the erotic sensation and she thought she might slide right off her seat.

Tiffany stirred in Tara's lap, and the game abruptly ended. Harry smiled at her, nodding his head and promising untold sensations if she'd stay with him. His look said they hadn't even gotten started yet. She wanted to correct him, knowing he was wrong for her, but her heart cried out, grab him! This is your chance of a lifetime.

By the time the movie ended, Tara had little more idea of what the movie was about than Tiffany, who'd slept through most of it. The child woke up when the lights came on, and would have been cranky except that Tara promised they were headed to dinner. Harry suggested a family restaurant, and he was so sincere in his wish to accommodate the children that she agreed, though the kids were all accustomed to five star restaurants and trained to act as adults. They were more familiar with escargot and calamari than most children were with chicken nuggets.

Yet dinner jolted Tara back to real life, bathroom breaks, helping cut Erica and Tiffany's steak, bargaining for later bedtimes if they were good through dinner. She was surprised Harry stuck with them through dessert and shocked when he finally said farewell.

"Can I come home with you?" He held her close next to the van, the children already in their seatbelts.

She stifled a nervous giggle. If Harry was in a romantic mood, it wouldn't last long. He had no idea of the chaos four children wreaked at bedtime. That would be one way to discourage him--let him think the kids were hers. But there were bigger issues than his dealing with children, specifically his dealing with women.

She shook her head, unable to look at him directly. "Stop by next quarter, or whenever..." She glanced at him. "The kids had a great time. I enjoyed meeting you."

"You can say, 'Goodbye, good riddance' just like that?"

"What do you expect? I'll never fit into your harem."

"I keep telling you I don't have a harem."

"Maybe not, but you have an infallible system that works perfectly for you and your women. I'd never fit into it. It would only make us both miserable because I'd nag you constantly and we'd end up hating each other."

He rested his lips against hers, tempting her with untold delights. Mustering her willpower, she pulled away. "Have a safe drive home. They're calling for snow, so be careful. Okay?"

He nodded. "You, too."

She couldn't even cry or she'd upset the children.

~ * ~

Harry usually listened to talk radio when he drove. Besides providing interesting fodder for his service calls, listening kept him alert. Tonight the weather bureau interrupted with dire warnings of heavy snow for the weekend, six to nine inches. No big deal. He was already well away from the area. His mind wandered as he drove, imagining Tara all alone in that huge house with four kids and heavy snow. A myriad of emergencies were possible. The electricity could go out, and how would she heat the house? She may have gas heat, but wouldn't she need electricity to circulate the heat? He shook the thought off. Not his problem. He was a self-proclaimed 'love 'em and leave 'em' kinda guy, and that's the way he liked it.

But within a few miles his thoughts jumped back to her plight. What if she ran out of food? Driving that big van on slippery roads? Scary.

He growled at his own thought and concentrated on a vision of Sybil, his next woman of the week. An image of Tara shoveling the driveway intruded.

Why didn't he get her phone number? He always got phone numbers from pretty ladies. Boy, maybe he needed a vacation.

Worrying about a woman was brand new to Harry. Oh, he had minor concerns about his mom now and then. Thank goodness she was healthy and strong. She worked in Fine Jewelry at a department store in a mall just a few miles from the house. His two older sisters lived nearby with their husbands and batches of kids, and checked on her daily when he was out of town. Harry's father had been a victim of a car accident years ago, when Harry was fifteen, so he realized how fragile life could be, and how fate could cheat innocent people. He turned the radio to a pop music station to belay the memories.

When he finally arrived home at one am, Dottie Howard met her son at the door of her thirty year old ranch house that she and Harry's father had bought as newlyweds. "Thank God you're home! Where have you been? I was scared to death something had happened to you!"

"Sorry, Mom, I got a late start." He headed for the refrigerator and grabbed a gallon of milk.

She followed him. "A late start? An hour is a late start. Seven hours is inexcusable. Why didn't you call?"

He had no choice but to lie. "My phone was dead."

"And all the pay phones were out of order the whole way from Chicago to Indianapolis?"

"I forgot, okay?"

"You forgot! You've never been so irresponsible. Did you lose your job?"

He shook his head and downed half the milk he'd poured.

"Did one of your accounts have an emergency?"

He shook his head.

"Are you ill? Was the traffic bad?"

"No more than usual. Can we just drop it?"

"You met a woman."

He met her eyes, unable to deny her accusation.

"You met a woman!" She all but danced around the room. "Tell me about her! She's pretty; I know she must be, to have attracted you. How old is she? What's her name? Where does she live?"

Harry started laughing, but she didn't stop.

"What does she do for a living? Where did you meet? When are you bringing her home to meet the family?"

How could he confess to his mother that the woman of his dreams had four kids by two different fathers, neither of whom she'd ever married? Or had she said, 'I'm not married,' which might imply that she was married when she had the kids. Wow. Divorced twice and she couldn't be more than twenty-five or six. Not good. Did she work? Did she go to college? Damn, he had as many questions as his mother and no answers for any of them. The more he told his mother, the more Tara sounded like a slut. Good thing he neglected to get her number. He didn't need the complications she carried. "I'm wiped out, Mom. Can we save this interrogation for morning?"

Dottie studied him with a wistful expression and opened her arms for a hug. "I'm so happy for you--if you're happy?"

"I don't know. Maybe I'm just tired."

"Get some rest. We'll talk tomorrow."

"I think the subject is closed. She was a momentary diversion. Love you, Mom."

"I love you, too, Harry. Get a good night's rest. Will you have time to do a few chores for me in the morning?"

"Sure." He sighed and headed downstairs to his bedroom. He'd framed out a portion of the basement several years ago when he'd finished the rec-room, built himself a private space. He realized that as his mother aged, she'd depend more and more on her children for odd jobs and support. His two sisters had both married men who knew their way around a workshop, yet every time a chore or project came up at Mom's place, it seemed they were in the middle of an odd job of their own or too busy with the kids.

Is that what he wanted? Harry asked himself, 'cause that's what he'd be doing if he got involved in Tara's life. From observing his sisters' lifestyles, raising children meant a never-ending cycle of sick kids and baseball and ballet and swimming and school conferences and shopping for shoes.

No thanks.

He wasn't too crazy about his responsibilities as it was, tonight.

Things never changed, never would...he could always count on his weekend list of chores. That should tell him that no way should he change his current, organized lifestyle or be available to someone like Tara with the responsibilities she carried. Someone like her wasn't a Monday through Friday kind of proposition.

His mother needed him. So would Tara...four times the amount. He couldn't handle the thought.

~ * ~

"Where exactly does your girlfriend live?"

Harry hadn't had even a sip of coffee yet and already his mother was quizzing him. "Chicago. Why?"

"That's where the worst of the storm is supposed to hit."

Despite only a few hours sleep, he jolted wide awake. "How much are they predicting?"

"Twenty-four to thirty-six inches. They're calling it the storm of the century."

"Considering we're only a few years into the new century, that's not saying much." He poured his coffee and joined his mother at the table. "They always exaggerate." His skepticism evaporated when he looked at the weather map. "Holy Shi--Crow."

"You were right the first time."

"I have to go back. She needs me."

"You just got here six hours ago. You can't make that trip again without proper rest."

"Of course I can. I'm young and strong. Isn't what you always tell me?"

"Surely she has family, neighbors to help her out."

"I don't know that for sure. She lives alone..."

"She'll be fine."

"Mom, she has four children."

"Four children!" She slapped her hand onto her heart. "Is she widowed?"

"I don't believe so."

"So where's the father?"

"Come on, Mom, I barely know her. As far as I know, the dads are in the Caribbean."

"Dads...as in...multiple fathers? Are they...gay or something?"

"I don't know. I just met her."

"Then you need to forget her real fast. You don't need weirdo relationships like that."

He heaved a deep, impatient sigh.

"Just think what you're getting yourself into, Son. Marriage is hard enough without asking for trouble. I thought you had more sense than getting trapped with a suspect woman--and all those kids!"

"I can't help it. I was standing next to her, totally unaware, and suddenly it just hit me. It was love at first sight."

Not exactly first sight, he realized. He remembered now the woman with the kids and how patient he'd been because he was so interested in the hot shop owner and wanting to know her better, actually, wanting to get into the shop owner's pants, but he couldn't tell his mom that. And that quick something hit him! He couldn't even remember the owner's name now, but if he lived to be a hundred, he'd never erase Tara Avery from his mind.

"I have to go back. She needs me." He saw the protest form on his mother's face. "And just as important, I need her."

Four

By mid-afternoon on Saturday, the snowfall was beginning to worry Tara. She'd heard the dire predictions and hadn't thought much of them. The news stations always exaggerated, tried to hype their forecasts to attract more viewers.

But it just kept piling up.

She took the kids out for errands early so there was plenty of fresh milk and eggs and all the essentials. At nine in the morning the lines in the grocery store had been halfway down the aisles. At home, the freezer was packed with meat, chicken and seafood; the refrigerator full of fresh fruit and vegetables; the cupboards stocked with canned goods, pasta, cake mix, cereal and cookies. She should have told the grocer that if the store ran out of anything, they could get it from her.

Late morning they shoveled the driveway and built a snowman, Baraboo romping in his element. She needed to get the little barrel you always found around St. Bernard's necks. By now the poor snow man was getting closer to the ground every hour as the snow continued to pile up around his bottom. His stove pipe hat doubled in height.

Kim and Erica tracked Tara down in the first floor office. "What'cha doing?"

"Trying to polish this book. It's due to my editor in another week, and I don't even have all the illustrations finished."

"Can you read it to us? We can help polish it."

"Thanks, but it's not suitable for sharing yet." Always a handy excuse when she lacked time and patience.

"Can we go out and play in the snow?"

"Did you clean your room?"

A pained expression crept over each of their faces. "That rule doesn't count on snow days."

"Yeah, it does. Matter of fact, you can help Tiffany pick up the stuffed animals in the nursery. I couldn't even walk through the room to make her bed. And remind Kevin to vacuum the couch. Baraboo was up there again." Tara made every attempt to rule her brother's home while he was away.

"Baraboo's always up on the couch," Erica pointed out. "Are you in a bad mood?"

"Of course not. I'm just reminding you guys to do your share. It'll teach you discipline."

"Why can't you just let us have some fun for a change?" Kim flounced out of the room, Erica on her heels.

Tara knew she was in trouble. If the girls were this bored already, after only seven hours of snow-falling, how would they get through the next couple days? Her brothers sure lucked out, scheduling their cruise during what turned out to be the storm of the century--up to now. It must have something to do with atmospheric pressure, she decided. She felt decidedly unsettled herself.

Part of it was being on deadline and knowing she hadn't finished the illustrations. They worried her. Thank goodness she was finished with the young adult series. After three books, all the pictures had started to look the same. Now that she'd switched to picture books, she needed a new style, but she hadn't discovered it yet. She put her head in her hands. She really needed some time off. Her editor disagreed.

Part of it was due to thoughts of Harry. He made her want...things. Love, excitement, a special man all her own. Things she'd probably never have. She'd have to be content with the family she had. Not that she didn't love every one of her family members...she did, she loved her two brothers and their wives and children, her mom and dad and various aunts and uncles and cousins. She just needed...Harry.

He wasn't a type she would have sought out; she had no need for a womanizer. What woman ever did? But how many women could resist? Ninety-nine in a hundred? That left her as one in a hundred. He wasn't even into children, though he seemed to tolerate them nicely enough. Surely he had some good points to counter the less than stellar qualities. He was thoughtful and kind. It was endearing that he took the kids to a family restaurant. Never mind that they sneered behind his back. He was drop-dead gorgeous. He probably got along with dogs okay. He loved women.

That was the kicker. He loved women so much that he maintained a revolving harem. He must not respect women totally or he wouldn't spread his favors so far afield. So how could she still crave being in his arms? She'd spent last night tossing and turning, wishing the kids' parents weren't on cruise and that she could be free to follow him to the ends of the earth

Her behavior shamed her.

Yet she ached for his touch.

Hell, she wasn't getting anywhere with her story, she may as well shovel the driveway--again--work off some of this sexual energy.

~ * ~

Harry pulled into the Avery driveway at seven o'clock Saturday night, thanking heaven for getting him here safely. After nearly twelve hours of driving, sometimes with traffic barely moving in blizzard conditions, he was achy and cold and bleary-eyed. He wanted a stiff drink, warm slippers and a hug from a special woman.

A foot of snow covered the sidewalk to the front door; he therefore rang the bell at the small door next to the double garage door. Surely with all this snow, he could assume informality was in order. While he waited, he saluted the two snowmen in the front yard. Tara must have kept the four kids busy...or more likely, they drove her crazy all day and she'd taken them outside as self-defense.

Wouldn't it be rotten luck to come all this way and find no one home? Lights were on inside, outside too, but that could just be a security measure. He counted off another minute and pushed on the doorbell until he heard a deep bark of a dog from inside the house.

Finally he heard the stirrings of people behind the door. "Who's there?" came Tara's voice.

"It's me, Harry!"

The momentary stillness scared him. What if she wouldn't let him in? He'd never find a motel room, not with the bad weather and stranded motorists, and he was too exhausted to drive back to Indianapolis tonight. He had no idea whether his Week #6 in his quarterly rotation down in Springfield would welcome him early and on a weekend. What if she had a date? Harry would feel like she was two-timing him. He'd rather not know.

The door swung open, Tara in front, four children peeking out from behind. The scratching of claws on cement warned him before the St. Bernard nearly bowled him over.

"Baraboo! Down!"

The dog wrapped his front legs around Harry's waist and danced his new partner around in a circle.

"I love you too, Mutt, but get down. I'm tired and cold." He caught Tara's eye. "Can I come in? Please?"

"Oh, you poor thing, of course you can come in. Baraboo, get down."

By then the dog was humping his knee.

"He remembers you. Baraboo, behave! He's fixed. I don't think he can actually--" She glanced at the kids and whispered-- "do anything."

"He's sure trying hard enough."

"You should see him when he doesn't like someone," Kevin said. "Just let him lick your face and he'll quit."

Feeling totally beaten, Harry leaned down and let the big dog slather his face. "I'll be glad to pay for obedience training."

"Been there, done that," Tara confessed. "Come on in."

"They have dog psychiatrists now."

She threw him a pitying look over her shoulder. "He doesn't have a problem with anyone else."

He followed Tara into the laundry room, where he left his boots and jacket, hat and gloves. As they went through the kitchen, she offered food and drink.

"I could use a drink or a hot fire. I'm frozen to the bone. The car was freezing up."

"You're lucky to have made it. I'll make you a drink. A hot toddy?"

"Sounds wonderful."

"Go on into the family room. There's a hot fire going."

He followed the kids to the cozy family room. He went immediately to the fireplace, rubbing his frozen hands.

One of the little girls, Erica maybe--he couldn't keep them all straight--joined him in front of the fire. "My hands and feet froze when we were out building a snowman today. I didn't cry though."

"That's hard. I want to cry now. Thawing them out is the worst."

"Yeah."

The little one joined them. "I freezed my feet one time. Yeah, I did."

"Poor little thing," he said. It seemed that the children were accepting him. Must be his irresistible charm. "Did it hurt?"

"Nooo." She shook her head. "I'm a big girl."

"Yes, you are. And a good girl, too."

"Not always," Tara said from behind him.

He turned to face her, accepting the tall mug she offered.

"How are you doing?"

One swig and he laughed. "Better already. A hug would help, and a pair of slippers." He laughed. "Never mind. That's just what I was wishing for when I was standing out on your doorstep."

"I might be able to find slippers."

He sobered. Men's slippers suggested a man somewhere in the vicinity. It meant she lived with someone. Typically people with four kids lived with someone.

When she came back, however, she carried a shoebox. "I got these for my dad for Christmas and they were too big. I can't remember how they got over here. I never got around to exchanging them. He didn't need another pair of slippers, anyway. I just couldn't think of anything else to get."

"Does he live here in Chicago?"

"Yes, fairly close by. Dad and Mom."

"That's nice."

"How about your dad? You mentioned your mom, but not your dad."

"My dad passed away when I was fifteen. A car accident."

"I'm sorry to hear that. Did your mother marry again?"

He shook his head, letting the subject drop.

The kids had already grown bored with the conversation and wandered away to the big screen television. They either had Premium cable channels or a CD going because it was a fairly recent release.

"How did the new plants fare?"

"They're still alive. Tiffany up-dumped her Norfolk Island pine and one of the branches broke off, but it's too soon to tell. I think it'll survive." Another silence fell between them. "How are your feet thawing?"

"Good, I guess, because they hurt like hell."

She flinched. "I'm sorry. Why did you come back?"

He'd asked himself the same question countless times in the last twelve hours. "I was worried about you, facing a blizzard with just you and the kids here, all alone. As far as I know, their father wasn't around to get you through this." He laughed self-consciously. "And here I was the one who got in trouble."

"That was sweet of you--more than sweet, driving all that way back from Indianapolis to make sure we were safe. You could have been stranded, or worse."

"I'm here now and close to total recovery, so watch out. I might jump your bones."

"Or die trying."

He laughed, though he wasn't sure she was kidding. When she didn't share his mirth, he sobered. "Okay...Now what can we talk about?"

"We could discuss your harem some more, figure out why you need so much variety. Does it have something to do with your father's death during your teenage years?"

"I told you, it's not a harem. I don't imprison anyone. I don't support them. I don't require that they live their lives around my schedule, except for one week a quarter. They're free to do whatever they wish for the other forty-eight weeks of the year."

"What other similarities are there among the dizzy dozen?"

"Hey, have some respect! Every one of my women is educated and independent, a health care professional in either a hospital or clinic. I have certain standards, you understand."

Tara giggled. "I can just guess what they are, too. 36-24-36..."

He laughed loud and long. "Don't I wish? With all the anorexia floating around these days, they're more likely 18-18-18."

She dipped her head, and he sensed that he'd insulted her because she had an average figure. "Hey, normal is good! Having a bust and hips is good. More than good. I love curves." He gave an exaggerated look at her curves. "Boy, do I love curves!"

She blushed, a pretty pink, and they were silent for a time. A laughter sound track from the TV covered the silence. Eventually, she turned to him. "It's not normal, one man and twelve women, no matter how compartmentalized the relationship. It's not right."

"As long as they don't mind, why should you?"

"It's none of my business, I know. I just can't accept your behavior, no matter how attractive I find you. I cannot be a party to your aberrant lifestyle."

"Thanks for giving me so much hope! I might as well turn around and drive home right now, for all the good that I've done worrying about you, making sure you're safe."

"I never asked for your help. As I said, it was sweet of you, but totally unnecessary."

He sat for a while, pondering the situation. "The storm isn't over yet. I might be of help to you yet."

~ * ~

Harry slept on a very comfortable king-sized guest bed in the second story of the house, directly above the family room. The house was bigger than he'd thought; there had to five or six bedrooms, in addition to the rec-room and family room and office or den and unnamed rooms scattered here and there, not to mention formal living room and dining room and the sun porch. Where did she find the finances to afford a house of such proportions?

He was on strike this morning. He refused to get out of bed until she dragged him out. He realized he might starve to death before she saved him. It was nearly nine o'clock before she finally ventured into enemy territory, otherwise known as the guest room, when he now lay. She didn't venture too close. The door jam was the closest she was willing to go. "You missed breakfast."

"I absolutely couldn't get out of bed after yesterday's trauma."

Rather than sympathize, she snorted, hurting him to the quick. "What?" he demanded.

"I give you credit for coming back, that was kind of Don Quixote-ish. But you see, we didn't really need your help...We're fine on our own, and I don't intend to vie for #13 Week in a twelve week quarter. Get the picture? Thanks, but no thanks!"

"No! I can't live without you! How can I convince you? What if I gave them all up? Every last one of them?"

"You'd do that for me? Give up all your women, the variety and reliability?"

"I might consider it, as a last ditch effort."

"Why? Why would you shake up your whole being for...me?" With each word, she came a foot closer, as if pulled by a magnet.

He waited until she was at the bedside, then popped up and caught her lips with his own, gently nipping and enticing her to enjoy their time together. "Where are the kids?"

"Watching the Weather Channel."

"How bad?"

"We had another foot overnight with 12 more inches expected today."

"Holy shit," he said. "It never quits. We should hire a service to clear what's out there."

"We have one. He hasn't made it here yet, but this is only the third day, if you count Friday when it started."

"Sheesh! I can think of something more reliable." He pulled her into bed on top of him.

"Like..."

"Me...making love to you."

"Maybe someday, if you're lucky."

"Why not now?" He shifted position so that he was on top. They fit perfectly. He nuzzled her neck while he sneaked his hand across her breast and his knee over her thighs. She was effectively pinned down, but with luck, she wouldn't even realize her vulnerability, simply accept his advances.

"I need you," he whispered in her ear.

"I need you, too..." she whispered back, "to take the kids out and run the energy off. I can't stand it anymore! Get up, get up!"

He laughed his head off, unable to resent her approach. Sex would have to wait until another time and place, preferably somewhere more private, and with a lot less kids around. For possibly the first time in his life, he admitted, she's worth waiting for.

Five

Never had Tara allowed herself to be knocked off her feet by any man, and certainly not a womanizer like Harry Howard. She needed to get him out of her house, out of her life, out of her...heart. The snow kept piling up, blowing and drifting, with a forecast of at least one more days of heavy snowfall. She was already going stir-crazy. The kids were taking the enforced confinement better than she.

Of course, Harry had something to do with her state of mind.

How could she get him out of the house, before any more damage was done?

"Let's shovel the driveway!" she announced to the four kids and Harry and Baraboo. At least the dog woofed his approval.

"It's cold out," Kimmy complained.

"We may as well wait for a snowplow to come past," Kevin suggested. "Otherwise, they'll just plow us back in."

"So how do you propose we get Harry back home today?"

"It isn't going to happen," the child genius proclaimed. Harry sent her a big smile.

"What does a six year old know?" she snarled.

"We can build another snowman," Erica suggested.

Tara shivered at the thought. "Honey, we're out of stovepipe hats and button noses."

Harry scratched the itch in his ear.

"Thanks, but 'No thanks'," Tara replied.

~ * ~

"So are you independently wealthy, or do you work for a living?"

"I work. I graduated from Northwestern, though I don't work in my major."

He'd found her in the office, off the central hallway on the main floor, working on the computer. Even on this Monday, the snow still fell.

"Do I get twenty questions?" Before she could refuse, he posed his questions. "What was your major and what do you do currently for a living?"

"That's two questions.

"I asked for twenty, remember?"

She sighed as if he was a pain in the ass. "I'll answer this time. I majored in early childhood education, but I write for a living."

"As in..."

"Children's books."

"Really? Have you sold anything?"

"Actually, yes. I lucked out and sold a series of children's science fiction books. The first is due out any day."

"Good for you. What's it called?"

"The Marlin Family Series."

"Holy shit! The one they're calling the next Harry Potter Series? Everybody I know is talking about it."

"I'm not in her league by any means."

He gawked at her for half a minute. "You're kidding me, right?"

She smiled. "Yes, of course, if it will make you feel better, I'm kidding you. Right now, I'm developing an early childhood series. Complete with my own illustrations."

He watched her out of the corner of one eye. "Who owns this house?"

"I sure don't."

"Can you please answer one simple question? Whose name is on the title to this house?"

She ducked her head. If she admitted the house belonged to her brother and the kids weren't her own, she'd have no defense against his charms. "Why can't you trust me?"

"But you really did write The Marlin Family Series." His tone suggested it wasn't a question, rather a reality. "I apologize. I thought..."

She assumed an amused look. "I know exactly what you thought." That she was having an affair with the owner of the house. "I'm not, so your impression that I'm a 'kept woman' doesn't bother me."

"What about the children's father?"

"Fathers," she corrected. "Two children apiece. I believe I mentioned they're on a cruise."

"Are they really in the Caribbean, or is that all fabrication?"

"They're really on a cruise ship in the Caribbean. They have no idea they'll receive roses from their children on Valentine's Day. It was totally the children's idea to send flowers to them on the cruise ship. "

"I shouldn't ask, but are the fathers gay? My mother wanted to know."

She laughed. "You're not even close."

They lapsed into silence. Finally Harry composed a new thought. "I'm very attracted to you; I have been since the minute I saw you. Unfortunately, I'm not rich. I didn't write the next phenomenal series for young people. Is there any hope for me to find a place in your life? Can I be of any service to you?"

She took a long time answering. "Harry, you're sweet and fun and know how to treat a woman, but as I told you already, I have reservations about your relationships. Even now, if you were to give up your dozen harem dancers so suddenly, I'd have to question your motivation. Truly."

"Guess I should have declared myself before I asked you to divulge your innermost secrets, huh?"

She nodded. "Yeah." She couldn't help smiling.

"But remember? I tried to put the make on you this morning, before you let it slip who you are."

"That you did, but then, isn't that typical of a man?"

"No! I was totally sincere, I assure you." He gauged her response, eyes slit halfway shut. "So do I have a chance?"

"Marginal, at most." She turned so he couldn't see her grin.

He moved quickly for such a large man, taking her breath away. "Don't play coy with me. We're both adults. I don't play games, and you seem too mature to tease a man. It's up to you whether we share something significant while I'm here."

"I don't even know you."

"Then let's get acquainted."

~ * ~

The four children lounged in front of the television in the family room that same Monday morning, already bored with television, no adults in sight.

"We should go build a snowman," Erica said.

"We already built two," Kim reminded her.

"Yeah, but there's enough snow out there for a hundred snow mans."

"Who would want a hundred snowmen?"

"We could have a snowman contest!" Erica said. "With different kinds, like the biggest, the scariest, the most creative."

"You guys will just get cold and wet and want to come back in ten minutes after we get out there," Kevin said. "Why bother?"

"Because it snowed, and it's perfect for making snowmen and we're kids and that's what we do. We play in snow when it falls." Kimmy sneered at them before flouncing off to the laundry room, which doubled as a mud room.

Kevin glanced after Kimmy in surprise. One minute, she didn't want to go out; the next, she was campaigning for kids' rights. "Women," he said with a huff.

Kevin helped Tiffany into her snowsuit and gathered her gear before starting his own. Kim and Erica followed, donning thick socks, snow pants, jackets, hats, gloves, boots and scarves. The snow had stopped falling, at least for now, but the wind blew bitter cold on their cheeks, and swirled the fluffy snow in their faces.

"I'm cold," Tiffany complained.

"We just came out," Kimmy protested. "You can't be cold yet. What about our snowman contest?"

"I don't care. It's cold out here."

"Yeah, it is," Erica agreed. "Let's go in and watch TV."

They were just outside the door stomping the snow off their boots when Erica spotted a white rabbit huddled in the corner next to the door. "Shh, don't move, look--a bunny rabbit."

"He looks cold," Tiffany said.

"Yeah, he's shivering. We need to take him inside and warm him up."

"Can we keep him?"

"Of course we can."

"How do we catch him?"

"Good question. Stay here, don't move. I'll get Kevin. He'll know."

"I'm cold."

"I know, Tiffy. I'm cold, too, but the bunny is even colder. I'll be back real quick."

She was good to her word, Kevin and Kimmy at her heels.

"Isn't he cute?" Erica exclaimed.

"He looks frozen to me. We're probably wasting our time 'cause I think he's too far gone to make it," Kevin said. "Let's all four make a barrier so he can't get past us. We'll move in real slow and I'll catch him."

"Why don't we open the door and herd him into the garage?" Kimmy suggested.

"Too many places to hide," Kevin protested. "We'd never find him again."

"But he'd be warmer than out here. At least he won't freeze to death. And if he doesn't have a chance of making it, what's the difference?"

"Yeah," Erica agreed.

"Yeah, Tiffany echoed.

Kevin threw his hands out. "Okay, okay. I'm out-voted."

He made sure everyone was in position and opened the door. The bunny hopped toward the relative warmth of the unheated garage.

"Don't let him get under the car," Kevin warned. "Herd him up the steps and into the laundry room so he can thaw out."

The bunny seemed to be attracted to the warmth, because he let himself be shooed up two steps and into the tiled flooring of the laundry room.

"Let's get him something to eat!" Erica said.

"We don't have any rabbit food," Kimmy said.

"We have fruit and vegetables, carrots and lettuce and green beans and apples and everything under the sun," Erica said.

Tiffany hunkered down to the frozen bunny rabbit. "We'll take good care of you, Bunny."

He wiggled his ears and pooped on the floor.

~ * ~

"And how do we get acquainted exactly?" Tara asked.

He'd followed her upstairs where she gathered dirty clothes to throw in the washer.

"Well, you know, sexual compatibility is very important in a relationship."

"Really? Is there a definitive test for sexual compatibility that I'm not aware of?"

"It's mostly trial and error, but I've developed a fairly reliable criterion. I haven't had a chance to patent it yet, since I haven't had the opportunity to field test it extensively at this point."

"What's it called?"

"Ah, duh...The Tingle Test!"

"Neat name. Triple T's."

"Right. That was intentional."

"And how does it work?"

"We analyze reactions to sexual stimuli."

"Ooh, sounds kinky."

"No, no, no. Not kinky. Scientific all the way." He drew back and pinned her with his most sales-oriented look. "Would you be interested in participating in alpha testing?"

"Does it pay well?"

"Not financially, at this point, but there may be residuals in the future."

"Still sounds kinky, although I'm not sure I like the idea of ...residuals." Residuals could be good, like payments long after services rendered, or bad, as in creating memories and conjuring up dreams that turn into pipe dreams. She had to keep reminding herself that any woman who interested him would be competing among a dozen others for his attention.

His voice drew her back to the subject at hand. "So, The Tingle Test operates exactly as it sounds. You submit to stimulus and we scientifically record reaction."

"Okay, I'm ready. I agree to your criterion. "

"You don't even know what it is yet."

"I know." She turned serious suddenly. "But you're driving me crazy. Do something beside make promises. You'd make a good salesman. Oh, I forgot. You are a salesman. Problem is, you don't deliver."

"Says who?"

"Me, except I don't have much experience. I didn't date much in college, I was too busy studying, and my brothers were always vetting my boyfriends, scaring them off. They can be big bullies sometimes, especially when they're determined to protect me. It was embarrassing, finally getting a date and having to sneak around. They still found out somehow, and would either get rid of him or they'd follow us around all night. I don't know which was worse."

Frown lines creased Harry's forehead. "They're not in the mob, are they? I hear they're all around in Chicago."

"Oh, goodness no. I had a lot of girlfriends though. They all wanted to date my brothers."

She could see the sympathy in his eyes, and that wasn't what she wanted. She wanted passion. She wanted to make up for all she'd missed growing up with overprotective brothers.

Now that he knew her story, Harry, too, seemed to be afraid she'd break. It was sweet of him to treat her so gently, especially with his Casanova reputation, except she didn't want sweet and gentle handling, she wanted passion, wild unabashed passion.

He scattered butterfly kisses across her face, tickling her skin, while she wanted him to lay the kiss of the century on her.

"Any tingles so far?"

"Minimal. I felt something, but it wouldn't register on the Howard scale."

He grunted. "Come here." He pulled her into his arms and toppled her on the bed. She giggled and tried to slide away. She couldn't resist smiling when he tiptoed his fingers across her midriff. She raised her eyebrows. He raised his hand to cover his breast.

"I'm feeling some tingles," she warned.

"How strong?"

"Come closer."

He moved just an inch or two, but it was enough to feel his heat and wonder how all that energy the heat generated would feel if he stopped treating her like fine crystal. Surely there was some way to unleash that power. She slipped her hand under his sweater and covered his male breast with her hand, kneading the flesh around his nipple with her fingertips.

"Are you feeling any tingles yet?"

Six

"Kevin? Kevin? Kevin!" Tiffany tugged on the boy's shirt when he continued to ignore her.

"WHAT!"

"The bunny turned into a cartoon people."

"What are you talking about?"

"Yeah, he did."

"I'll be there in a minute. I'm trying to get him some food." He took the bowl of fresh fruit and vegetables in one hand, a bowl of water in the other and headed for the laundry room. "Now let's see what's going on."

"He's not there anymore," Tiffany informed him.

"He must be hiding behind the dryer or in the closet. He couldn't have got out."

"He's in the family room."

"He can't be. How could he get over the gate I put up? Did you let him out?"

"I told you! He turned into a cartoon people."

Kevin marched across the kitchen, sloshing water from the bowl, and crossed the hall to the family room. He stopped dead.

"She's right, you know," the cartoon character bunny said, straightening his right ear. It had the tendency to flop over when he was relaxed.

"Hi, Bunny," Tiffany said.

"Hello, cutie pie. You're a very good girl for rescuing me from a certain death out there. It's colder than a witches ti-- Sorry."

"This is not happening, I am dreaming, I am hallucinating," Kevin chanted.

Baraboo woofed and licked the bunny's hand.

"Hey, boy," Bunny warned Kevin. "Don't drop the food. I'm real and I'm starving."

"Cartoon characters do not exist."

"You're right, but the Easter Bunny does, and I'm him."

Kevin gingerly placed the two bowls on the table. Backing away, he said, "I'm going back to bed so I can finish my nightmare."

Kimmy walked into the family room. "Oh my God, it's the Easter Bunny," she said.

"You said God's name in vain," Erica said, echoing her mother's common comment. She sat at the table and continued to color as if nothing of note were happening. "You can't swear or you'll go to hell."

"Forget about hell. The Easter Bunny is here! For real!" Kimmy said.

Now that the shock was over, the children gathered around the table and sat in the presence of the most famous fuzzy rabbit on earth. "You're early, Bunny. It's not Easter for months," Kevin said.

"Did you bring chocolate and colored eggs?" Erica asked.

"Where's Cupid?" Kimmy asked.

"That's the problem, Guys," Bunny admitted. "Cupid is in trouble this Valentine's Day. He had a little problem with his archery last week and created some...mismatched couples, let's say."

"You mean like Tara and Harry?" Kevin asked.

"Huh?" the girls all said.

Bunny blushed. "You mean they're here? Together?"

Kevin looked at the other three children. They all giggled. "Yeah, but they're not getting along too good," Erica admitted. "She says he's a wo--womanizer."

"That's good. We can't let them get along," Bunny said "They're not meant for each other. I promised Cupid I'd help fix his mess."

"You know we saw you and Cupid on the wall at the florist shop," Erica said.

"Really? Transmission signals really got screwed up if you could see us."

"I'm glad we did." Kevin said. "Otherwise we wouldn't believe you were even here right now. So what can we do to help you?"

"Keep them apart, keep them fighting. It's only one more day until Valentine's Day, and then the spell will be broken."

"I kind of like Harry," Tiffany said. "He took us to a movie."

"You slept through it," Erica said.

"That doesn't matter," Kimmy said in Harry's defense. "He still paid for our tickets and popcorn and soda. And he took us to dinner, too!"

"Very generous of him. He must have been shot hard," Bunny observed, munching the fruit and vegetables down with gusto. "Very tasty. Would you have a cold beer to rinse that down?"

"We're not allowed to touch alcoholic beverages," Kevin informed him.

"Oh, too bad."

"Isn't that what caused this problem in the first place?" Kimmy observed.

Bunny's ears twitched but he didn't comment.

"How are we supposed to hide you while you're here?"

"Easy, I'll shift back into animal form. You need a litter pan in there though. Sorry about the mess."

"There's a bag of litter in the trunk of the car!" Kevin said. "Dad put it in there in case we ever get stuck. I think there's a plastic pan somewhere around, too."

"What about Baraboo?"

"We'll keep the gate up."

"But his water bowl and food dish is in there," Kimmy said.

"I can take care of the mutt. He won't bother me. We're best buds, right, Baraboo?" Bunny looked down at the floor next to his feet, where the St. Bernard lay, tail thumping with his unspoken promise to preserve the magical bunny.

"Yeah, see? We're cool."

~ * ~

Upstairs in the bedroom, things were heating up. Tara had Harry's sweater off and his shirt unbuttoned, and her sweater was pushed up around her shoulders. He lathed one hardened nipple with his tongue through her bra while trying to ease his hand into her pants without scaring her off. Her eyes were closed and her head thrown back as if held in ecstasy, making him feel like He-Man. He only hoped that she wouldn't pull a She-Ra number and draw her sword.

Her little story about her overprotective brothers pounded through his mind. Surely any woman with four children by two fathers would be wise to the world by now. So far she seemed to enjoy his advances. His shirt and shoes were off, and he ran his toes up and down her jean-clad leg. She inched closer to him and he let his leg rest on top of hers, bringing them close together. Intimately close, he soon realized, as his jeans tightened in the crotch.

"You're getting awfully close," she warned.

"Any closer and I'll be inside you."

"That's not a good idea."

He groaned, wanting her so badly he couldn't take any more. "Let me help you with those jeans," he offered.

She stilled and he knew immediately that he'd rushed her. He moved away a bit.

"This is where I remind you that we've only known each other a few days," she whispered.

"I'm aware of that, but thanks for the reminder."

"And there are four kids downstairs who might come clomping up the stairs any minute."

"We better hurry up then."

He slid his hand down across her belly. Her eyes flew open, and he smiled to reassure her. "Relax for me. I won't do anything you're uncomfortable with."

She remained still and watched him, eyes at half mast.

He backed up, sensing he needed to get her hotter. With his fingertips he pressed against the mound of her breast, tiptoeing around her nipple. "How does that feel?"

"Tingly."

"How far up the scale?"

"Maybe...six and a half."

"Come on, it should be an eight, at least."

He covered her nipple with his mouth and sucked gently.

"Eight!"

"You're welcome to try the Tingle Test on me, too." While she was distracted he eased his lower half marginally closer. She noticed.

"You don't play fair."

He laughed. "That's why I'm so popular with the ladies."

She froze and he realized he'd made a major blunder. "Don't leave. That was a joke!"

She pushed against him, and he fought her escape, nipping her belly, her nipples, shoulders, shushing her and pleading for her forgiveness. She bit him back, and he pinned her bottom-half down with his legs, working his mouth down her belly, popping the snap on her jeans. She stilled for a long moment, then fought him, bucking and kicking.

Let her fight. She'd love it, and it really turned him on. There would be no more teasing, he was fighting for his destiny. "You're mine, and I'm damn well going to claim you."

"Listen to me, Harry! Stop! I thought we talked this out before, I'm not ready for this."

Her words finally penetrated his brain. "Oh my God, what am I doing? Tara, I'm sorry, so sorry." He hid his face against her breast.

Even though he was horrified at his behavior, passion still throbbed within him. It wasn't likely to go away with her lying next to him. Reluctantly, he sat up and swung his legs off the bed. She stirred, and he spotted her sweater on the floor. He handed it to her.

She jerked the sweater out of his hands. "The kids are downstairs, probably tearing each others' hair out by now."

He really didn't want to hear about the kids. He wanted to find some way to explain his behavior. There wasn't any, so he kept to her subject. "They're well-behaved kids. You do a good job with them."

"They have their moments," she said, sarcasm heavy in her voice.

"We all do." He sighed heavily.

"You're having a guilt trip, right?" she guessed. "I still don't understand what happened. You have a dozen women that you service in quarterly installments, and Number One, you try cheating on them with me, and Number Two, you try forcing me."

"I said I was sorry. I just lost control I'm not used to a woman refusing my advances."

"Obviously. You're such a twit, you can't even be loyal to your twelve regular partners." She flounced off the bed, picked clothes up off the floor and threw Harry's items at him. "What does that say about me?"

"You have no reason to feel guilty. I forced you."

"I probably gave you mixed signals. I should have stopped long before I did."

"What's that supposed to mean?"

"That I let myself be a victim, and I don't like the way I feel. That I don't respect you, but I want you; that I know I should stay away from you, but I can't seem to help myself."

He walked to her and pulled her in his arms. "I know exactly how you feel. I'm in the same boat. But we'll get through this. When the snow quits and the roads are open again, I'll get out of your life. As soon as I know you'll be safe."

"That's pretty funny, because as long as you're around, I don't think I'll ever be safe."

~ * ~

"We have something to show you," Erica the peacemaker told Tara.

"If it's alive, I don't want to know about it, okay?"

"It's not bad! We were good Samaritans this morning and rescued the sweetest little bunny rabbit from certain death. Tiffany found it."

"Where is it now? Pooping in the laundry room, I'll bet."

"No, he's quite civilized," Kevin interrupted. "He uses a litter pan."

"Which we don't have," Tara pointed out. She closed her eyes, wishing she could get out of this bad mood.

"We're using a makeshift one," Kevin assured her. "Remember when Dad had the ankle injury and had to soak it so many times a day? I found the basin he used."

"I'm impressed. Where'd you find litter?"

"In the trunk of the car."

"I won't even ask." Tara knew when to fight battles, and this didn't come close to qualifying. "You may keep the rabbit as long as I don't need to feed it or empty the litter pan. And please use gloves when you clean the litter pan. You don't know what diseases they carry."

"Rabbits are clean," Kevin protested.

"They're probably cleaner outside, if you get my drift."

"He was freezing outside!"

"Kevin, I know you're young but you're also smart and realistic, even more so than I am. Did you ever hear of 'Survival of the Fittest'?"

"No! I mean, I understand the concept, but it doesn't apply in this situation."

"Okay," she said in a dismissing voice. "Enough said. I trust your judgment. Introduce me to this phenomenal rabbit."

Kevin picked the white rabbit out of the dog's bed that had been Baraboo's when he was just a pup. Hard to believe he'd ever been that small. Kevin placed the furry white ball in Tara's arms, and the bunny seemed to sense that it was crunch time, that he had to behave or risk dire straits. He melted into her figure, rubbing his head against her breasts, her nipples in particular. Repeatedly.

"Hey, Rabbit, watch it or you'll be out on your ear. What a fresh little creature you are." She turned to Kevin. "What does Baraboo think of him?"

"He's cool about it. He seems to protect Bunny."

"That's sweet. I've heard of big dogs doing this, taking care of family pets, or family members. We should buy him an extra box of Milk Bones next time we go to the grocery store."

In the meantime the Bunny Rabbit seemed more interested in Tara's curves than in future Milk Bones awards.

"Bad bunny," she chastised.

Seven

Valentine's Eve dawned clear and cold, about 30 below zero. The highway department blamed the slippery roads on the bitter cold since the road salt only worked to temperatures above 15°.

Needless to say, Harry wasn't going home or anywhere else today or anytime soon.

"What's your hurry?" she asked suspiciously.

"It's a new workweek and I already missed a day yesterday because of weather.

"Where are you scheduled this week?"

"Springfield."

"And what's her name?"

"Don't."

"As in Dont Iluvhar? My, what an unusual name."

"You know what I mean. My life outside this house is my own, totally separate from you. Don't mix the two."

"How can I not? You're ready to walk out on me for whatever her name is. How can I not be jealous? How can I not be disturbed?"

"You knew when you met me that this is my lifestyle. You have no business interfering now."

"I'm not interfering. I don't even care."

"Good. Then there's not a problem."

"Exactly. No problem. So why won't you tell me her name?"

He heaved a big sigh. "Her name is Sybil."

"Sounds cold, very off-putting. What does she look like?"

"She's five feet, five inches, blonde hair, blue eyes, slim but with a curvy figure. Big boobs, I'm not sure they're natural, but that's okay. She works in the X-Ray department at the hospital, she's single, no children, lives alone. Is that enough details?"

"How old is she?"

"I don't...Old enough to know better. Twenty-two."

"You're kind of robbing the cradle, aren't you? You're thirty already."

He snorted. "I knew you'd find something to criticize."

"So if I got a boob job, would you be interested in me?"

He backed her into a corner, intimidating her with his height. "I'm already interested in you. You're the one with the problem."

"You came onto me like a steamroller. How can you blame me?"

"I can't help it. The kids put me off my stride. I rushed it. They're a major stumbling block."

"That's not fair. They were good yesterday while we were...upstairs."

"True, except you weren't in your bed last night when I paid a visit."

She gasped. She'd assumed he wouldn't be interested in her any more, not after the unpleasant...incident. "Tiffany had a nightmare."

"Exactly my point."

"You need to grow up. Kids require responsibilities from their parents or whoever takes care of them. It might not be romantic, but that's what parenthood is all about-- being there when they need you, nor necessarily when it's convenient."

"You don't get my point. I'm not 'into' kids and responsibilities. I've managed to avoid those so far, and I intend to keep it that way."

"Then why are you here? You sure don't fit into my idea of the hero and father figure in my fantasy."

"Really? Well, that's good, because I'll be outside, shoveling my way out of guaranteed disaster."

"Well good," she agreed. "I hope you freeze your selfish backside off while you're at it."

"Nothing on earth compares with the vindictive wrath of a woman scorned."

"Isn't that the other way around? Sybil, my ass."

"I'm out of here."

"Well, good." Let him go out and freeze his ass off. "I wouldn't want you to think I'm jealous because you have all these women that lure you back, come hell or high water. What do they have that I don't have?"

"Maybe...loyalty or genuine caring. I'm an event for them each quarter, and they know how to make a man feel special."

"That's easy for them. They only have to deal with you a week each quarter. I pity them, pining for you the rest of the time."

"That's not the case. If I'm not there, as far as I know, they don't grieve for me. They don't worry about me or try to apply their principles to my behavior. They accept the person I am."

"Go ahead, you can say it: While I try to change you."

"I realize that you do it for what you think is my own good, but sometimes, I'd like to be me, forget the warts."

"I'll just tell the kids you had better things to do."

"You can tell them I love them, and that I wish I could be with them tonight."

"What a crock. Talk about loyalty and genuine caring."

"You bother the hell out of me, lady."

"Yeah, then why don't you do something about it?

"Like what?"

"Stick around. Find out what a real relationship can be like. You don't have to leave to prove a point, Harry, but I won't beg. Never mind that I planned a special dinner. I planned to put the kids to bed early, make the evening special for both of us. But it doesn't matter."

"Well good." He shrugged as if he had a choice.

Unfortunately for him, the roads were still closed.

"I'm going out to shovel. If I get the driveway done, I'll start on the street and work my way to the county highway, just in case I want to go."

~ * ~

Tara wasn't beneath begging. "I need you four to have a nice, early supper."

"Five," Erica corrected. "Bunny wants to eat with us."

"It's a rule in this household, no animals at the supper table."

"He doesn't count. He's not totally a bunny."

"Fine, I don't care, but I don't want to step in bunny poop on my way to the dining room. That would ruin the romance real quick."

"Romance...Really?" Kevin perked up. "With Harry?"

"I'll never tell," she told him, but who else but Harry was in the vicinity?

"Do you two have adequate protection?"

"Kevin! You're not supposed to know about birth control at age six," Tara told him.

"It's never too early to learn. If we want to control world population, we need to start young."

"I have more immediate goals, like erasing his extensive database of available females from his memory. Any ideas how I can achieve that?"

"Maybe you're right. Sex has its appeal in certain situations."

"You know, hon, I feel for you when you finally grow up. You'll be so blasé about love and romance by then, there won't be any excitement left for a couple in love. Who knows if couples will still fall in love? Maybe they'll simply be matched, and that would be a tragedy."

As always, Kevin had a comeback. "Or maybe by then, we'll discover a system to identify compatible couples and eliminate divorce and separation."

"As in reverting to the old system of the forties and fifties before divorce came into vogue?"

"Interesting theory," he allowed.

"Do you know if poor Harry is still in the whirlpool after all that shoveling?"

"I think he fell asleep in there."

"If I asked you to take him a glass of wine, would you promise not to taste it?"

"I can't promise."

"Hmmm. I guess I better deliver the wine myself. Can you all try to be good while I take a glass to him?"

"Depends on what's for dessert."

"Make-Your-Own-Dessert-But-Don't-Make-A-Mess."

"There is no such dessert," Erica said.

"There is in this household," Tara said. "Emergency only, okay? Oh, by the way, it's permissible to interrupt us--in an emergency. We won't be doing anything that would embarrass you, except maybe kissing...if he ever forgives me."

"Is Harry leaving us?" Tiffany asked.

"Can we afford to lose him?" Kimmy asked.

"We can't lose Harry," Erica agreed.

Their concern swelled within her heart. She didn't want to lose Harry either, and she'd do everything in her power to keep him here--short of going against her principles. She didn't want to involve the kids, though. That would be blackmail.

"Let's not over-analyze this situation, guys. And let's not get too attached to Harry. As soon as conditions improve, he'll return to his normal life. I'd like to say he'll fit us into some part of his life, but I can't guarantee that. Most likely, if the roads are clear tomorrow, Harry will be long gone. We don't fit into his lifestyle, but even without him, we'll survive."

"Why would he leave us?" Erica asked.

"His normal life may be too busy to fit us in."

Tiffany sniffed. "How can he not love us?"

"He does love us, in his own way. Sometimes guys just can't recognize it, or admit it. So we just have to enjoy the time he's here. He was fun, wasn't he?"

The children sat listlessly, each attempting to accept this lesson in human behavior in their own way. Tara regretted opening the discussion to begin with, but it was never too early to learn the way of the world.

~ * ~

Harry finally emerged from the hot tub when he felt more like a jellyfish than a sponge. He'd enjoyed the exercise of shoveling today. He seldom did physical work any more since he'd finished the basement in his mother's house. Occasionally, one or both of his sisters would have a project going on a weekend while he was home--usually if one did, the other was close behind, and outdid it bigger and better than her sister.

He threw on a pair of jeans and a sweater and made his way downstairs to see what happened to Tara. She'd promised to join him in the spa as soon as she fed the kids.

He followed the sound of voices to the eat-in kitchen, but hesitated before entering. Tara and the children were talking about him, and it sounded like she was teaching them a life's lesson in the process.

"Let's not over-analyze this situation, guys. And let's not get too attached to Harry. As soon as conditions improve, he'll return to his normal life. I'd like to say he'll fit us into some part of his life, but I can't guarantee that. Most likely, if the roads are clear tomorrow, Harry will be long gone. We don't fit into his lifestyle, but even without him, we'll survive."

"Why would he leave us?" Erica asked.

"His normal life may be too busy to fit us in."

Tiffany sniffed. "How can he not love us?"

"He does love us, in his own way. Sometimes guys just can't recognize it, or admit it. So we just have to hope for the best."

He felt like a heel, mostly because she was right on. Tomorrow when the roads opened, Valentine's Day be damned, he'd leave her and her family with promises to keep in touch--and maybe he would for a while, as long as it was convenient.

Not that he didn't care about Tara and her brood of four, but he had a carefully-crafted schedule that was established and worked well. Sure Tara was tempting, but she'd never integrate into his lifestyle. As lovely and sexy as she was, she'd never fit his requirements.

Without revealing his presence, he turned on his heel and headed back upstairs. He'd wait for Tara to find him there, not letting her know that he ever ventured out of the comfort of the watery retreat.

~ * ~

"Are you a raisin yet?" she asked when she entered the master suite's spa.

"I'm just about ripe," Harry answered.

"You kill me. You never show physical exercise, or any response to anything. Anyone else would look pecker-pink, and you sit there as nonchalant as a James Bond character."

"I watched a lot of James Bond movies growing up. I may have had it rubbed into me."

"He was always flitting from one woman to another, too."

"Maybe we should watch some of his movies together. Might give you some ideas. You can practice on me anytime."

Harry felt like a heel knowing he wouldn't be around tomorrow to provide the unparalleled sex that she desired. Surely if he promised he might be back someday, she'd welcome him into her bed before he left.

Eight

Harry tried, he really did expend every effort to make Valentine's Eve special. Tara had fed the fearsome foursome, plus the dog and rabbit ahead of time, so he assumed she'd be relaxed and attentive over dinner. Yet she seemed distracted throughout their meal.

"Something wrong?" he asked her.

"Everything's wonderful. The food was good, the music you chose is exceptional. Even the kids and animals went to bed on time, and without one protest. Do you realize how unusual that is?"

"You're good with the kids." He smiled, remembering the excuses they'd come up with in order to delay their bedtime, checking the plants, brushing the dog, finding a snack for the rabbit.

"They're good with me, too. A lot of it is simply respect for one another and their feelings, don't you think?"

"You sound like a teacher."

"Ouch! That sounds like an accusation."

"I didn't mean it that way. My memories of high school aren't all bad."

As for the bad ones, he'd buried the worst of them.

"Maybe you forgot, I was a teacher until I started writing. I guess once a teacher, always a teacher. I had to give it up when I sold the young adult series. I don't have time to teach and write seriously."

He refilled the champagne in her glass. "Where do you fit 'you' in there?"

"Someday, I'll figure it out. For now, I'm grateful for what I have. I can't wait for the first book in the series to come out. My life will change, I know. I dread going on tour. It sounds glamorous, but I've heard so many horror stories. I don't travel well, you see. I tend to get tired and need a nap; otherwise I get really grouchy. Can't treat fans that way."

"So get a manager."

"Are you volunteering?"

"I can't get away that long." For just a flash of time, he saw himself doing just that.

Being on tour could be fun and exciting, but it would mess up his whole system. Maybe for just one quarter, he could consider the position. Nah, what was he thinking? That would only give Tara false hope of a future together. "Will you take the children along?"

She shook her head. "They might enjoy going to a local book signing occasionally, but it would put too much stress on everyone concerned to travel with children. A special event on occasion is another story, maybe a signing at a school depending on the location, but from what I hear, the book signing circuit is no life for a child."

"Do you think that's fair to them?"

"I don't why that would be a consideration. Naturally, if they need me to help out, I'll do whatever I can."

Harry pushed back from the table, unable to contain his agitation. "I'll get another bottle of champagne."

He paced back and forth in the kitchen, even considered going outside to cool off, but it was bitter cold out there and it wouldn't change anything.

"What's wrong, Harry?" she asked when he returned.

He blew out a long sigh. "How can a mother choose her career over her family?"

"There's not always a choice. What's the problem?"

He swirled the liquid in his glass, as if the bubbles would provide an answer. "I thought you were different, that kids and family came first, the way I remember my family when I was growing up."

"I should have realized you'd be a male chauvinist to match your women of the week mentality. Not every family has such an ideal existence."

He frowned. "There was never an 'ideal existence.' We were a normal family. There were arguments, mostly my two sisters bickering, but they were minor spats."

"All families bicker. It's part of living together. You should hear me and my brothers."

A flash of memory blindsided him. Loud voices...his parents arguing in the kitchen, their anger carrying through the wall to his bedroom directly behind the kitchen. He grabbed his forehead to ward off the memories. It didn't work.

"What is it, Harry?" Tara asked with gentle concern.

His mother's bitter words came back, 'You get rid of that woman, or I'll leave you. We don't have money for new school shoes for the kids and here you are, out drinking and carousing with that woman every night! I won't stand for it anymore, I tell you. You'll never see your children again.'

"All these years, I've blocked the memory out of my mind. My dad was having an affair. She was with him when he crashed the car."

"Did she...survive?"

He shook his head. "They covered the affair up, said my dad offered to give her a ride home because she'd had too much to drink. She was divorced."

"I'm sorry." She patted his hand.

"I don't know how my mother made it through all that. The bar closed at two a.m. and they crashed around four, so there was no excuse for them being together that late. It was unreal--all the rumors and juicy tidbits. I was a sophomore in high school and all the girls teased me, 'Are you a lover like your dad?'"

"How cruel. I'm sorry. It must have been horrible for you."

"Yeah, it was. I got wild for a while, skipping school, drinking every night, drag racing. I was only fifteen, didn't even have a license. That whole year, I think I had a death wish."

"You had nobody to turn to?"

"I probably could have; I chose not to. My mother ended up crying every time she tried to talk to me, my sisters washed their hands of me, their friends wanted to date me. Did you ever hear of James Dean?"

"Sure. He was a movie star. 'Rebel without a Cause.' He died in a car crash in real life. You look a little like him."

"Oh. The girls sure liked him, even though he was dead. They said I reminded them of him."

"So what happened? How did you turn yourself around?"

He shook his head, not sure he wanted to continue the conversation but knowing he'd have to give her enough to satisfy her curiosity. "We got a new police chief in town. I don't know why, I think he had the hots for my mother, but he took an interest in me. He kept stopping by the house, trying to interest me in sports and activities around the neighborhood."

"And..."

"And nothing. I just gradually turned around."

"Just like that.'

"Yep. Just like that."

"I don't believe you."

He reached for the bottle and filled his glass. "I don't really care."

"Oh, come on! It can't be that bad!"

"What the hell do you know?" he gulped down half the champagne he'd poured. "You want to know how bad it was? When he wasn't getting anywhere with me, the chief locked my sorry ass in the slammer overnight. The bastard left me alone with a muscle bound, horny fag, taught me a lesson I'll never forget!"

"Oh my God. He raped you?"

"Multiple times."

She came around behind his chair and hugged him from behind, laying her face against his. "I'm so sorry. What did you do? You pressed charges, didn't you?"

He spat out his disgust. "Lot of good it would have done. That next morning, before he released me, the chief gave me a brief but to-the-point lecture. I had a choice to continue facing the consequences if I chose to walk on the wild side, or to put the past behind me and turn my life around before it was too late. I learned a bitter lesson, but I cleaned up my act real quick. I suppose I should be grateful to the chief for his interference." The memory of the brutal night haunted him even today, nearly fifteen years later.

Tara returned to her chair and they lapsed into silence for a long while, sipping the champagne, reflecting on life. Finally she spoke. "So that's why you can't latch onto one woman. You're afraid you're like your father and can't stay faithful to one woman. Or is it because you think no woman would stay faithful to you? You're afraid to be hurt, so you spread your attentions to multiple women in an organized and creative manner."

"That's bullshit."

"Maybe you need the validation of multiple women to prove you're not homosexual."

He'd never hit a woman in his life, but he almost lost control this time. "Just stop trying to analyze me, okay?"

"But it makes sense. No man balancing affairs with a dozen women at once would ever have to question his masculinity."

"I don't."

"Right. It works for you. You have the variety you crave, possibly inherited from your father, and if one of your women backs out, it's simple for you to find a substitute."

"You make it sound deviant."

"Trust me, Harry. It is definitely deviant behavior. I'll bet you're always on the lookout for potential material, aren't you? It's convenient that you sell medical equipment. You have all those pretty young women in the hospitals to pick from."

He scowled at her. "So far it hasn't disappointed me."

"Oh, and I bet with schools buying defibrillators for sports, you have a whole new market, not only for business but also for pleasure!"

"You're making fun of me now."

"You bet I am. All those young female teachers! They tend to want more permanency, though, than medical workers, don't they? They're probably a little more traditional, kind of like me."

"Let's just change the subject. We started out talking about you and your lack of responsibility toward the children. You managed to turn it around so that I'm the bad guy."

How dare she criticize him and pretend to be traditional? He did not appreciate her cavalier attitude toward responsibilities. Four children and no wedding ring in sight? Willing to leave for weeks or months on end to publicize a book, never mind her children's needs? Maybe the fathers--both of them--had an arrangement or custody agreements. Perhaps they did their thing and then switched while she did hers. He laughed out loud. She had the same reservations about him.

"How can we want each other so bad when we don't approve of each other's lifestyle?" he wondered out loud.

"I guess we're a perfect match."

"Opposites attract?"

"Maybe. But surely we can come up with a compromise."

Feeling better about life in general, he poured more bubbly. He stared into the fire and the scent of wood smoke was redolent of camping with his dad when he was still alive. The dining room shared a wood fireplace with the formal living room, as did the family room with the den or office, while the master suite upstairs had a gas fireplace.

He looked up when he realized he'd been daydreaming. "Sorry. I didn't mean to ignore you." Her wide smile warmed his heart, made him feel so welcome he never wanted to leave her.

"I enjoy watching the fire, too, though I seldom bother building one. I'm always busy doing something with the kids when I'm here, or writing--staring into a computer screen. I should find a screen saver that's a fireplace. That would be more interesting than shooting stars, though it lets me think without distraction."

"What do you think about?"

"Lately, you," she admitted. "You're on my mind constantly, it seems."

"I'm not sure how good that is. I confess I'm attracted to you. I want to take you to bed, but I refuse to promise anything permanent. You know how I operate."

"I don't know, for sure...but I don't think I could live with that. Except I want you so much, it's driving me crazy. Should I take what I can get...for now?"

"For now," he protested. "That's what scares me; that you want more than I can give."

She shrugged, "That's my problem, not yours." She shoved her chair back and grabbed her place setting. "See you in the morning."

"You don't need to get mad. I'm just trying to be realistic."

"Don't bother next time."

She turned to leave. He grabbed her arm from behind, stopping her. She tried to shrug his hand off, but by then he curled his other arm around her waist, sweeping up her midriff to her breasts, where he slowed his pace. She leaned back against him, savoring the sensations of his exploration.

He took the place setting out of her hand and set it on the table. She reached back and stroked his thigh, searching for more intimate territory. He did the same, teasing her hardened nipples with one hand, the other just short of the juncture between her legs. From her reaction, he knew she was very aware of how close he was to her private space. "Are you going to let it happen this time?"

"I don't think I have a choice."

"I promise to stop if you freak out again. Okay?"

She nodded.

"We have too many clothes on," he whispered against her ear, his warm breath on her skin giving her shivers.

She angled her head to allow access to her neck and moaned when he took advantage. "You're multi-talented," she told him.

"Could you relax a little? You feel like I left you out in the cold too long."

"That's not very romantic. I'll try to do better."

"You're doing just fine."

She took a deep breath and visually relaxed. "How's that?" she asked.

"Wonderful, except if one of the kids comes downstairs, we're toast," he reminded her.

"Shut the door. That way we'll hear them before they find us."

"Don't count on it. Kids are crafty. I was one once."

She giggled.

"Much better," he praised her. He left her briefly to follow her order, though, and turned the overhead light out at the same time he closed the door. When he came back, he pulled her to him, his hands on her buttocks. They both drew in a shaky breath at the intimate encounter, and he looked down at her trusting expression.

She surprised him by unlatching his belt buckle. Never mind that her hands shook.

"Oh, baby, go for it," he teased and matched her initiative by unbuckling her belt. "What do you want to tackle next?"

"Umm, the snap," she said, her breathing ragged.

He flicked her jeans snap. "That didn't take long. Zipper next, okay?"

She nodded and inched his zipper down. He could barely hold in a sigh. He waited until she finished before he started on hers, ignoring the urge to rearrange his erection inside his jeans. With luck, he'd have plenty of room within minutes.

Following her lead he unzipped her jeans slowly, but he also managed to trail his fingers down the silky material of her panties, then past where the zipper ended. She stood up straighter, he figured to allow him extra room, but he withdrew his hand and gripped the bottom of her sweater. Slow and easy was his mantra, knowing he'd scared her off the last time he put the make on her. "All right?" Harry prided himself on his patience at all times, but right now all he wanted to do was rip their remaining garments off and rut like a bunny rabbit.

She smiled and nodded.

He inched the cashmere sweater up similar to his technique with the panties, letting his fingers ease up her body, this time, lingering on her breasts. God, he felt like a sixteen year old again, trying to prevent himself from losing control. He wanted her so bad, it was worse than painful. He was caught in a torture chamber.

"My turn," Tara announced as soon as the fabric cleared her ears.

"You getting impatient?" he asked, hoping she'd urge him to turn up the pace.

"Who, me? Never," she said.

He loved her for being so brave, all the while groaning against his need. How embarrassing for his reputation if he lost control. She was sexy as sin in her silk pink bra and open jeans.

She lifted the hem of his sweater, but instead of pushing it up, she felt for the button on the shirt he wore underneath. Her fingers crept up his chest. Under cover, she opened all seven buttons in slow motion, copping a feel of his male nipples along the way. The feel of her hands flicking over his sensitive flesh nearly sent him over the top. The lady had an imagination; she sure turned him on. His erection threatened to burst his zipper, sending tingles throughout his body. Too bad the Tingle Test didn't exist. He would have made an A-plus.

She took care of peeling off his shirt in slow motion and knelt in front on him. He sucked in a breath, unsure what she was up to. One could only hope. He sighed when she untied his shoes and couldn't suppress a laugh.

"Get your mind out of the gutter," she warned.

He seldom laughed when he was putting the make on a woman. To Harry, sex was serious business. That was another reason they couldn't be together on a permanent basis; they had different philosophies about sex. She had no respect for the serious nature of making love and doing it properly, if her behavior so far this evening was typical of her technique.

Though he had to admit, this was fun for a change.

She also skipped his socks, shocking him by tugging at his jeans. "Hey, I didn't do your shoes."

"I just have slippers on. I can kick them off any time you want."

"I guess that's okay." He rubbed her shoulders. "Come on up here. You need a kiss."

"In a minute." She tugged his jeans down over his hips and lower, taking his breath away. "Kick them off for me," she said.

"Gladly," he agreed, thanking his dedication for untold hours spent in gyms across three states. But she was rushing it. He was accustomed to controlling the pace.

She continued to ease his jeans down, and it was a choice of breaking his neck trying to fight her, or finally stepping out of them. He chose the latter, but this wasn't going well. He was in danger of losing control as she reached for his privates. His family jewels shrunk in defense.

"Stand up here," he tugged on her arm. She ignored his request and made short order of his underwear, but then she seemed to freeze. Maybe she wasn't accustomed to someone his size. He puffed up his chest, proud of her efforts, and provided advice. "Cup me with your hands. Feel my desire."

Oh, yes, she caught on quickly. "Kiss me there," he urged. "Take me into your mouth."

She followed his instructions, cradling his sex in her hands, as if urging him to fulfill her dreams and expectations of him. Oh yeah, he sighed as she flicked her tongue over his tip. He'd gladly fulfill her every wish, if she'd just suck him. He said it out loud. "Suck me," he pleaded.

He watched while the tip of her tongue again touched the tip of his shaft, teasing him,

tracing his length, withholding what he most wanted. "Tara, baby, take me in your mouth or I'll die." He wasn't exaggerating. He would seriously die if she didn't satisfy his need.

"What do you need?" she finally asked.

"I ache for you. Take me in your mouth. Love me."

When she followed his request he drew in a huge breath, willing himself to savor the sensation. Eyes closed, he rocked gently against her mouth, urging deeper penetration.

Her hair camouflaged her features, and his only image of her was her hands, her lips surrounding his sex. So erotic was it that he'd see it in his dreams. Hot sensation flooded him, and unless she stopped very soon, he threatened to lose control, not to mention losing his pride. He frowned, knowing she was missing some of the best sex in her life, but he was incapable of stopping her. He throbbed with need, promising himself to fulfill her every wish once she took the edge off. He had to balance his swaying body with both hands on her shoulders. As much as he enjoyed the sensation, he wasn't pleasuring her, and he prided himself on pleasing his partners.

Finally when he could stand no more or he'd explode, he pulled her up to him and held her close. Big mistake. That only brought her skin to skin against his erection. "I'm gonna go if we don't stop. I don't want it to end that way."

He bent down to grab his wallet out of his back pocket, and panicked. There was nothing but money in there. "Shit! I don't have any condoms on me! I have a gross of them out in the car, but by the time I wade through snow, we won't have need for them anymore."

Her face fell.

"Do you have--"

She shook her head.

"Are you on birth control?"

Another shake of her head made him want to kick something.

"I'm not leaving you hanging," he said and dropped to his knees. Within seconds, he whipped her jeans and panties off. His hands on either side of her hips, he slowed his pace, kissing her belly, teasing her sensitive skin with his tongue. He felt like a heel, pushing her climax in anticipation of his own. At first she pulled back with reluctance--surely not innocence--but soon he had her swaying with pleasure, flicking his tongue inside her to coincide with each stroke. Judging by her quiet moans, she appreciated his technique. He pulled her closer, his hands on the silky skin of her bottom, tilting her toward him

Pulling her delicious secret area closer, he inhaled the woman scent of her, musky, sexy, arousing. His nostrils flaring, he nicked her with his teeth, then kissed her 'owie.' She moaned, begging for release. With his fingers, his tongue, his lips, he teased her until she whimpered for mercy, pulsated against his persistence, and shuddered with release.

Her pleasure triggered his needs. Spasms of lust gripped him, tearing him apart inside with hunger, burning him with greed. Unable to control himself, he grabbed his shirt to his crotch and spilled his seed. He lay with his head on her stomach, mouth open above her core, for endless minutes until his rapid breathing slowed. She finally urged him up to lay beside her, as if she needed reassurance after the mind-blowing sex they're had together.

Which brought him full circle. He could fall for Tara hard, yet she was such an enigma he'd never figure her out.

Nine

Still trembling with emotion long after their lovemaking, her legs so weak she knew better than to stand, Tara pulled Harry up to cuddle close to her. She'd never been aggressive with a guy, nor had she ever been out of control. "No wonder you have a harem of women seeking your favors."

"I keep telling you I don't have a harem." His words were slurred, as if he was half asleep. "I don't contribute to their support, except if I buy groceries when I stay there, or take them out to dinner or a movie. It's a lonely life, being on the road all week."

"I never thought about that. I suppose a lot of men are tempted to seek solace when they're away for a long stretch."

"Not only men." He slid his hand up her back and swore suddenly. "What the hell! I never took your bra off? Boy, am I off my stride today."

"Our minds were on other matters. I never even noticed."

"I owe you a marathon orgy. It would be better if the kids weren't around at the time though."

"I agree with you on that." Strange that though she was blown away by his expertise and killer orgasm, her body wasn't satisfied. Why?

"Any chance you could pawn them off on a friend or relative tomorrow so we can enjoy Valentine's Day?"

"I doubt it. Not many parents are willing to take an extra four children for an overnight, especially on Valentine's Day and on a school night." She thought briefly of her parents, who lived close, but they were still in Florida for the winter.

"When do parents with lots of children have a life?"

"I think the children are their life. What's the saying-- Life begins at forty? That's probably why."

"Yeah, I suppose my sisters are like that. They each have a couple kids, and most of their life revolves around the kids, school and boy scouts/girl scouts, sports, birthday parties. They're always busy."

"And that's good. Wholesome, all-American fun."

"But what about you? When do you have time for you?"

"I have friends and family. I lead a normal life. Date occasionally. It goes in streaks. Sometimes life is busier than others."

He winced at her words but she didn't bother defending herself. With his woman of the week lifestyle, who was he to judge? How dare he be jealous that she dated occasionally?

"It's getting late," she said. "I don't know if there will be school in the morning. I doubt it, but I need to get up early."

"Can I sleep with you?"

She tilted her head, weighing the pros and cons. She would love to curl up with him and feel cherished. She could feel his hands on her already. They'd end up having sex, real sex with protection this time, and they wouldn't be able to restrain themselves. What if the kids heard something and came to investigate? "No, the kids often wander into my room overnight. It wouldn't set a good example."

"I want you. You're on my mind every minute of the day. I even dream about you."

She curled into him with relief. "That's how I've been ever since we met. I swear, if the kids weren't around, we'd be in trouble 'cause we'd never get out of bed to eat."

"Other than the kids, there's nothing keeping us apart," Harry said, a note of wonder in his voice.

"You're forgetting something. You have to break it off with your twelve women. Would a mass-mailing be too insensitive? I'll pay the postage."

"Break it off? I can't do that."

"Yes, you can. You said I'm on your mind every minute of the day. You even dream about me."

"That's true, but I can't give up my Lucky Twelve. They've been loyal to me, some of them for years."

"You actually call them your Lucky Twelve?"

"No, of course not. I think you turned the phrase, and it sounded appropriate. Maybe we could let them graduate out naturally."

"Graduate out," she snorted, "like you offer them an education on relationships?"

"I hadn't thought about that, but it fits."

"I don't think so. The only education they get on relationships from you is how to survive a bad one."

"How can you say that after the wonderful lovemaking we shared?"

"Harry! We couldn't even complete our pseudo-lovemaking because we didn't have birth control--or should I say disease control? That would be more like it, with all the women you sleep with. To me that's not lovemaking. That's pure and simple sex."

His chin went up. "What's wrong with good old fashioned sex?"

"You mean like pirates on the open seas, marauding and ransacking?"

"Damn, you have an answer for everything. I can never win."

She patted his face. "That's because you're wrong."

He pouted for a minute. "Does that mean you don't love me anymore?"

"No, of course not. I can't help loving you, but I don't like your lifestyle very much." She laughed without mirth. "Very much? I don't like it at all."

"I may as well go to bed."

"Yes, you may as well. That way you can get up early and shovel your way out. And then you can be gone, back to your woman of the week. She missed a day already for the quarter. Do you stay through Saturday in that case?"

"Stop teasing."

"I'm not teasing. I can't love someone I can't respect, and your lifestyle turns me off...It makes me sick because you're such a nice man. You could make someone a wonderful husband and father."

"That's never going to happen so I'll just leave right now."

"Good. The sooner the better."

"I agree."

He grabbed his clothes and shoes and left the room.

As annoyed as she was with him, she watched his nicely curving butt exit the dining room door, muscles rippling with indignation. She scurried out to the wide hallway, hoping for a last glimpse of his front when he started up the stairway.

Tara suddenly realized she still wore only a bra. He could at least have found her panties for her.

She gathered her clothes and dressed, then carried the dishes and leftovers into the kitchen, remembering the erotic sensations Harry had introduced her to...scattering kisses on her toes, blowing his warm breath on the back of her knees, kissing his way up her thigh...all the while she craved fulfillment. She wanted more.

Harry hurried through the kitchen, glared at her on his way to the garage. He was dressed for cold weather. It seemed he meant it when he said he couldn't wait to get away from her.

She put away the leftover food, filled the dishwasher and wiped all the counters. Still agitated with restless energy, she swept the tile floor, checked the kids and dog upstairs and the rabbit in the laundry room. He gave her the creeps tonight the way he watched her, as if he knew what was going on with her and Harry. Would a rabbit disdain sex?

Hardly!

Well, hell, she wouldn't be able to sleep anytime soon. She may as well go out and help him shovel. Her boots and ski jacket were in the laundry room, along with gloves and hat and she was soon dressed and opening the outside door.

Freezing rain greeted her. Over the top of the snow, the icy glaze turned everything into a crystal wonderland. "How beautiful!" she said.

Her comment must have surprised Harry because his feet went out from under him and he landed on his back with a thud. His curse reverberated through half the neighborhood, disturbing the peace.

"Did you hurt yourself?"

"I think I broke my pelvis."

"That'll put a crimp in your love life." She couldn't help laughing. She walked over to where he still lay and looked down on him. "Poor boy. Do you need a hand up?"

As she leaned down to help, he slapped his arm against her foot and that quick she was on her back next to him.

Apparently his mood had improved because he laughed until he held his sides.

"Very funny," she said. She grabbed a handful of slush and rubbed his face. "Now who's laughing?"

He was on top of her before she could protest, his hands pulling at the zipper of her coat, under her sweater, inside her pants. His gloves were ice cold and tickled her and she laughed until tears came to her eyes. "Stop, stop," she pleaded.

He sobered. "I take it you don't like my technique."

"You need to work on it a little." She carefully stood up. "Don't forget the gross of rubbers in your car. Tomorrow's Valentine's Day. Maybe you'll get lucky."

He waggled her eyebrows at her. Incredible how they fought, loved, swore not to have anything to do to each other ever again, and two minutes later they not only made up, but were in each other's arms again. It was like they were caught in the middle of a magical spell.

~ * ~

Valentine's Day dawned clear and bitter cold. "Colder than a witch's tit," Harry pronounced.

All four kids giggled and repeated Harry's phrase, "Colder than a witch's tit!"

"That's enough," Tara warned and turned her back to hide her smile.

"You got that from Bunny," Erica accused him.

"How in the world could he get a saying from a bunny?" Tara asked.

"Whoops, sorry," Harry said in earnest. "I'm not used to being around kids that often."

"None of your women of the week have children?"

"No way. I don't get involved with anyone with children. It's not my scene."

"You seem to be holding your own the past few days."

"They're good kids, like little adults."

"Be careful with the compliments. They'll get big heads. By the way, kiddlings...is it time to water your plants yet? Are they still alive?"

"Of course," Kevin said. "We check them daily. The sun hasn't cooperated since we brought them home. Go figure. Just when we need sunshine, it disappears."

"That's the way of the world," Harry agreed. "Life sucks."

"Harry, mind your mouth! You can't talk like that in front of kids. You're demonstrating a negative attitude."

"What did I say?"

"Life sucks!" the older kids chimed in, breaking into giggles. Tiffany and Erica glared at them since they didn't understand the joke.

"See?" Tara glared at him. "What were we talking about? Oh yeah, the plants."

"We should have bought heat lamps when we were at the florist," Erica said. "We need fertilizer, too, and bug spray and...what was other stuff Lindsey recommended?"

"We'll ask her when we stop back, maybe tomorrow. The florist shop will be mobbed today. I'm sure the plants will survive another day."

"They better," Kimmy said, "You paid a fortune for those plants. Dad's going to be hoppin' mad."

"Hey, silly girl, your dad would spend his last penny if he knew you wanted something, 'cause that's how much he loves you. As it is, I paid for those plants by myself, 'cause I love you and your sister, and your cousins, so your dad has no business worrying about the cost. And you can tell him I said that."

Harry looked confused.

"I will if the subject comes up," Kimmy said. "Maybe even if the subject doesn't come up."

"Ooh," Tara cooed.

"We need to get ready for school," Kevin reminded her.

"Ah, gee. Bad news. School is closed again today due to inclement weather. No school today!"

Everyone cheered, whether they were due at school or not--everyone but Kevin.

"You're kidding!" Kevin said with alarm. "They can't do this to me. I've been stuck here at home for three days, and they deny me my God-given education?"

"I'm sure you'll catch up an hour after you return to school, most likely tomorrow." Tara said. "Deal with it."

"It's not fair."

"Life isn't always fair. Like I said, deal with it."

"Now who's being negative?" Harry asked.

The six-year-old sighed heavily.

Harry poked her with his elbow. "Is he for real?"

She nodded reluctantly. "Unfortunately. I know it's not normal, but then that's Kevin. You know how families are, you take what you get. Sometimes they turn out to be geniuses."

Harry nodded, satisfied with the answer.

Ten

Unfortunately, Harry didn't have the luxury of skipping work another day. He commandeered the den as his office for the morning since Tara was in the office finishing her illustrations. He set up his laptop and cell phone and started calling the accounts which were scheduled for him to call on for Monday and Tuesday. Even if he left for Springfield now, which was impossible, he'd never catch up this week. In addition to the phone calls, he'd stop in at his biggest accounts later in the week. They were his bread and butter.

His approach was always similar: ask about the kids by name or the golfing or whatever was most important in the contact's life and tell a joke. He named all his jokes and always kept track of which one he told where. Then it was down to business, what problems were they having, how the equipment was working, what their needs were for the future. And he listened, that was his biggest asset, listening to what the clients told him.

Funny how that technique didn't work with Tara. An image popped into his mind at the thought of her, naked on the dining room floor, his mouth sucking her sweet nectar from within her. He shifted in his chair to accommodate his sudden erection. He pushed her image away as his call went through.

"Yeah, I heard you got a little snow in Chicago," everyone teased when they heard where he was stranded.

Early afternoon, before he quit for the day, Harry called Sybil, his Lucky Lady for the week. "Harry, I've been so worried about you! Why didn't you call me sooner?

"I've been snowbound, and you know how weather can interfere with cell phones." It wasn't a lie, necessarily, except he could have called earlier if he'd remembered.

"I miss you. When will you get here?"

"I'm not sure I'll make it this time around."

"But you still have to service your accounts." Her emphasis on 'service' showed him where her mind was. "Won't you be here next week?"

"I don't think I'll make it this quarter at all, but I'll keep in touch, and of course, if you need anything, call me."

"Oh, I need something, all right."

"What's that?"

"Harry, is something wrong? I meant sex. You're not acting like yourself."

"That sounds... interesting."

"Too bad you're not here. I'm in my office with the door closed and I'm wearing those red string bikini panties today. Remember you wanted to rip them off me last time you were here?"

Harry cleared his throat. "I remember. Isn't that the pair that matches the bra, the one with the nipples cut out?"

"One and the same."

He should buy Tara a set like that. That quick, he had to adjust his crotch again. Not that either of them needed extra stimulus when they were together.

"Harry, are you still listening? Are you still there? Harry?"

"I'm still here." He glanced toward the door to find Kevin standing there. How much of the conversation had he heard? "I have to go. I'll be in touch."

Thank goodness he didn't engage in phone sex in earnest on his side of the call or Kevin would have probably reported the behavior to Tara.

"Do you need something?" Harry asked the boy.

"We have a problem. We're out of fresh fruit and vegetables. We need to go to the store."

"Where did it all go? The refrigerator was stuffed full on Saturday when I came here. There's only six of us in the house. No way could we have devoured all that produce in three days,"

"That was before the rabbit arrived."

"How much can a rabbit eat in three days?"

"You'd be surprised."

"No way." Harry envisioned the compact furry bunny that lived in the laundry room. "There must have been twenty times his weight in the fridge in fresh vegetables alone."

"Probably, in bunny form, but when he morphs into human form, he has an appetite that doesn't quit."

"Whoa, wait a minute. What are you talking about, changing into human form?"

Kevin nodded, convincing Harry that the child believed the incredible story he told. "He's a changeling," Kevin said. "Sometimes rabbit, sometimes human, or like a cartoon character, apparently at will."

"I don't believe you."

"I've seen him change, He's the Easter Bunny! He can do whatever he pleases, take whatever form he wishes. He's magical!"

"There is no such thing as magic. You've read too many Harry Potter books, or whatever Tara calls her fairy tales."

Kevin shook his head, just like his mother, as stubborn in his beliefs as Tara.

"Where is the rabbit? I'll straighten him out. He won't dare attempt to change in my presence or I'll wring his neck."

The bunny must have heard them or sensed danger, because he made a break for the street the minute the door opened. He was in cartoon human form, and Harry realized Kevin spoke the truth. People, characters, whatever, really could appear in alternate forms, even one Harry was unfamiliar with. He yelled out, "Bunny, come back!"

The skittish rabbit ignored him, running into the street at exactly the same time a county salt truck went by. Rabbit never had a chance. The salt truck flattened him. Literally.

Harry and the kids rushed to the scene and observed the carnage. The bunny--which had switched to animal form--lay in the snow-covered street.

No sign of hope.

"He's dead," Kevin pronounced, his eyes round with disbelief.

"He can't be dead," Erica sobbed. "He's the Easter Bunny!"

"You killed him," Kimmy accused Harry.

"I didn't do it on purpose."

Tiffany spoke up, "Does this mean we don't get any chocolate for Valentine's Day?"

"Ah duh," Erica confirmed.

"It wasn't our fault," Erica said, sniffling.

"No, it was Harry's," Kevin confirmed. "Harry killed the Easter Bunny. Should I go get Tara? Maybe she can help."

"Wait," Harry said. "I have a machine in my trunk. I might be able to save him yet."

Thank goodness he had keys in his pocket. His hands shaking with the emergency, he pulled the defibrillator from the trunk. He looked around for an outlet, and Kevin yelled, "There's an outlet on the light post." He pointed to the corner of the drive.

Harry knew the human's charge would kill the little rabbit, so he switched the machine to the lowest possible setting. He rubbed the paddles together, touched the paddles to the white fur and said, "Clear," just like on ER. The rabbit jumped involuntarily, then lay still. "Once more," Harry warned. "Clear!"

Renewed life ripped into the rabbit, and he sat up. Looking around him as if disoriented, he shook his head, making his ears flop, hopped once, twice, then headed toward the driveway.

"You saved him," one of the girls said. "You saved the Easter Bunny!"

"Not hardly," Harry protested. "It was my fault he ran out into traffic."

"Yeah, but you brought him back."

They all cheered, and if they'd been older and stronger, they would have carried their hero through the streets of downtown Chicago on their shoulders. They settled with swinging linked-hands up the driveway.

~ * ~

"Do you think we can get one of the cars out so we can offer fresh fruit and vegetables for Rabbit's dinner?" Tara asked later. "I don't think he'd like frozen veggies."

"Absolutely," Harry agreed. "Anything for the Easter Bunny."

The roses began arriving mid-afternoon while Harry and the kids were at the grocery store. The florist truck stopped with a dozen-dozen roses, each dozen in separate boxes. Tara ran out of vases immediately. There were only six in the house. She called the florist for emergency vases.

"When did you order these?" she demanded at Harry on his return.

"The same day I met you. Remember I went back inside to complete my order? I asked them to change all twelve orders to your address."

"You knew we'd be together for Valentine's Day even them?"

"You bet'cha."

"One dozen would have been adequate. Two dozen would have blown me away. Instead, you sent twelve. I don't know what to do with them all."

"We'll find something," he promised, wiggling his brow. If they didn't have thorns, she would have expected to find them between her sheets tonight. Maybe Harry would take the time to pluck all the petals off their stems. It sounded kind of kinky, warm bodies on soft, fragrant petals. She distributed the six vases of long stemmed roses to different rooms in the house, family room, her bedroom, Erica and Kim's room, the nursery for Tiffany, Kevin's bedroom and the guest room so Harry could benefit from his largess--if he stayed. When the florist delivered the extra vases later, she'd cover the rest of the downstairs rooms.

That afternoon the florist van pulled into the driveway again. This time, in addition to the extra vases, he delivered a dozen roses to Tara from Harry, and a single red rose to each of the four children. They were thrilled. Tara was especially thrilled at Harry's thoughtfulness. For someone unfamiliar with child behavior, he was doing everything right. She immediately started snipping off the thorns.

"I wanted to make sure you know this is from me to you," he told her, "not just one piece of an order for twelve women, redirected."

"How could you hide your feelings like that? All this weekend, you led me to believe that I was in competition with your twelve favorites, and lacking."

"You have been in competition, and--" he drew in a deep, calming breath, "--you won me over."

She couldn't resist a play of words. "Like the bunny wabbit who really was 'won over.' Get it? Huh? Huh?"

He groaned at her dumb joke. "I'm so confused since I met you. You make me laugh, and that's novel for me. I've been trying to decide all week what to do about my life. I have to admit, I've been lonely being on the road lately. Each week is the same as the one before, only the beds change."

She looked up from her task. "Do they all look the same--not the beds, but your women of the week? Do they all have big boobs and blonde hair?"

"Pretty much."

"Do you change pictures in your wallet to match the right woman every Sunday before you take off for the week?"

"No, I don't go that far any more. I did in the beginning, until I forgot one week, and wouldn't you know, she went through my wallet. She said it was to see if I was married. I had to replace her. A shame." He sipped his cappuccino. "Are you about done with the twenty questions?"

"Not yet. I have one more." She gathered all the thorns and threw them in the garbage compactor. "Are you willing to give up all twelve for me?"

"I don't have an answer for you. I wish I did."

"What are you still doing here with me then?"

"But you need me as bad as I need you. What about the driveway? Who will clear it? I just shoveled enough to get my car out so we could go to the grocery store."

"I'm sure the snow removal service will show up sometime soon. You don't need to worry about us. We're not your responsibility, but thank you for all you've done." She walked past him to set a second vase of roses on the long kitchen table. "Harry, I don't mean to hurt your feelings, but we don't need you here. I enjoy your company, but we'll do fine on our own."

"If that's the way you feel, I'll get out of your way. I only stayed because I thought you needed me."

"I did appreciate your support. I would have been lonely on my own," She offered a teary smile. "I had fun."

"I'll pack my bags then and get out of your way."

"That's good. I'm glad you've finally made a decision." She kept her head lowered so he wouldn't see her lips wobble. She really didn't want him to see her cry. For some reason, she felt they were each playing a role on stage, reciting words written in a script, but neither of their hearts was in it. She searched for something to deviate from the prescribed plot. "Oh! You can't leave yet. The kids planned a celebration dinner for the rabbit. You saved him, so it wouldn't be right if you weren't here."

"Of course. I wouldn't miss it."

The big smile on his face convinced Tara that Harry was relieved, too.

"You don't mind him sitting at the dining room table with us, do you?"

"Not a bit. This is so bizarre, I'd agree to anything at this point."

Eleven

For the second night in a row, Tara set the formal table in the dining room; though this time she laid out seven place settings, instead of two. She seldom had the opportunity to entertain on her own, usually it was with family. She'd put a roast of lamb in the oven hours ago and made a salad the likes of which Bunny wouldn't see for many times to come. All the fixings were ready and waiting. She wanted this night to be perfect since Bunny's visit was so special.

"Bunny, can I get you a glass of wine?" He was in human-esque form tonight, standing up straight on legs, but with fur and his bunny ears.

"I'm partial to beer." His nose twitched when he talked.

"Oh... sure... but if the children come in--"

"I'll hide the beer. I promise. We children's heroes must never set a bad example."

"I knew you'd understand, Bunny."

"You can call me Eddie."

"Really? I never thought of you're having a name."

As soon as she reached the kitchen, she got a cold can of beer out of the refrigerator.

"Yeah, it's Eddie Rabbit. People don't think of us as real."

She raised her brows. She must have hit a sore spot. "Do you use a glass?"

He held up his furry paw. "The can is easier."

Tara realized how difficult it would be for him to hold a slippery glass with his silky fur. Once she opened the pop top, he hunkered down so he could see her expression. "Why so down in the mouth?"

She flashed a quick smile. "I'm fine, but you'll be leaving, and Harry--" She squeezed her eyes shut to stop the tears that threatened.

Eddie eyed her closely, making her feel like he could see into her mind.

"What about Harry? Is he going somewhere?" he asked.

"Well, yeah. He travels all week and lives in Indiana. He can't stay here forever."

"He could if he wanted," Eddie said softly.

She burst out crying, and he offered his wide shoulder. The thick, soft fur was so comforting; she wished she could stay there forever.

She was suddenly aware of a growing bulge against her belly, and she realized Eddie was living up to the rabbits' reputation as a horny animal. She pulled back at the same time he pushed away.

"Sorry about that. I seem to be living up to my image."

Face as red as a valentine, she kept her eyes on the messages on the refrigerator door. No way did she want to let her gaze drop.

He continued as if it was no big deal. "I thought you two were getting along famously."

Careful where she looked, she met his eye, surprised that he'd noticed anything between Harry and her. She should have known all those times she felt him--in rabbit form--watching her. She shivered and answered his question.

"We are... or were." She heaved a big sigh. "He's afraid to trust his heart to one woman, afraid I'll hurt him. He'd rather spread himself around as insurance, I guess. There seems nothing I can do or say to get through to him."

He ducked down so they were eye to eye. "Would you like me to talk to him, man to man."

She giggled at the term, considering his fur.

"Okay, how about male to male?"

"If someone else has to convince him, then he doesn't really love me."

"Not true. Men have all kinds of strange complexes. Not us rabbits, of course."

"Of course," she agreed with a smile.

Once again supporting her shoulders, he told her, "Missy, I have the ability to release one or both of you from the spell."

"You mean it truly is a spell?"

"Yeah, Cupid got in the cups and missed. He was aiming at that flower lady and Harry."

Her mouth dropped open. "Glenna? He was meant for Glenna?"

"They would have been a good match. They're both kind of shallow about feelings."

"I knew it wasn't normal, falling in love like that. I pegged him as a playboy the minute I saw him," she said out loud.

"It's tough if just one person wants out, because the other one will pine away. But if you're sure that Harry will make you miserable, if you're sure there's no hope of his loving you as you deserve to be loved, you might want to think about...getting rid of him."

She drew in a shocked breath.

"Not 'get rid of him' in Mafia terms. Get rid of the spell."

"Oh, thank goodness." Still, her heart pounded in her chest so hard, surely the bunny could hear it. How could she give up hope of capturing Harry's heart? How could she bear the hurt of his not loving her in return? "I don't know what to say. I love him, I always will."

"I'll have a talk with the misguided fool." He dropped his paws from her shoulders and turned away. "Could I bother you for another beer?"

"Oh, of course." She got one out of the refrigerator and popped the top for him. "Is there any way Cupid might join us for dinner?" she asked as she handed him the can. "We could eat later."

Bunny shook his head. "I'm sure he'd love to be here, but because of the time zones, he just can't get away tonight. This is his biggest day of the year."

"I understand," she said thoughtfully. "Bunny? If I have to rely on a magic spell to keep Harry, it's not worth it. I want a man to love me for myself, for the two of us together and the children we might have someday. I don't believe in magic." Tears sneaked out from under her lashes. "Go ahead and break the spell."

From the corner of her eye, she caught movement. She looked in that direction, only to realize that Harry stood at the door of the kitchen. "Come on in," she said, her cheeks burning. "I assume you heard everything I said."

"Some of it. Enough to know you want me out of your life."

She sighed in one big huff. "You can't even hear right when you're eavesdropping. I just admitted I love you, and no magic spell will change my love for you. So what about you?"

"I think we need the safety net. If it's available, why not use it?"

"I suppose you want a prenuptial agreement, too."

"Probably wouldn't be a bad idea. If your book series is as successful as I imagine it will be, you'd want some insurance so I don't steal you blind."

She wished she had a two-by-four handy so she could clobber him. "Must you always look for the worst in people, including yourself?" It suddenly hit her that if he was talking divorce, that meant marriage first. "Oh my God, are you proposing?"

"I might be, later tonight."

She opened her mouth to say something, but the shock of a possible marriage proposal plucked the thought from her mind. She leaned a hip against the counter to maintain her balance. "Why wait for tonight? Eddie Rabbit's here now--"

"Who?"

"The Easter Bunny. We have a celebration dinner all set to go. Makes sense to announce the breaking news while he's still here."

She turned toward the rabbit, but he was already walking toward the family room.

"I'll check on the kids. You need your privacy for now."

~ * ~

The Easter Bunny left shortly after the fine dinner, with his gratitude for their hospitality. He promised to bring Cupid to the wedding, though having a cartoon character and a mythical god at the reception might start a stir among the guests, especially with the amount of spirits the two of them were reputed to consume. Tara didn't care; she was so grateful for their matchmaking that she'd allow them to appear naked, if that was their choice.

Harry helped her clear the table. He loaded the dishwasher while she put the food away and fed the dog.

"Baraboo will be lonely without his new friend," she said. "Maybe we should get him a pet, a rabbit or kitten."

"You really think he'd tolerate a little critter?"

"Of course. Most large dogs are incredibly gentle with babies, human or animal, depending on the species, of course."

He shut the dishwasher and wrapped his arms around her from behind. She melted against him, resting the back of her head against his neck and wanting to stay here with him forever.

"What about most men?" he asked.

"What about them? Yes, most men like dogs and kids. Sometimes they're not too partial to cats. I can't say why. And they shoot rabbits for sport."

"That wasn't my question. I wanted to know what they most like, in your opinion."

She crossed her arms over his and jiggled her bottom against him. "You mean sex?"

"Now we're on the same wavelength."

"Finally."

He rested his forehead against the top of her head. "You know what's going to happen. About the time we walk upstairs and shower and change into our 'jammies,' and finally meet up in one of our bedrooms, one of the four children is sure to wake up with a nightmare or a thirst or a bellyache."

"You may be right."

"Why don't we just do it? Right here, right now," he said.

"We're in the kitchen."

"What's wrong with that?"

"I don't know, exactly, but most people do it behind closed doors," she said. His breath tickled her ear and she shivered.

"There's a door between the kitchen and hall."

She whispered, "I don't know if it locks."

"I bet'cha it does," he whispered back. "Why are we whispering?"

"We don't want to wake up the kids."

"We do want to do it here then?"

"I guess I'm game, though it seems kind of premeditated."

He laughed. "What do you consider sex in a bed? Predestination?"

"Very funny. Let's get on with it."

He inched the zipper of her jeans down in response to her challenge.

"Oh, I guess we're starting."

He pulled her sweater over her head and unhooked her bra. "I'll be damned if I'll forget something important this time."

"Do you have a condom on you this time?"

"Seven."

She giggled. "Why seven?"

"I counted all the positions I want to do it with you, and that many readily came to mind." As he spoke he pushed her jeans down her legs.

"I don't even know seven positions."

"Honey, you haven't lived."

"I sure would like to."

"Step out, hon." He helped balance her while she stepped out of her jeans. "Stay here a second." He strode across the room and closed and locked the door, then dimmed the lights.

Nervous energy hit her and she didn't know where to look, what to do. It really would happen this time, and she felt suddenly shy, knowing their lovemaking would be premeditated.

She ducked her head instead of facing him as he crossed the kitchen. "I should tell you something."

"Not right now. I need to kiss you."

Oh, what a kiss. It heated her blood and stirred sensations she wasn't aware existed, and finally she was sure she wanted this and knew how to proceed. She started on his excess of clothing, peeling off layer by layer while she could still function. He had her so hot, so fast, she could no longer think of anything but joining his sex to her body. He lifted her onto the countertop, the tile cool on her heated flesh. He kissed her deeply and teased her open with his fingers, taking her breath away. Stopping to sheathe himself, he slid inside her, slowly, tenderly.

"What's going on?" he said suddenly. "I can't get in."

"Oh, yeah, that's what I meant to tell you. I've never done this before."

"What do you mean, you've never done this before?"

"I'm a virgin."

He leaned back to see her expression and laughed incredulously. "You have four kids. You cannot be a virgin."

"They're not my kids." She shook her head in denial. "I'm just baby-sitting for my brothers."

"Ah, jeez, I can't hold it." He lost control, coming partway inside her but providing no pleasure for her. "Ah, son of a bitch."

Apparently providing no pleasure for him, either.

~ * ~

They'd dressed and were now watching a fire in the family room, Baraboo at their feet.

"I'm sorry if I misled you. I didn't realize you thought I was the kids' mother..."

"Tiffany even called you that."

"Oh, little kids don't know the difference sometimes. They call any caregiver mommy or mother."

"So whose house is this?"

"My brother, Eugene's. Albert lives a couple blocks away."

"Are your brothers really on a cruise in the Caribbean?"

"Yes, of course. Eugene and his wife Karen. They have Kevin and Erica; Albert and Jill have Kim and little Tiffany."

Harry watched the fire with a frown and he didn't seem to be processing half the details she'd told him.

"There's no big conspiracy. They needed some time away after football season, so I said I'd watch the kids. Mom and Dad would have kept them, but they winter in Florida and the kids are a handful for them."

"Football..." he said. She could almost see the wheels turning in his brain. "Eugene and Albert...Avery...Gene and Al Avery! Tackles for the Chicago Bears! Are you fucking kidding me? Gene and Al Avery are your brothers?"

"All my life."

"I can't believe this. I thought you were a kept woman."

"How could you make love to me if that's what you thought?"

"I couldn't help myself. It must have been the spell Cupid put on me."

"Us," she corrected.

"Whatever."

"Do you still want to be with me? I have to warn you, I want marriage."

"Absolutely. Oh, Jeez, my mother! She'll be relieved. All this week she thought you were unmarried with four kids."

"You told your mother about me already? You better call her and let her know you're safe. Unmarried with four kids." She chuckled.

"Did you tell your parents about me yet?"

"Are you kidding? They'd have a fit if they knew I let you stay here for the past four days without a chaperone."

"I think the kids provided adequate chaperonage," Harry said.

"Ho, ho, tell me another one. How many times did we play house in the past four days? At least two of the four."

"We might make #3 this evening. And the other six positions I plan to try."

"Harry," she ducked her head and spoke softly, "what about your Dirty Dozen?"

It was his turn to duck his head. "Remember you suggested a mass-mailing? I guess a marriage announcement will suffice."

She hugged him close, knowing his difficulty to commit to the change in his lifestyle. "You're such a wonderful man, deep down. Do you anticipate a long engagement?"

He pulled back and peered suspiciously at her. "No... why?"

"Well, I thought that as long as we're this close and I'm still officially chaste, maybe we should save it for our wedding night. Wouldn't that be special?"

"You're kidding me, right? I'm giving up twelve experienced women for a virgin, and you want to save it for our wedding night?"

"Just a thought..."

"It's a dumb thought." He stared at the fire for a bit. "How many days would I have to be celibate before we can marry?"

"Oh, the Avery clan is notorious for throwing a wedding together in no time. Six months, seven, maybe... Oh, but then it would be football season again. How about this time next year?"

He leaned his head against hers and sobbed. "I'm gonna call that Bunny back here, and entice Cupid to visit, too, and then I'm gonna wring both their necks. They did this to me and I'll make them pay for it."

"I love you, Harry."

"I love you, too, dear. But if you think I won't kill them anyway, you're wrong."